SHANNON
SAGA

# Angel of Mercy

SHANNON
SAGA

# Angel of Mercy

## TRACIE PETERSON
### and
## JAMES SCOTT BELL

BETHANYHOUSE
MINNEAPOLIS, MINNESOTA 55438

TRACIE PETERSON is a popular speaker and bestselling author who has written over forty-five books, both historical and contemporary fiction. Tracie and her family make their home in Montana.

Visit Tracie's Web site at: *www.traciepeterson.com.*

JAMES SCOTT BELL is a Los Angeles native and former trial lawyer who now writes full time. He is the author of several legal thrillers; his novel *Final Witness* won the 2000 Christy Award as the top suspense novel of the year. He and his family still reside in the City of Angels.

Jim's Web site is *www.jamesscottbell.com.*

# Books By James Scott Bell

*Circumstantial Evidence*
*Final Witness*
*Blind Justice*
*The Nephilim Seed*
*The Darwin Conspiracy*

# Books By
# Tracie Peterson & James Scott Bell

SHANNON SAGA

*City of Angels*
*Angels Flight*
*Angel of Mercy*

# Books By Tracie Peterson

*Controlling Interests*
*Entangled*
*Framed*
*The Long-Awaited Child*
*A Slender Thread*
*Tidings of Peace*

WESTWARD CHRONICLES

*A Shelter of Hope*
*Hidden in a Whisper*
*A Veiled Reflection*

RIBBONS OF STEEL*

*Distant Dreams*
*A Hope Beyond*
*A Promise for Tomorrow*

RIBBONS WEST*

*Westward the Dream*
*Separate Roads*
*Ties That Bind*

YUKON QUEST

*Treasures of the North*
*Ashes and Ice*
*Rivers of Gold*

*with Judith Pella

*The quality of mercy is not strain'd,*
*It droppeth as the gentle rain from heaven*
*Upon the place beneath: it is twice blessed;*
*It blesseth him that gives and him that takes.*

—SHAKESPEARE
*The Merchant of Venice*

*Part One*

# Chapter 1

"THE BIBLE IS BOGUS!"

The deep, resonant tones of Clarence Darrow, the famous attorney, filled the Morosco Theater. Kit Shannon, sitting on the stage, looked out at the solid sea of faces. Not an empty seat in the house. *Must have been like this back when they threw Christians to lions*, she mused.

In fact, Darrow was often called the "Lion of the Courtroom." Kit could well understand why. His physical presence was commanding, his voice imperious. No wonder it was said he could put whole juries in his pocket—despite the evidence.

Darrow, speaking without notes, raised his arms to the rapt audience. "When I say bogus, ladies and gentlemen, I refer to the Bible when viewed as some document dictated by a deity. Friends, this is 1904! We are not a backward people living in tents in the shadow of the gods. We are an advanced, thinking people. And Americans are people of courage. That is why we must be courageous enough to look at the evidence, wherever it leads. . . ."

*Despite the evidence*, Kit thought. On her left sat Dr. Edward Lazarus, who would speak next. While not an atheist like Darrow, he was also a critic of the Bible as the divine Word of God.

That left Kit Shannon as the one defender of the Bible on the dais. She felt her heart flutter. Of the three speakers, she was least qualified in the area of critical studies. How had she gotten herself into this?

Her own Irish temper, she had to admit. But when she heard Dr. Lazarus, a leading clergyman in Los Angeles, call into question the divine inspiration of Scripture, she felt compelled to say something. And she did so twice: once at his church, and once at a Women's Club tea, when Kit had interrupted his talk.

Now she was being forced to defend her position against this scholar and, perhaps worse, Darrow. He had been in Los Angeles to defend the loathsome Heath Sloate. Successfully, too. Then Darrow had invited himself to this debate. Two against one!

Kit began to pray, asking God for the strength and wisdom to defend His Word. She did not want to back away. This was a necessary defense. Traditional Christianity was being attacked from many sides in the new century—Darwinism challenged Genesis; higher criticism questioned Scripture; even the divinity of Christ was being attacked by men, like Dr. Lazarus, who wore the cloth. God's people had to make a stand.

She gripped her father's Bible, her most beloved possession on earth, and slowly ran her hands over the worn leather cover. Somehow, some way, God would see her through this. Papa had taught her that lesson over and over.

Darrow paced as he continued. He looked uncomfortable in his high starched collar and tails, but his voice betrayed none of it. "Few men who are important in any community retain the old conception of the Bible, of a God, of hell, and of immortality, such as was once believed. In the cold light of science, we must now give up our childlike faith in the pleasant poetry of the book and see it for what it is. A collection of writings from a backward and super-stitious people."

A faint rustling arose from the audience. Kit wondered what they were thinking. Most of them looked well-to-do, and she recognized some of the cream of society. Mrs. Eulalie Pike, the mortified hostess of the tea Kit had disrupted, was here to witness Kit's humiliating defeat.

Aunt Freddy was not here, however, and Kit knew why. The debate had been splashed across the two leading newspapers—the *Times* of General Harrison Gray Otis and the *Examiner* of William Randolph Hearst—and Freddy was too nervous to witness yet another public spectacle made by her great-niece.

Kit swallowed as Darrow continued. "The books of the Old and New Testaments were written ages before the world had any knowledge of our science. To those old authors the world was flat, the sun moved across the sky, and the stars were stuck into the firmament like diamonds in a blanket."

His rhetoric was designed to manipulate, and to Kit his strategy appeared to be working. Many a head nodded as Darrow outlined his case against the Bible.

Finally, he came to the close of his address. "The evidence shows, then, that our life must be lived by our wits alone, and not by instructions handed down from God. Emotionally, perhaps I will act as others do at the last moment of my existence. But intellectually, I am satisfied that life is a serious burden, and we must do the best we can with all the courage we can muster. We cannot have that courage if we continue to hide behind a book of old stories. I thank you."

The applause was robust, meaning Mr. Darrow had woven a

masterful web. No wonder he had managed an acquittal for Heath Sloate, who was as guilty as any public sinner ever was.

Now Dr. Edward Lazarus was introduced. He rose and took center stage. Like Darrow, he was also an accomplished speaker, the result of years in the pulpit. Unlike Darrow, he was rather thin, with hair perfectly combed. He filled out his evening clothes like a man who posed for magazine artists.

"I thank Mr. Darrow for his remarks," Lazarus began. "I find I am in substantial agreement with him about the Bible, though not with his ultimate conclusions. While I do not think the Bible is a divine book, there is something about it that we can respond to. It can point us to a better life."

Kit listened carefully to the argument of this theologian. It boiled down to this—the ancient stories and myths of the Bible represent man's longings. Those longings are for good things. So man, through the efforts of his "better self," can bring about good in the world. And so the world will be saved. There was no mention of hope to be found only in Jesus Christ. That rankled Kit, for that was her father's constant message. She believed all Christian preaching should be so centered.

When Lazarus sat down the moderator introduced, "Miss Kathleen Shannon, attorney-at-law, for the conservative position."

There was only a smattering of applause from the assembled gallery. Kit smoothed the lace cuffs of her white muslin gown. She had thought to wear her most severe business suit, then at the last minute, changed her mind. Earl Rogers had once told her that the unexpected was far more effective. Darrow and Lazarus would expect her to come at them all fire and brimstone. Instead, she felt the very picture of femininity and grace. Her light auburn hair had been caught up in a delicate fashion with tendrils falling artfully to frame her face. A simple but completely respectable hat, fashioned to accentuate her gown, perched atop her head to further reiterate her womanly appearance.

Kit cleared her throat, stood, and walked to the podium, her father's Bible in hand. But as she did, she realized to her horror that everything she had prepared to say was suddenly gone from her head.

———

Big Ed Hanratty was in a foul mood.

And why not? There was plenty to be foul about, starting with Burt, the barkeep at O'Reilly's, who was serving warm beer. Burt had said it was the iceman's fault. *Not likely,* Hanratty thought.

The taste of the beer was as sour as Hanratty's outlook. It seemed like only yesterday that his captain, McGinty, had dressed him down in no uncertain terms. To be honest, Hanratty had to confess he deserved it. He had played fast and loose with the truth in that Chavez trial. He could have been drummed off the force. And McGinty let him know that would have been his own preference.

But for some reason he was given another chance. Hanratty shook his head and took a long gulp of beer. Should he even continue to take that chance?

Being a cop in Los Angeles was no bag of gems. You got a lousy hundred-fifty dollars a month and had to buy your own gun and uniform to boot. Then you had to go out and try to bring order, every day and night, to a town that still wanted its wild side to go unhindered. And did anybody ever thank you for it? Not on your flat feet.

The worst thing of all was knowing that Kit Shannon had knocked him all over court. The thought had oppressed him ever since the trial ended. But it was more than that. Something about the way she looked at him. It was like she saw into his soul. He didn't want anybody looking there, especially a gal attorney. Yet her stare was incisive, like she not only saw but also understood him.

He hated her for that, but he had to admit one thing. She was about the best lawyer in town. He'd seen Earl Rogers in action and thought there would never be anyone to match him. But this Shannon woman might. Someday.

"Hey, Burt!" Hanratty bellowed.

The roly-poly bartender, his sleeves rolled up to reveal massive arms, strode over.

"Gimme another," said Hanratty. "A cold one this time."

"I already told you—"

"I don't care what ya told me! *I'm* tellin' you!"

Burt smiled—he was missing his two front teeth, the result of a fight with a drunken cop a few years before—and said, "You can always take your business somewheres else."

Big Ed Hanratty sighed. The world was a dark, dreary place, with no friends and no cold beer. Outside, where night had fallen over Los Angeles, it was more of the same. He had a wife and children waiting for him at home, but he was in no mood to go there. It wouldn't be good for the girls to see him this way.

Burt drew him a warm one and set it on the counter. "Ed, we've known each other a long time, right?"

Hanratty looked into the suds of his beer. "So?"

"I know cops. I know what it is that's hammerin' your head."

Ed Hanratty looked up, seeking a sympathetic eye.

Burt continued. "And I know what you can do to get your train back on the right track."

Hanratty took a gulp of beer, then said, "What are you driving around, Burt?"

"You need a good collar, is all."

"Ah, a collar is a collar."

"I'm not talking about rounding up some rum hound. I'm talking about something that'll make the papers. Make you out a hero."

Hanratty chuffed. "If I could pick 'em, sure. But you never know about those things beforehand."

"Maybe some do." Burt had that canary-in-the-mouth look to go with his catlike eyes.

"Maybe you better quit beatin' around the bush and tell me what you're thinkin'."

"Will you nevermore give me any pain about my beer?"

"So it's a deal we're makin'?"

"To be sure—and you get a promotion and a raise."

That sounded good. Oh yes. His family could use the extra. "Talk to me."

"What if I told you there's some out-of-towners down at the Braxton Arms?"

"At Hill and Fifth?"

Burt nodded. "And what if I told you the same are wanted in Indiana on robbery charges?"

"I'd ask how you knew about it."

"Priests and bartenders is always the first to know."

A bit of wisdom Hanratty did not dispute. "But unlike a priest, a barkeep ain't got to be keepin' it between himself and God. Is that it?"

Burt's lip quivered with the slightest hint of a smile. "Most of what I know, I keep between me and God, but this time I figure it can do us both a bit of good."

"So why ain't they been collared yet?"

"That's something I can't say. All I know is they're out-of-state fugitives and they're sitting like ducks. And you're a Los Angeles police officer. Our city needs to keep away the criminal element from outside our borders."

*True*, Hanratty thought. The city valued its reputation as an emerging, vibrant center.

"So what are you waiting for?" Burt said.

Hanratty downed his beer with a long gulp, slapped the counter, and stood up. "Braxton Arms?"

"That's right."

With a swipe of a sleeve across his mouth, Big Ed Hanratty turned toward the barroom door.

# Chapter 2

THE AUDIENCE STARED EXPECTANTLY at Kit Shannon. The silence was as ominous as a deathwatch.

Kit gripped the sides of the podium. Never before had this happened, not even in the direst circumstances in court. While she had sometimes been unsure of what to say, her mind had never been so completely blank—like a sheet of white paper drifting on the wind.

*Oh, God, help me now,* Kit prayed. *What do I do?*

For a moment there was nothing. And then, suddenly, a thought flashed into her head. This was all about evidence, and she had spent countless hours studying the evidence code. *Use it.*

"Yes," Kit said aloud and then realized she was talking to herself. To the confused looks in the front row she said, "Yes, I am quite pleased to speak on behalf of the Bible. We have heard it prosecuted tonight, by the able Mr. Darrow and the erudite Dr. Lazarus. I now rise to its defense. What we have in these ancient writings, ladies and gentlemen, is testimony. The testimony of witnesses. Witnesses to the works of God. And I am sure I will get no objection from Mr. Darrow if we put their words to the same test, under the rules of evidence, that Mr. Darrow uses each time he steps into a courtroom."

She turned then and looked at Clarence Darrow. The legal warrior graciously nodded, as if to say, "Show me what you've got."

"I shall focus my attention on the testimony of the Gospels," Kit said, "for one important reason. If the Gospels are reliable concerning Jesus and His divine nature, then what Jesus himself said is reliable. And Jesus taught that Scripture is the very Word of God. If the Gospels are reliable concerning His resurrection, as I will attempt to show, then Jesus is divine and His word is truth. The Bible is no mere human book."

With that she gave Dr. Lazarus a glance. He scowled.

Feeling the energy she always did when impassioned by an argument, Kit stepped away from the podium. She wanted to face the audience as she would a jury, without any hindrance between them.

For the next half hour Kit vindicated the witnesses to Jesus under each standard of the evidence rules. She demonstrated their competence—their ability to correctly observe events. She proved their credibility by showing no motive for fabrication. Indeed, several died by sticking to their story. Finally, the manner in which their accounts agreed—corroboration—was proof beyond a shadow of a doubt that their message was reliable.

As she spoke it occurred to her that God was presenting her with an opportunity. She was not here merely to defend the Bible, as had been the original purpose. She was here to share the truth of Jesus Christ with everyone in the hall. She had often contemplated God's will in bringing her to this city. But a city, anywhere, is merely a collection of people. And all people had the same need.

"The Gospels are without question reliable accounts of the life of Jesus of Nazareth. And that is truly good news for all of us." She turned again to Dr. Lazarus. "If we pick and choose in the Bible, we human beings will never know what, if anything, is inspired. That makes the Bible just another book. And it makes Jesus just another man, a man whose life may have been nothing but a terrible deceit, for millions have died in His name."

She whirled back to the gallery. She held her father's Bible in the air. "But we have an inspired Word from God himself, and the Savior He sent to dwell among men, to die in our place on the cross, and to rise again into glory. He is listening to us at this very moment. But more than that, He is listening to each heart. Ladies and gentlemen, the final verdict is in your own hands. Come to the Savior; embrace Him as your own. And never, ever, be in doubt about the Holy Bible again."

With that she resumed her chair, to the sound of silence.

———

The stairs creaked under the big shoes of Ed Hanratty. The desk clerk at Braxton Arms, a little weed of a man, hadn't been any trouble. One look at Hanratty's uniform and badge, and he was a fountain of information.

There were three of them—a wife, husband, and son—in Room 202. The desk clerk said their name was Chausser. *What kind of name is that*, Hanratty wondered. *German? Do they have Germans in Indiana?*

No matter. Big Ed knew bagging a threesome on the run from the law, single-handedly, would be just the right medicine for his downtrodden spirit.

Hanratty paused and pulled out his gun. The celebrated Harrington Police .38 had served him well. He opened the breakaway cylinder and checked the ammunition.

The weapon danced a little in front of his eyes. That was the beer, he knew. But he could handle his liquor. He always had. Snapping the cylinder back into place, Hanratty gripped the rubber stock securely and started up the stairs again.

Suddenly Hanratty felt like a fool. No, someone who had been made a fool *of*. What if this was all some sort of elaborate joke? What if Burt, maybe at the behest of some other cop, was just having a little fun at the expense of Big Ed Hanratty?

Hanratty looked at his .38 again. "If he is," he said, "I'll kill him." He smiled at the mental picture of his big hands around Burt's neck, scaring the stuffings out of that whiskey spouter until he owned up to what he had done.

A thump sounded on the stairs. Hanratty spun and looked up, instinctively raising his revolver.

A wide-eyed man in a starched collar put his hands in the air. "Don't shoot," he said.

Hanratty quickly lowered the gun. "What's your name?"

"Balsam, sir."

"Put your hands down."

Balsam, sweat droplets popping out on his forehead, did as he was told.

Hanratty took a step up, going nose to nose with the man. "Don't ya know better than to be sneakin' around like that?"

"I was just going out for a moment," Balsam said, his voice warbling.

"I don't need your life story," Hanratty said. "Just go on about your business."

"Yes, sir." Balsam scurried down the stairs.

Hanratty waited until Balsam disappeared and then went up to the second floor. There were ten rooms here, five on either side of the hall. At the end of the corridor was a window that opened, according to Hanratty's calculations, onto Hill Street.

Room 202 was just off the stairwell. Hanratty paused at the door. He heard voices inside. Two men. And the talk was heated. One of the men, who seemed to be the younger, said, "They'll catch on for sure."

So there really was something to Burt's tip. Hanratty strained to hear more of the conversation but couldn't make out all the words. Was this the father and son? Or was somebody else inside with them?

Maybe they had met up with another criminal. Maybe they were forming a gang. There was no way to know from out here.

Hanratty, feeling slightly dizzy, decided the direct approach was best. No time to lose. Give them a Big Ed Hanratty special. He was still a presence to be reckoned with, by golly, and nobody was going to tell him any different. To the devil with that Shannon woman and her fancy, educated ways. He had the gun to back him up. There would be no trouble with the direct approach. They'd be scared and they'd talk.

Ed Hanratty hadn't broken a door down in some time. He was out of practice. But one thing a good kick to this door might do is clear the head. Get the blood pumping. Put a little drama into the arrest about to unfold.

Clearing his throat, Big Ed Hanratty took one step back. He readied his gun. Then he lifted his right foot and, with one mighty thrust, splintered the door of Room 202.

# Chapter 3

AUNT FREDDY, looking a bit plumper these days, poured coffee from the silver pot and handed a fine china cup to Kit. It was late in the evening, but she had insisted on Kit visiting after the great debate. "Better to hear the report from you," she had said, "than read about it in the papers."

Kit was happy to oblige. She did not get to spend as much time with her great-aunt as she would have liked. Now they were comfortably seated in the library of the Fairbank mansion, Kit's favorite room in the house. It was an affection that began when she had lodged here upon her arrival in Los Angeles.

"Was Eulalie Pike in attendance?" Aunt Freddy said. "Was she wearing that ghastly Poiret gown? Oh, do tell me."

"Of course she was there," Kit said matter-of-factly. "She was, after all, the one who set up the event."

"Hoping you would disgrace yourself," Freddy said.

"Perhaps."

"Perhaps nothing! And you acquitted yourself well?"

"The audience was respectful."

"I could not bear to have Eulalie turning her nose up at us. You are still my kin, even though you have more of your father's Irish in you than is respectable." She seemed to study Kit for a moment, then added, "Still, you are very correct in your appearance. Your gown is most fashionable, and your hat, while a bit small, is still completely stylish. I find society will often overlook a person's breeding if their appearance is in keeping with that which is acceptable."

Kit could only smile and nod. No use arguing with Aunt Freddy over matters of family blood or respectability.

"Was anyone else of note in attendance?" Freddy said.

Kit thought about it and was sure several people who would meet Freddy's notable list were there. But Kit did not know them and didn't care to. "One interesting gentleman approached me afterward."

Freddy quickly put down her cup. "Gentleman? Do tell. Was he handsome?"

With a slight laugh, Kit said, "I did not notice. He is not that sort of gentleman."

"What sort?"

"The marrying sort."

"My dear, what other sort is there?"

"What I mean, Aunt Freddy, is that he may already have been married. I do not know. His approach was in a professional capacity."

Freddy's ruddy cheeks turned a little redder. "Come, come, what was this man's name? Perhaps I know him."

"He is English."

"I know some Englishmen."

"I don't think you know this one," Kit said coyly, playing with her aunt. "He is a minister."

"What was that? Minister? An English politician, you say?"

"A minister of the Gospel."

"Oh!" Freddy sat back in her chair.

"His name is G. Campbell Morgan."

Freddy waved her hand in the air. "Never heard of him."

"Nor have I, but he said he is in America on a lecture tour."

"On what subject?"

"The Bible."

"Oh!" Freddy said again. Her cry came out like a yelp.

Kit shook her head slightly, praying silently for her aunt. She was in so many ways a dear and loving woman, but when it came to religion she had blinders on. Or, rather, glasses that only saw the latest psychic fashions that cropped up in Los Angeles like weeds. Her bed table was stacked with literature and books that favored all manner of palm and tea readings and the power of séances. Kit hoped her companionship and influence would lead her aunt to the Savior.

"Yes," Kit said, "he said he was impressed with my defense of the Bible. You would have been, too."

Freddy took up her cup and sipped quickly. "Well, tell me how you are getting along these days as a . . ." her voice trailed off.

"Lawyer?"

"I cannot even say the word!"

"Fine, Auntie. I am making enough to pay the rent."

Freddy put her hand on her breast. "Able to pay the rent! My heart . . ."

Kit patted her aunt's knee. "You worry too much."

"I have much to worry about."

"Such as?"

"Such as you. I had so hoped you would be married to that nice doctor by now."

Kit closed her eyes. That "nice" doctor, Jeffrey Kenton, had been a liar and deceiver, his Christianity a sham. And Kit had almost run off to marry him. How had she, a woman of logical, reasonable thought, given herself so completely to such an illusion? Her pride still smarted from the encounter; her heart still ached from the loss. Not the loss of the man himself, but the loss of what she thought she'd found. "Jeffrey Kenton has fled the city," Kit said. "That should tell you all you need to know."

Freddy took a sip of coffee and eyed her niece. "Why don't you come with me to see Professor Stillwater?"

"Professor who?"

"A wonderful psychic. He can see both the past and the future."

Kit shook her head. "I do not condone mystic cranks."

"Cranks! Why, you have not even met the man."

"I don't have to, Aunt Freddy."

"You are, if I may say, behaving quite narrow-mindedly."

"This city is full of spiritual charlatanism. I don't like to see people falling for it."

"You think me a fool?"

Kit took her aunt's hands in her own. "Aunt Freddy, tonight I defended the truth of Christianity to a packed theater. Even as I did so, I felt the power of the Gospel more strongly than I ever have. Perhaps this is part of God's plan for me. He has placed me here, in part, to bring His message to Los Angeles."

"Which is?"

"That the grace of God through Jesus Christ is man's only hope. And yours, Aunt Freddy. And mine."

"Do you really believe God is telling you this?"

"Yes, I do. And I will follow His lead. If I am to confront spiritual quacks, even publicly, then I suppose I will just have to do it."

"Oh dear." Aunt Freddy put her hand on her heart once more. "I was afraid you'd say that. Hasn't enough harm been done in the name of God?"

Kit felt a sudden heat. "Harm?"

"If you would listen to Professor Stillwater. He is such a learned man, he knows history, psychology . . ."

"And he believes Christianity is harmful?"

"He wants to free our minds."

Now the heat was developing into anger—at this confident man who apparently had her great-aunt's ear. "The only thing he will free you of is your money," Kit said on impulse.

Her aunt visibly reacted. "How do you presume to talk to me that way? You care so little for your Aunt Freddy?"

"No, Aunt Freddy. I care so much."

"Then do not speak this way again. I can take care of my affairs. Just as you think that you can take care of yours without my help."

"But—"

Freddy raised her plump hand. "No more is to be said. You are as stubborn as the Irish coast. Very well." She lowered her hand with a wave.

Kit felt the wave was dismissive, in a way Aunt Freddy had never been before. It had to be this Stillwater fellow, and she determined to find out more. Her aunt may be enamored of the learned professor, but Kit was going to protect her Aunt Freddy whether she liked it or not.

# Chapter 4

LIKE EVERYONE ELSE in the *Examiner* building, Tom Phelps felt the excitement. This morning the big man—William Randolph Hearst himself—was here.

Phelps, like all the reporters for the paper, knew the Hearst story well. He was the only child of George and Phoebe Hearst and heir to an immense fortune. Expelled from Harvard, the young Hearst took over his father's failing San Francisco newspaper, the *Examiner*. Aggressively hiring—some said stealing—a talented staff, Hearst went head-to-head with the established *Chronicle*. With an instinct for finding—some said creating—sensational news, the *San Francisco Examiner* soon surpassed the *Chronicle* in circulation.

That success prompted Hearst, in 1895, to try the same thing in New York City, where he purchased the *Morning Journal*. In what came to be called "yellow journalism," Hearst used his sensation-seeking ways to win the newspaper war against Joseph Pulitzer's *New York World.*

Then, a year ago, he set his sights on Los Angeles. Phelps, in fact, had been working for the city's established paper, the *Times* of General Harrison Gray Otis. But Hearst's *Los Angeles Examiner* made him an offer he could not refuse.

Phelps felt immediately at home with the *Examiner.* With its loud headlines and gaudy illustrations, the paper was redefining what news looked and smelled like. It was an exciting time to be in the newspaper game.

Hearst had only visited the Los Angeles paper on two occasions. One was for the newspaper's debut, and that had been a circus. Phelps never even got to shake his hand. The other time Hearst came in, Phelps was on assignment in San Diego. So he had never met the king, but now he would have his chance—the managing editor, Archibald Crowley, had summoned Phelps to his office for a meeting with Hearst.

"I've heard good things about you, Mr. Phipps," Hearst said in greeting.

"Phelps," the reporter said, swallowing. Hearst was a robust man, around forty, Phelps guessed. Dashing in a way.

"Very good things," Hearst said.

Arch Crowley motioned for everyone to take a chair. "Mr. Hearst is concerned about the circulation numbers."

"I thought we were doing well," Phelps said.

"We are," Hearst said, "but not well enough. That old goat Otis is proving a worthy adversary."

"And so we have to turn up the heat," Crowley added.

"I saw what you wrote during that Mexican trial," Hearst said. "That's just the ticket."

Phelps looked at the floor. His coverage of the Chavez case, and

Kit Shannon, had been an *Examiner* job all the way. Sensational. Provocative.

"We need something big like that," Hearst continued. "Something that will stick a finger in Otis's eye. You have any ideas, Mr. Phipps?"

Phelps did not bother to correct the man. "I am sure we can come up with something," he said.

"What are some of Otis's pet projects?" Hearst asked.

Crowley said, "He hates organized labor."

Hearst nodded impatiently. "We know that. We have already captured the common man."

"He is head of a real-estate syndicate," added Crowley, "along with E. H. Harriman."

"Hopes to make a killing when Los Angeles gets a water source, eh?"

"That's right."

Hearst stood and began pacing. Phelps watched him for a moment, then said, "The police."

Hearst spun on his heels. "What about the police?"

Phelps cleared his throat. "A lot of the cops in this town are dirty. That's something that's come out in these trials I've covered. But Otis keeps defending them. Even when it's been proved they are lying."

"Police, eh? That's promising. Have you got a lead on any bad cops?"

"Not at the moment," Phelps said, "but it wouldn't be difficult to find one."

"Why don't you do that?" Hearst said. "Find us a good case. We can play it up as a terrible civic scandal. I like it." Hearst spread his hands in front of himself. "Dirty Cops Stain City. *Examiner* Vows to Get at the Truth."

Phelps only nodded. If Hearst liked it, that settled it.

"Are you up to the task, my boy?" Hearst said.

"Yes, sir," Phelps said.

"There will be a nice, fat raise for you if you carry it off, right, Arch?"

Crowley smiled at Phelps. "No question."

"Then go at it."

Phelps and Crowley nodded.

Hearst slapped Tom Phelps on the back. "I like you, Mr. Phipps. Good luck."

————

June was going to be hot, even by Los Angeles standards. To Kit it seemed as if the sea had grown tired and simply decided to give up on breezes.

It did not help matters when Kit opened the window of her law office at 238 W. First Street. She resigned herself to having her dress stick to her skin today.

"You will need a bath, I think," Corazón said with a grin. Her former maid, now friend, had come with cool oranges for an afternoon snack.

"I would adore a bath," Kit said.

"Let us go to the hotel. I will make one for you."

"Thank you, Corazón, but I must at least *pretend* I'm going to have a client come through that door."

"You have no one now?"

"No one. All of Los Angeles seems fat and happy."

"*Sí*, and the president is coming!"

That was the report. According to the papers, President Theodore Roosevelt was set to visit the city soon. Kit hoped Aunt Freddy would take the news well. She was not an admirer of the progressive chief executive.

But as a sign of the coming of age of Los Angeles, Roosevelt's visit was a great step forward. With a population of well over one hundred thousand, the City of Angels was feeling optimistic, and the influx of new residents continued unabated. New buildings were springing up all over, and streets were constantly being widened and lengthened to accommodate the increased traffic of horses, carriages, and even gas-powered automobiles. Originally lacking a first-class harbor, the city had nearly finished construction of one at San Pedro. Now the world could sail to its shores as well as ride the Southern Pacific Railroad to its depot.

Yet none of this excitement filled the void Kit felt, a feeling something like a wound. Apparently her face was transparent, for Corazón said, "But your heart is hurt, I think."

Kit and Corazón had no secrets from each other. Corazón knew all about what had happened with Jeffrey Kenton and Ted Fox. The two men Kit had loved—and lost.

"I'll get over it," Kit said. "In time."

"Do you think God will find you a man?"

"Right now I would be happy if God found me a client."

"What kind of a client?"

"Handsome, strong, Christian, and innocent."

Corazón laughed.

"You are my best friend in the world," Kit said.

"And you for me."

They finished one orange, then Corazón peeled another. The office filled with the lovely scent of citrus, a smell Kit had come to love in this land. Growing up in a Boston orphanage, and later living in New York City, Kit had not known the fresh scents Los Angeles offered in such abundance—ocean air, orange groves, magnolia blossoms. In many ways these were the smells that made Los Angeles a home for Kit.

A knock sounded on the office door, and Corazón rose to answer it. A man in a tweed suit and derby stepped inside.

"Miss Shannon?" the man said.

Kit stood to greet him. "I am she."

"I have something for you." He walked to her, removing a folded paper from his coat. He handed it to Kit and quickly added, "Good day."

He wasted no time hoofing it out of the office.

"What is this?" Corazón asked.

Kit unfolded the paper and read it.

"Is bad news?" Corazón said.

"Yes," Kit said. "I am being sued." Kit felt her cheeks getting hotter by the second.

Corazón's eyes widened. "You are angry?"

Kit slapped the paper on her desk. "*Angry* doesn't even begin to describe it."

"But who could want this?"

Through clenched teeth Kit said, "Do you remember Elinor Wynn?"

# Chapter 5

JOHN DAVENPORT, the district attorney of Los Angeles, looked again at the front page of the *Los Angeles Examiner*. For two weeks after the shooting of Jay Chausser, the city of Los Angeles barely took note of it. The story had not made the front pages of either the *Times* or the *Examiner*, and both papers only gave it one-day coverage. Both papers intimated that it was a police shooting of a suspect on the run from the law.

That was certainly how Davenport saw it.

Then, this morning, a Hearst bombshell was dropped on the city in the form of a front page spread:

*Los Angeles Examiner*

**POLICE MURDER AT BRAXTON ARMS!**
*Examiner* Uncovers Tale of Rogue Policeman
Innocent Lives Shattered
by Tom Phelps

*The killing of Jay Chausser at the Braxton Arms Hotel was not, as first supposed, an act of self-defense. The questioning of witnesses at the time of the shooting reveals a much more sinister story.*

*According to witness statements, Mr. Chausser was gunned down by a Los Angeles police officer without provocation, leaving behind a widow and son. One witness says, "It was cold-blooded murder, that is for certain."*

*As pieced together from witness statements, the story that emerges is that on the night of June 7, Officer Edward Hanratty went to the Braxton Arms on an uncorroborated tip-off about a fugitive from Indiana. The tragic events that followed . . .*

Davenport lowered the paper and sighed. He looked at the chief of police, Horace Allen, who had come to Davenport's office after reading the same story. "Nothing to be done, then?"

Allen shook his head. "This is no longer a departmental matter. You will have to take it from here."

Davenport said, "What is your official statement going to be?"

"I will vouch for the department as a whole. I will admit there are some bad policemen, but that we are actively engaged in seeing to it that every policeman in the city follows the law."

"And about Hanratty?"

"I won't even mention his name. The city knows who he is. I will say that I am working hand-in-hand with the district attorney."

"The two knights in shining armor, eh?"

"Naturally."

"Don't you feel a bit like Judas Iscariot?"

Allen's eyes narrowed. "You are a blunt man, Mr. Davenport."

"I prefer plainspoken."

"Then I will speak plainly, as well. You are as ambitious as I am, perhaps more so."

"Such is your opinion of me?"

"Let us just say I would not feel comfortable with my back to you."

Davenport smiled.

"We both know this matter has become the personal crusade of Mr. Hearst," Allen said. "He has decided the police department must be made clean. We can be for him or against him, but not in between. Personally, I choose for him."

"A wise decision, since it's the governorship you're after."

Allen shook his head in wonderment. "Nothing gets past you, does it?"

"I take pride in my vision. And that vision tells me we both ought to be on the side of Mr. Hearst. Besides, a new governor may handpick his lieutenant."

Horace Allen laughed. "By heavens, you are a man after my own heart."

*Perhaps literally*, Davenport thought. He took out his pocket watch and opened it. "I suppose now is as good a time as any."

"For what?" Allen said.

"To have a couple of your boys place Hanratty under arrest. A night in jail might be good for his soul."

# Chapter 6

ON THE WAY to the courthouse Kit couldn't help but think about Ted Fox. Where was he just now? Was he even alive?

Ever since he'd left Los Angeles, Kit had prayed for his return. But most of all, she'd prayed he'd open his heart to the truth. God's truth.

As Kit walked toward Temple Street by way of Spring, her cheviot walking dress swishing along the sidewalk and her large-brimmed Arlington hat shielding her from the oppressive sun, she wondered what Ted would think of this outrageous turn of events. Elinor Wynn suing Kit for alienation of his affection! What gall. Kit's face began to heat up like the sidewalk.

At the courthouse she found the predictable mob of curiosity seekers and reporters. This entire affair was a juicy social scandal. Kit pushed through without a word to anyone. She would do all her talking in the courtroom.

That courtroom belonged to Judge Franklin Adams. All she

asked was that he be fair. An open-minded judge could never allow Elinor Wynn's ridiculous lawsuit to continue.

Yet there sat Elinor with her lawyer, Barker Wesley. Both of them had a look on their faces that Kit could only describe as smug. Wesley, a dapper man in a three-piece suit, casually fiddled with a gold watch fob as he waited for the judge to call the case.

What did he have up his sleeve? Kit's copious research had found no legal basis for Elinor's claim. How, then, could they appear so unconcerned?

Elinor Wynn, of course, was all dressed up for her moment in the sun. Her blue etamine gown, with two circular flounces terminating at each side, was something more befitting an evening at the opera. And the full blouse waist trimmed with stitched bands and embroidered ornaments was something only a social peacock would wear to a proceeding like this. Topping it all off was the most ostentatious hat Kit had ever seen—a blue silk affair virtually exploding with ostrich plumes.

The picture of lawyer and client was one of supreme confidence. Kit felt tendrils of anxiety creeping around her. Earl Rogers, who had offered to defend Kit for no fee, had told her that a lawyer who represents himself has a fool for a client. She had refused, confident the judge would throw this lawsuit out. So why was she feeling foolish all of a sudden?

Judge Adams took the bench. He was an intelligent-looking man in his fifties, with short-cropped black hair. He rapped once with his gavel and said in a clear, no-nonsense voice, "Wynn versus Shannon. We are here on a motion to dismiss the case brought by the respondent. Is the respondent ready to bring her argument?"

Kit stood. "I am, Your Honor."

"Proceed."

"Your Honor," she said, "the court must dismiss this case for one simple reason. There is no cause of action under law, either civil or common. What is being foisted upon this court is a waste of time."

Kit strode to the center of the courtroom to address the judge directly. He did not indicate anything by his expression.

"The tort of alienation of affection, Your Honor, was first recognized in New York in 1866. The case is *Heermance v. James*, and I note that it was not cited by my learned adversary." Kit nodded at Barker Wesley. He smiled.

"This cause of action actually began, that court notes, as a property right. A master had the right at common law to bring action when someone enticed his servant away, thus depriving him of services. Under early common law, since a wife was seen as a servant of the husband, this tort of alienation was gradually recognized."

The words almost stuck in Kit's throat. The idea of a wife as property, still rippling through the law, appalled her. But this outrage was, ironically, the strength of her argument.

"There is no such action recognized for a wife, Your Honor. While many of us might take issue with the view that a woman can ever be owned by her husband, there is as yet no basis for a wife to sue for alienation of affection."

Kit paused and glanced at Elinor Wynn. She was looking straight ahead.

"Even if there were," Kit continued, "the fact is there was no marriage here. Miss Wynn and Mr. Fox were engaged to be married. They had not yet entered into a recognized union. If, for example, Mr. Fox were to bring an action for alienation, it would be thrown out on that same basis. In short, Your Honor, there is no cause of action here because there is no law to support it. I would therefore request Your Honor dismiss this case and assess the plaintiff with the sanction of paying my legal fee."

As Kit sat down Judge Adams said, "You may respond now, Mr. Wesley."

The well-appointed lawyer stood. "Your Honor, my worthy opponent has actually outlined our argument for us. I believe she just said there is not *yet* a basis for a wife to sue for alienation of affection. Miss Shannon, being the shining example of progressive womanhood that she is, would like, I am sure, to see that very thing remedied."

With a polished smile, Wesley bowed toward Kit. A few titters arose from the gallery.

"And isn't that what the courts of justice are for, Your Honor? Where there is injustice they stand as shining beacons to the great, oppressed masses seeking only the redress of the grievous harms done to them."

The words *ham actor* raced into Kit's mind. But the judge was listening intently. He wasn't truly considering this, was he?

"This is 1904, Your Honor! Women like Miss Shannon have every right to practice law. How can we deny them the rights of the law itself?"

Kit felt her hands clenching. It was a powerful argument Wesley was making, and he was painting her into a corner. How could she stand and argue, in effect, against herself?

"I ask this court to recognize the social changes that are upon us at this moment in time and to consider the terrible loss my client has suffered because of the purposeful allurements of Miss Shannon. Were it not for her, my client would be happily married by now, even now perhaps bearing a child and contributing her part to ensure the survival of this continuing enterprise we call civilization."

Kit's head was starting to throb. Was it these overripe words or the fact that the judge was nodding his head?

Then the judge said, "Mr. Wesley, even if this court were to agree with you about a cause of action on behalf of a wife, is it not limited to one who is married?"

"I do not see why, Your Honor. In either case the damage is the same—the loss of the affection and companionship of that special person with whom one expects to spend the rest of one's life."

Nodding again, Judge Adams said, "Any response, Miss Shannon?"

What response could there be, other than the legal one? "Your Honor," she said, "no such right has ever been recognized. This is a matter for the legislature."

Scowling, the judge said, "Justice is always a matter for the courts, Miss Shannon. If this is a matter of common law, I can certainly look to see the intent of it and rule accordingly, is that not correct?"

"Correct, but—"

"That is all I need to know. You agree on that point. And I am going to agree with Mr. Wesley. There is a cause of action here for a very real injury. It is not up to me, but to a jury, to assess fault and damages. So my ruling is that this matter may proceed to trial."

The audience whispered loudly. Elinor Wynn was looking at Kit now, her face the very picture of self-satisfaction.

It was all so ludicrous! How could the judge have possibly ruled this way? It was almost as if there had been a back-room deal between Adams and Wesley.

"Will there be anything else?" said the judge.

"Yes, Your Honor," Kit said. "I would like to amend my motion to make it one for summary judgment." A summary judgment argued that there were no facts sufficient to make any sort of case. Since her legal argument had failed, this was her last hope to get the case dismissed before a trial.

"It is my contention that even if the law is changed—excuse

me, accepted—by this court as has been stated, there are no facts under which a cause of action may be sustained." Kit was not at all sure how this was being formed in her mind, but it sounded good and logical, and she felt inspired. "The plaintiff has not alleged the fundamental elements for a cause of action."

"We most certainly have, Your Honor," Wesley protested.

Seeming momentarily confused, the judge began looking at the copy of the complaint that lay before him. Kit took the opportunity to grab her own copy from her briefcase. "If I may," she said.

"Go on," said Judge Adams.

"The basis for liability is the intentional interference with a relationship, not merely negligent conduct. There are no facts in this complaint that establish intent."

With more consternation than anything else, Judge Adams looked at Wesley. "What say you to that, Mr. Wesley?"

"I . . ." Wesley groped for words, then suddenly appeared to have an idea. "If Your Honor please, we can take care of that right now. I am willing to put Miss Wynn on the stand for the sole purpose of giving us the facts necessary to take this to a jury."

"I protest," Kit said. "The complaint is insufficient."

For some reason, Judge Adams looked relieved. "Miss Shannon, this court allowed you to amend your motion to one for summary judgment. Fairness requires that we allow Mr. Wesley to amend his complaint now by taking the statement of Miss Wynn. I will allow it. Miss Wynn, if you will please step forward and be sworn."

Her haughty smile still in place, Elinor Wynn stood up and began to glide, in perfect social form, toward the witness stand. In her bearing was the confidence of someone who considered herself better than most others, especially a common lawyeress who had grown up on the wrong side of any track worth mentioning. Even more troubling, Elinor Wynn seemed to possess some secret knowledge.

Kit watched helplessly as Elinor was sworn as a witness.

————

Carrie Hanratty was thirty-two, but to Big Ed she looked a decade older. Today, at least. Tears had streaked her cheeks for the last twenty minutes. Ed understood. She was, after all, looking at him through the unforgiving bars of a cell at the county jail.

"Why won't they let you come home with me?" Carrie asked, for the tenth time.

"I told ya, honey. They have to bring me to a judge."

"But it's not true, what the papers say!"

"It's Hearst. He don't care if he rips me apart."

Carrie fixed her large brown eyes on her husband. "Did you . . ." She cut herself off and looked at the ground.

"No," Hanratty said softly. "I didn't do it the way they say, if that's what you're thinking."

"I'm sorry for even having the thought."

Hanratty reached through the bars of his cell and took Carrie's hands in his. They were soft and warm. She was so much younger than he. She looked scared and vulnerable.

The jailer, watching from his table at the end of the corridor, rapped his stick on the hard floor. "Now, Ed, none of that."

Hanratty kept his grip. "See here, Will. We've known each other a long time."

"Rules is rules, Ed."

"Will, you're not turning rat on me, are you?"

The guard looked embarrassed. Carrie slowly took her hands away. "Let's not make more trouble," she said.

Ed looked warmly at his wife of eight years. "How are the girls?"

"They're afraid. Rebecca cried herself to sleep last night."

The news caused Hanratty to grip the bars until his knuckles were white. He shouted, "No!"

Will was up in a blink, banging on the wall with his nightstick. "That's enough, Ed."

"I got to get out, Will!"

"You have to see the judge."

"How long?"

"I don't know that."

Ed Hanratty breathed in and out, rapidly, like he'd just taken a long flight of stairs. "Carrie, I need a lawyer."

"Who should it be?"

Ed did not hesitate. He had been thinking this over for a long time. "Get me Kit Shannon."

# Chapter 7

"YOU WERE ENGAGED to be married to Mr. Theodore Fox?" Barker Wesley said.

"I called him Teddy," Elinor Wynn replied, her voice catching in her throat.

Teddy? Kit had to bite her lip. What an accomplished liar Elinor was. But Judge Adams had seemed rapt from the moment Elinor took the witness stand and batted her eyes at him.

"Mr. Fox was your fiancé, is that correct?"

"Oh yes," Elinor said, nodding. The ostrich feather on her hat danced.

"How long were you engaged to Mr. Fox?"

"Almost a year, but he pledged himself to me a year before that."

That was a lie, too. But how was Kit going to disprove it? All Elinor had to do was convince the judge these were possible facts.

That was a very small threshold to cross before allowing an entire jury to hear the case.

"And were you in love with him?"

"With all my heart."

"And was he in love with you?"

"Objection," Kit said. "That calls for hearsay."

"The witness can tell us her impression," Judge Adams said. "Overruled."

"Very much in love with me," Elinor said.

"How did he show his love?"

"Through many kind acts. Through his words."

"Did he tell you that he loved you?"

"Many times."

"What else did he do?"

"Brought me flowers and gifts. Took me to romantic places for dinner. All of his attention was upon me. That is, until . . ." Elinor glared at Kit.

"Until what, Miss Wynn?"

"Kathleen Shannon arrived in town."

The crowd in the courtroom buzzed. Judge Adams made no move to silence them.

"What about wedding plans?" Barker Wesley said.

"Oh, we made them. We spoke about them constantly. Teddy wanted a large wedding. He wanted the whole city to know about our love."

Kit grabbed the arms of her chair and squeezed. *Steady,* she told herself. *Don't let the court see your emotions.*

"When did you know that Mr. Fox's heart had changed toward you?"

Elinor took a dainty handkerchief from her sleeve and dabbed her eyes with it, even though Kit could see clearly they were dry. "The very first moment I caught her flirting with him. It was shameless. I was attending a party at the Fairbank home. Teddy was to join me there. When the hour grew late, I went to look for him. I found Kathleen Shannon trying to cast a spell on him in a deserted hallway."

Kit shot to her feet. "Your Honor, must we continue with this?"

"Take your seat, Miss Shannon," the judge said.

"But, Your Honor—"

"Now, Miss Shannon."

She sat. But from that moment on she did not take her eyes off of Elinor Wynn's face. She wanted to study every powdery twitch.

Wesley questioned Elinor for another few minutes, eliciting enough of a story to satisfy legal requirements. When he turned the witness over to Kit, she knew if she did not rip a major hole in the fabric of Elinor's testimony there would be a very public trial.

"Miss Wynn." Kit did not attempt to hide the contempt in her voice. "When did you concoct this story?"

"I did not concoct anything," Elinor Wynn said.

"It has been nearly a year since some of these alleged incidents occurred, isn't that right?"

"I am not certain of the time."

"Have you lost your ability to count?"

"Objection," Barker said.

"Sustained."

Kit bore in on the witness. "Surely you remember your testimony in the murder trial of Mr. Fox? Do you recall that?"

Elinor Wynn shifted slightly. "Of course."

"Do you recall my cross-examining you?"

"Yes."

"Do you recall testifying that it was you who broke the engagement?"

"Yes, I do. But it was because Ted no longer loved me."

"I can produce the transcript if you like, Miss Wynn. You made no mention of Ted's affections shifting to me at that time, did you?"

"I did not see the need."

"But all of a sudden you do now?"

"Objection," said Wesley.

"Sustained."

Kit took a breath. "Why did you wait so long to file this action against me?"

"I was grieving," Elinor said.

"Were you grieving during Mr. Fox's murder trial?"

"I beg your pardon?"

"When you lied, on the stand, under oath?"

"Objection!" Barker Wesley said. "Incompetent, irrelevant, and immaterial."

"Sustained."

"Sustained?" Kit said. "This goes to her truthfulness, Your Honor."

"Sustained, Miss Shannon," the judge said. "I will assess Miss Wynn's credibility in this proceeding. Have you any more questions?"

"I take exception to Your Honor's ruling."

"Noted for the record."

Kit felt like all the air had been let out of her body. If she could not emphasize Elinor's perjury, there was nothing else with which to challenge her veracity. All that would be left was her version of the facts. That was all Elinor needed in this proceeding.

Kit looked helplessly around the room, scanning her mind for some further avenue of cross-examination. But it was useless. She was sure the judge was part of this scheme, going through the motions for the benefit of the public.

The fix was in.

---

An angry shroud enveloped Kit all the way back to her office. Now she had yet another non-paying client—this time herself—to take through a trial. There was nothing to do but get to work.

She was vigorously taking down notes of the proceeding when someone knocked on her door. It was a plain woman in a simple brown walking dress. Her face was etched with distress.

"My name is Carrie Hanratty," the woman said.

Kit invited her in to sit down. "Are you Officer Hanratty's sister?"

"His wife."

The news surprised her. Somehow Kit had never thought of Hanratty as being married. Rogue cops did not seem like family men.

More intriguing was why she was here. Mrs. Hanratty had to know it was Kit who exposed her husband's lies during the Chavez trial.

"My husband needs the services of an attorney," Mrs. Hanratty said.

"There are good ones in the city."

"He asked for you."

"Why would he—"

"That's all he told me. 'Get me Kit Shannon,' he said. Can you help him?"

"Mrs. Hanratty," Kit began, choosing her words carefully, "I don't think that I am the right person to represent your husband."

"But why not?"

"A lawyer must be able to present a zealous defense of a client."

"Can't you do that?"

"As you know, your husband was the arresting officer against a client of mine."

Mrs. Hanratty looked at her hands, clasping and unclasping them.

"There are lawyers who are very able to—"

"No one will want to defend him."

"I am sure that's not true."

Carrie Hanratty looked unconvinced. More, she looked lost. But Kit knew she could not take on this case. She had pledged only to defend those she was sure were innocent. And knowing Big Ed Hanratty, the odds were very much against that.

"He is not a bad man," Mrs. Hanratty said. "I know he's done some things in the past he shouldn't have. But I also know he is good deep down. If you could only see him with our children."

"How many?" Kit hadn't meant to sound so surprised.

"Two little girls. I cannot believe he would do what they say he did. Murder a man in cold blood! Never that, Miss Shannon. Never that . . ." Carrie's voice trailed off in a stifled sob.

Kit found herself wishing she could believe this woman. Though she did not know her in the slightest, she had a feeling about her. There was something good in her. But Kit quickly reminded herself that it was Ed Hanratty, not his wife, sitting in a jail cell accused of murder.

"Won't you at least see him, Miss Shannon?"

"I—"

"I know you are a woman of faith," Carrie Hanratty said. "The papers say. I have prayed for someone like you to represent my husband."

"Like me?"

Carrie Hanratty nodded. "He needs more than a lawyer, Miss Shannon. He needs to find his way to God." She paused, bowing her head, then said, "Will you see him? I have money. I can pay you."

Kit looked at the woman for a long moment, feeling her

anguish. She knew then she could not turn a cold shoulder to her. "I can't promise I will take his case."

"But you might?" Carrie Hanratty said, a thin tone of hope in her voice.

"I'll talk to him."

"Thank you," Carrie said. "Oh, thank you, Miss Shannon. That is all I ask."

# Chapter 8

SMILEY, AS THE CHIEF JAILER was known to all the lawyers in Los Angeles, was so named because his huge teeth could not be contained under mere lips. They were like piano keys, and gave the impression of a constant grin. But it was difficult to tell when his smile was friendly or acrimonious. A lawyer knew his standing with Smiley only by how the jailer chose to address him—a first name being a sign of approval.

Thus, when he nodded and said, "Good afternoon, Kit," she knew she had reached another pinnacle in her legal ascendancy.

"How are you, Smiley?" Kit said jauntily.

"I got the world on a string," Smiley said. "And the jail on a ring of keys. So what low form of life has brought you here this fine day?"

"May I remind you that those who are locked up are innocent until proven guilty?"

"And I'm the King of England."

"Very well, your highness. I'm here to see Edward Hanratty."

Smiley's eyebrows raised. "Indeed?"

"Just an interview."

Smiley stood up from his desk and reached for a large key ring. "I likes you, Kit. You been a square dealer with me. But let me give you a word of advice." He leaned toward her and whispered, "Don't go near this one. He's as good as dead."

A quick shiver ran up Kit's arms. Something in Smiley's voice bespoke of information that was more than mere rumor.

"Are you saying you know he's guilty?" Kit said.

"I will say this and say no more. Big Ed's going to swing for the good of the department. They'll see to it."

"Who?"

"That's all I can allow. And you never heard this from me. Come along then."

Kit followed Smiley through the big door that led to the cells. She noted that most of them were occupied. The smell of liquor was pervasive; half the men had no doubt been locked up on some sort of public drunkenness charge.

The deputy jailer, Will, stood up. "Give Miss Shannon ten minutes with Hanratty," Smiley said. Will nodded.

Ed Hanratty's cell was at the end of the row. Kit grabbed a wooden stool and set it in front of the cell.

"Thank God you came," Ed Hanratty said. His eyes were haggard, his shoulders sloped. This was not the same policeman who had once brazenly boasted about his ability to beat men into submission.

Kit sat on the stool, feeling an odd mix of contempt and pity. She was sure of only one thing now: She shouldn't have come. What possible good could her visit do but to offer him false hope for a few minutes?

"You saw my wife?" Hanratty said. He dragged his own stool

to the bars so he could sit close to her.

"I did."

"Then you'll take my case?"

Kit cleared her throat. "I told your wife I would see you. That's all."

"You mean you haven't . . ."

"Officer Hanratty, I told her I would offer her advice about whom to hire in your case—"

"But I want you."

"Frankly, I am surprised—after the Chavez case."

"That's why. I know how good you are."

"Officer Hanratty, I need to explain something to you. It is not my desire merely to be a successful trial lawyer, to win at all costs. I feel I must be on the side of truth . . . always."

Hanratty put up his hand. "You don't have to say more. You think I did it, don't you? You think I'm a murderer."

Kit could not dispute him. In her heart that is exactly what she thought.

"I can't blame you for thinkin' it," Hanratty said. "But I want you to know something here and now, Miss Shannon. I am a lot of things, but murderer ain't one of them. It was self-defense. I swear it."

"But according to the paper, witnesses—"

"Witnesses! Bought and paid for by Hearst himself!"

A fantastic story. Kit wondered how a jury would react to the idea. She found herself watching Hanratty's face as she would a hostile witness. She decided to treat him like one. Press him. See if his story held.

"Are you saying all of these people are lying?" Kit asked.

"Yes."

"There isn't a chance one of them could be telling the truth?"

"No chance."

"It is possible they heard things and reported them in a way they think is accurate?"

"But it's not like the paper says. He shot at me first."

Kit did not relent. "Did you go to the Braxton Arms with the intention of shooting Jay Chausser?"

"No, ma'am."

"Why did you go?"

"To arrest him."

"On what charge?"

"He was wanted in Indiana."

"How did you know this?"

"Because . . ." He looked down.

"Yes?"

"I was given a tip."

"By whom?"

"I can't say."

Kit shook her head. "Officer Hanratty, you will have to say."

"All I can tell you is it was a good tip. The *Examiner* reported it was true about Chausser being wanted."

"This is not about Chausser's background anymore. It's about your state of mind at the time of the shooting."

"And I'm tellin' you, in my mind I wanted to arrest him. That's all."

"Your mind was absolutely clear?"

Hanratty swallowed. "It was."

Kit was not at all sure. And if she had doubts, she could not defend him. A jury would see her doubts, and conviction would follow.

"Officer Hanratty, I came here at the request of your wife. I told her that I could not promise to represent you. And I cannot. I am—"

Hanratty slapped his big hands together. "Miss Shannon, I have never said this before in my life. But now I am. I am begging you. Please."

She looked at him and couldn't help thinking about the many men accused of crimes who might have begged Ed Hanratty not to hurt them. She thought about what Carrie Hanratty had told her, of her husband's spiritual need. "Are you a praying man?" she asked.

He looked at her. "Not since I was boy."

"It is not too late to start again."

The big policeman shook his head as he looked at the floor. "It's like I told my wife. I just wouldn't know how."

"Very simply. Like a child."

Hanratty said nothing. Confusion clouded his eyes. But in that confusion Kit saw a hint of sorrow.

"I will make you a deal, Officer," Kit said. "You pray. On your knees. And I will make an inquiry. I will come back at six o'clock this evening and we'll talk again. If I believe by then that you are telling the truth, I will be your lawyer. Agreed?"

"Pray?"

"On your knees."

Hanratty wiped his palms on his pants. "You will come back?"

"At six."

"All right, then, Miss Shannon. I agree."

Kit nodded and stood up. Outwardly she tried to look calm. But her spirit was anything but peaceful. She'd made a deal with Ed Hanratty because he asked her for mercy. But at the moment she had none to give.

---

The *Examiner* city room was a cacophony of voices and clacking typewriters. Kit did not bother asking if Tom Phelps was in.

She found him ensconced at his desk, tapping at his typewriter like a two-fingered madman.

"Busy?" she said.

Phelps looked up like he'd heard a gunshot. "Deadline. What brings the legal genius of the Western world around?"

Kit chafed at the sarcasm. Ever since Phelps had written some overdrawn stories about the Juan Chavez trial there had been a barrier between them. At one time she might have considered him a friend. But now she had come to accept there would always be adversarial tones in her relationship with the newspapers.

"I want to ask you about Hanratty."

Phelps looked incredulous. "You going to be his mouthpiece?"

"I have not made any commitment."

"How could you even think of it? He tried to bury Chavez. He's a bad cop."

"Is he?"

Phelps paused, snatched a cigarette paper from a tray on his desk, and began tapping tobacco into it. "You wouldn't be questioning the accuracy of this city's finest paper, would you?"

"It wouldn't be the first time, would it?"

"We will dig for a story no matter how deep it goes."

"I have heard it said that a Hearst paper will often dig beyond a story. Or around it."

Phelps licked the edge of the cigarette paper and rolled it in his fingers. He stuck the finished product in his mouth and lit it with a wooden match. "You got a particular story in mind?"

"Do you really think Ed Hanratty shot Jay Chausser in cold blood?"

"That's what the witnesses say."

"There were no eyewitnesses."

"How do you know?"

"Because it wasn't in your story. And I always believe a Tom Phelps story."

Phelps issued a plume of smoke. "If I didn't know you better, I would swear you were making sport of me."

"Give me the names of the witnesses, Tom."

"Can't do that."

"Off the record. Just so I can talk to them."

"Sorry, Kit, but the D.A. . . . ."

Kit almost jumped. "What about the district attorney?"

"Nothing. Forget I—"

"Is Davenport in this with Hearst?"

Phelps said nothing.

"Tell me."

Slamming his fists on the desk, Phelps stood up. "Where do you get the idea you can give me orders?"

"I want the truth."

"Read the *Examiner*."

"I said the truth."

"Listen, Miss High and Mighty, I report the news. It's all there. If you want more, you'll have to get it on your own. But if you want my advice, you'll stay as far away from Hanratty as possible."

"Why is everybody trying to warn me off him?"

"Because he's dirty. Between you and me, the D.A.'s got an airtight case. Besides, aren't you the one who said she couldn't defend someone unless she thought he was innocent?"

Kit nodded. "And when I walked in here today I didn't think that. But after this little conversation, I'm not so sure."

"I'm warning you, Kit."

"Another warning from the *Examiner*?"

"You'd be taking on one of the most powerful men in America. And I don't mean John Davenport."

"Hearst is not the judge or jury, Tom."

"Don't be so sure."

"You won't help me, then?"

"This isn't the case for you. If you think you can be some David against Goliath, I have to tell you you're crazy."

Kit studied Phelps. He was adamant. She turned to leave.

"Where are you going?" Phelps said.

Kit looked over her shoulder. "To find five smooth stones."

# Chapter 9

JOHN DAVENPORT'S SECRETARY sat at a desk in the anteroom of the D.A.'s office. When Kit gave her name and asked if she could see Davenport, the secretary's face turned grim.

"Do you have an appointment?" she said.

"No," Kit said. "This is a legal matter."

"I am sorry, but Mr. Davenport is unavailable."

"Would you mind telling him it concerns Officer Hanratty?"

The name stopped the secretary for a moment. Then she rose and went through a door behind her desk. A short moment later, John Davenport appeared.

"Miss Shannon," he said. "What a pleasant surprise. Come in."

The secretary, her face cold, huffily resumed her seat.

Kit entered Davenport's office. It was tastefully appointed, with two walls filled with books. It had an authoritative feel. This was the inner sanctum of the justice system of Los Angeles, for it was the district attorney who chose which cases to prosecute.

"My girl tells me this concerns Officer Hanratty," Davenport said. He sat in a swivel chair behind a large oak desk.

"It does," Kit said.

"And what, may I ask, is your interest in this matter?"

"I may represent him."

"May?"

"An agreement has not been reached."

Davenport entwined his fingers over his waistcoat. "Then I am under no compulsion to speak to you, am I?"

"That is true," Kit said. "But I was hoping that an exchange of information might be forthcoming."

"Why should I agree to that?" Davenport said.

"This city has just gone through one distressing trial."

Davenport's face tightened. "This is nothing like the Chavez case."

"It may be. The police force is on trial."

"No, Miss Shannon. One policeman is on trial. A bad policeman. He will be tried, convicted, and removed. We are committed to cleaning up the force one officer at a time."

"When was this commitment made?"

"What do you mean?"

"It certainly was not present during Juan's trial."

For a moment Davenport looked as if he had been slapped. Then cold steel swung back to his eyes. "You certainly have a jaundiced view of the district attorney's office."

"I only meant—"

"I know exactly what you meant. And I know about you. You have the idea that you are on God's mission here, don't you? Well, what makes you think we are not? Are you the only instrument of justice on God's earth?"

Kit was silent. Was that what he thought of her? Was that truly what she thought of herself?

"I am the District Attorney of Los Angeles County," Davenport said. "It is my duty to see that justice is done in every case I prosecute. So pardon me if I am a little offended at the suggestion that you are the only one with that interest in mind."

"I did not mean to offend."

"Didn't you?"

Perhaps she had. And it wasn't right. "I am sorry, Mr. Davenport."

Davenport grunted. "I accept your apology. I think you are a fine lawyer, Miss Shannon. I never thought I would say that to a member of the fair sex, but there it is. You serve your clients with zeal. But if I may give you a word of advice?"

"Yes?"

"You must temper that zeal with wisdom. It is for the good of your clients that you do so."

Kit felt he wanted to say more, and so she waited.

"I will tell you what would be wise in this matter," Davenport continued, "though I do not have to say a word to you about the case. Let's just call this a matter of professional courtesy, shall we?"

"All right," Kit said.

"There is a change in the wind, Miss Shannon. If this city is to take its place at the table of civilized society, we cannot allow the police, the enforcers of the law, to flout the very rules they are sworn to enforce."

Kit could have said those very words. But she sensed there was another angle in Davenport's mind.

"Now, we know Mr. Hanratty is a dirty cop," Davenport said. "He is not the only one, but he is one who has been caught. He must be made an example of. For the good of the city. I am personally going to send him to the gallows."

There was no doubt in Kit's mind that Davenport meant to do that very thing. And if Hanratty had committed murder, that would not be an unjust result. But she thought of Carrie Hanratty and his two little girls . . .

"This case is as compelling as any I have ever seen," Davenport said. "I don't mind telling you there are several witnesses who will testify against Hanratty. The lawyer who takes this case is going to lose it. But the right lawyer might be able to salvage something."

"What would that be?"

"His life." Davenport walked to his window and looked out at the city. "Who was it that said confession is good for the soul?"

"The thought, if not the exact expression, is found in Holy Scripture."

"Quite so. Then let us do what is right for Mr. Hanratty's soul," Davenport turned back to Kit, "by convincing him to do what is right under the law. If he will confess to his deed, I will not seek execution. I will recommend life in prison to the judge."

Kit mulled this over. On the face of it, this seemed the perfect solution. Hanratty would be spared. His wife and children would at least be able to visit him in prison. The police department would have a much-needed housecleaning. And perhaps the people of Los Angeles would start to trust their policemen.

Yet something pulled at Kit which she could not understand. There was some troubling aspect to all of this that she was unable to name. Was it merely a matter of trusting Davenport? She did not fully do so, but his offer seemed reasonable.

"What do you say, Miss Shannon?" Davenport asked.

Kit stood. "Have I your word on this? That if Officer Hanratty confesses, you will seek prison only?"

"You have my word as an officer of the court."

"Then I will convey your message to Officer Hanratty."

Davenport smiled. "Yes, you are a fine lawyer, Miss Shannon. And getting better even as we speak."

---

"Never!" Hanratty bellowed.

"You must consider it," Kit said.

"I will not confess to a crime I did not commit!"

Kit tried to keep her voice calm. "If you go to trial, they will hang you."

"I want my day in court."

"That is what I am concerned about."

Hanratty's eyes darkened. "I never thought you would sell me out."

"I would never—"

"I kept my part of the bargain," Hanratty said. "I got on my knees before Almighty God. For the sake of my family I asked for His help. I thought you would be the one to bring it to me. But I see now I was wrong."

"Officer, I—"

"Go on. Leave me be."

"Won't you—"

"I said leave me!" Hanratty turned his back on her and walked to the other side of his cell. His head hung low, his chin resting against his chest.

Kit felt a hand on her shoulder. It was the young jailer, Will. "Time to go, miss."

# Chapter 10

DARKNESS WAS UPON the city by the time Kit returned to her office. But instead of entering her own room, she walked down the corridor, where she saw light coming from under the door of the office of Earl Rogers. She let herself in.

The light was from a single oil lamp on the desk. Rogers, his tie loosened, was alone, vigorously writing notes. He did not see her, so intent was he on his work. She looked at him for a moment in admiration. Yes, he was a skilled orator and brilliant thinker. But he worked harder than any man she had ever known.

"Earl?"

He looked up, startled. "Why, you little church mouse! What are you doing sneaking around like that?"

"May I speak with you?"

Rogers set his pen down. "For you, Kit Shannon, my ear is always ready."

She sat down across from him. "I have a matter that confuses me."

"Welcome to the world, my dear."

"I would like to know what you would do."

"Get paid up front."

"Earl."

"What is it?"

"It concerns Ed Hanratty."

Rogers threw his hands in the air. "I knew it! Kit Shannon, the angel of mercy, out to save all mankind. Even a lousy cop."

"You don't understand."

"Don't I? Kit, I've understood you ever since you bumped into me on the courthouse steps. Remember?"

"Of course."

"You had the look in your eye of the true believer. And to be fair, that has served you well to this point. But to represent Hanratty?"

"I am not representing him."

"Perhaps you had better explain."

"I went to see the district attorney today."

"You saw Davenport himself?"

"Yes."

"And what did the Prince of Darkness have to say?"

"He seemed reasonable to me."

"Don't fool yourself. Put eyes in the back of your head when you deal with the devil. Why did you see him?"

"To talk about Hanratty. I went to see Hanratty in jail at the request of his wife. He swears he is innocent."

"Of course. I haven't met a guilty man yet who didn't swear he was innocent."

"So I went to see what Mr. Davenport had on him."

"And?"

"He sounds confident of his case."

"He should, if the *Examiner* stories are any indication."

"He said he would seek the gallows, unless I were to convince Officer Hanratty to confess. Then he would give him a life sentence in prison."

At this, Earl Rogers grew solemn. He put his fingertips together, as he often did when thinking deeply. Finally he said, "I hate seeing anyone executed by the State. Even if it's a murdering cop. What did Hanratty say to all this?"

"He absolutely refused to consider it. He says he will never confess to something he did not do."

"And what do you think, Kit? Do you think he is guilty as charged?"

Kit was about to say *yes*, but she stopped. "I don't know. I honestly don't know. Part of me thinks he is."

"And the other part?"

"I suppose there is a chance he's telling the truth."

Rogers eyed her steadily. "Then take this case."

"Take it?"

"Oh, I know about your scruples," Rogers said. "You won't defend the guilty. Well, it's time you grew up a little."

Only Earl Rogers could talk to her this way, like a father. In a sense that's what he was, her father in the profession of law. She would not be practicing were it not for his help.

"You are a defense lawyer, Kit, and our system depends on you. When you have a client accused of a crime, it is your job under the Constitution to defend him."

"But if the evidence is strongly against him?"

"Then you let the jury decide. But when the State proposes to execute a man, or take away his liberty, they must prove their case beyond a reasonable doubt. If we don't give a vigorous defense to make the State prove its case, then the innocent will truly suffer.

The State will begin to prosecute people just because it doesn't like them. Maybe they don't like a man's politics. Or the color of his skin."

Kit thought of Juan Chavez, how close he had come to being imprisoned unjustly.

"We are essential, Kit. Every time a lawyer puts the State to the test, he makes justice a little more secure."

Still torn, Kit pondered his words. What Earl Rogers said went to the very heart of the criminal justice system. As flawed as it might be, she knew from history it was the best yet devised by man. And at the very center of it was dignity for the individual. That was also the heart of the Bible. "What do you think I should do?" she said.

"I'll tell you what I would do. Try the case at the preliminary hearing."

*The preliminary?* That was when the prosecution presented only a minimal case in order to convince a judge there was enough cause for a trial. Rarely did the defense put on its own case at that time.

"Here is why," Rogers said. "First, juries here don't like the cops. They see them as perjurers, Simon Legrees, flatfeet. Second, you'll catch Davenport before he can manufacture anything. Third, you'll have a chance to see the evidence full on, and so will your client. And then Hanratty will not be able to deny it. Nor his wife. He can then change his plea to guilty, and you won't have to proceed to a trial.

"That's one way to go. The other is that you might be able to prove his innocence. He's probably as guilty as sin, but even a cop should have the benefits of a citizen when he's being tried for murder."

Rogers got up from his desk and sat in the chair next to Kit. "In the old days, cases would be tried on the field of honor. The judges would leave it to God to sort out who was guilty and who was not. We don't use lances anymore. We use the law and the presumption of innocence. You can try this case at the preliminary, Kit, and let God do the sorting."

Yes, that was the heart of the Bible, too. God was in control. "Then that is what I will do," Kit said.

# Chapter 11

ON MONDAY MORNING, after a weekend spent in jail, Officer Ed Hanratty appeared in court for his arraignment. As it always seemed when Kit Shannon was involved, the spectators and press were out in full force. It was, in fact, going to be what the new major league baseball teams called a doubleheader. In the afternoon Kit would be picking a jury in the Elinor Wynn lawsuit. The press could simply follow her from courtroom to courtroom, scribbling stories as they went.

The judge in Hanratty's case, Gerard Stuart Reems, was relatively young for a presiding magistrate. In his early forties, he had an intelligent face and a sense of fairness. Kit had tried a simple one-day trial before him two months before. After the close of the prosecution's evidence, on her motion, he had dismissed the case for lack of evidence. She wondered if lightning could strike twice.

After welcoming the lawyers, Judge Reems got down to business. A deputy sheriff brought Ed Hanratty into the courtroom, his hands shackled in front of him. Kit saw Carrie Hanratty in the first row, trying to control her emotions.

"All right," Reems said, "in the matter of the People of the State of California against Edward Hanratty"—the judge looked at the policeman—"you are being charged, sir, under Penal Code section 187, murder, the unlawful killing of a human being, with malice aforethought. This is a charge of murder in the first degree. You understand the charge against you, sir?"

Ed Hanratty said, "I do."

"To the charge of murder in the first degree, how do you plead? Guilty or not guilty?"

A stillness fell over the courtroom. "Not guilty," Hanratty said.

As the court erupted in voices Kit put her hand on Hanratty's arm. Reems was gaveling for order even as Davenport was shouting, "Your Honor!"

After more pounding with the gavel, silence returned. Reems said, "You wish to be heard, Mr. Davenport?"

The district attorney gave Kit an angry glance. "I was under the impression that we had an agreement with the defense."

"Agreement?"

"A plea agreement, Your Honor."

"Is that so, Miss Shannon?"

"No, Your Honor," Kit said. "The offer was made and was rejected by my client."

Davenport made some huffing sounds, like a train leaving a station.

"If there is no agreement," Judge Reems said, "then I must accept the plea of not guilty and set this matter for preliminary hearing. Any further objections? Then the preliminary will be three weeks from today."

"One request, Your Honor," Kit said.

Judge Reems looked at her.

"In the matter of incarceration," Kit said. "I ask that my client be released forthwith to return to his home and family."

"I object," Davenport said firmly.

"Your Honor," Kit said, "Ed Hanratty is a family man. His wife is sitting in the first row. He has two little girls. He is not going to flee this city. He wishes to have his day in court."

"This is a dangerous man," Davenport said. "He has not only killed in cold blood, he—"

"Allegedly, Your Honor. Mr. Davenport surely knows an accused is innocent until proven guilty."

"Nevertheless, Mr. Hanratty has a past record of behavior that can only be described as reckless."

*And which you did not object to before today,* Kit thought bitterly.

Judge Reems reposed a moment. "Seeing as how this is a first-degree murder charge, Miss Shannon, I cannot take the risk of allowing your client to roam free. I will, however, set bail at twenty-thousand dollars. If there is nothing else, court is adjourned."

There was nothing else. Ed Hanratty was taken back to his cell. Kit knew there was no way he or his wife could afford bail. Ed Hanratty would be spending the next three weeks in jail.

———

At one-thirty, Kit Shannon picked a jury.

She was seething, trying as best she could not to let her anger become apparent to the jurors so that they would be prejudiced against her. But the very idea of having to defend herself in a trial against such a scurrilous charge was not helping her temper.

The courtroom of Judge Franklin Adams was predictably filled. There were even spectators standing against the back wall. The *Examiner* had turned this into another juicy public event. Kit had heard the story was being run in the Hearst papers in New York, San Francisco, and Chicago. So she had become a national name, like Clarence Darrow, only this wasn't for her work as a lawyer.

Jury selection took only one hour. Kit accepted the first twelve men who were seated. She wanted them to know she didn't need to engage in a lengthy *voir dire.* The message she sought to send was that any twelve men, good and true, who heard this nonsense could not fail to reject Elinor Wynn's preposterous case.

So she prayed. She would get no help from the judge, she was certain. Her only hope was with these twelve men—and the appellate court, if need be.

Barker Wesley called Elinor Wynn to the stand. Once again, she was dressed like some European diva. This time she wore a gown of white crepe de chine with puff sleeves and lace frills. Her hat of silk velvet was dominated by a wide band of white satin from which sprouted feathers. She could have been auditioning for the leading role in some Clyde Fitch play.

Barker Wesley once again led Elinor through her story. Kit sat back and said nothing. Wesley seemed a bit surprised, as if he expected Kit to object at various points. She did not, and his examination was finished in less than thirty minutes.

"Your witness," he said as he returned to his seat.

"No questions," Kit said.

The courtroom spectators gave murmuring voice to this surprising twist. Even Judge Adams looked shocked. "You have nothing for this witness?"

"No, Your Honor."

"Then, I suppose, the witness is dismissed," Judge Adams said.

There was a moment's pause, when no one seemed to quite know what to do. Then Barker Wesley stood and said, "The plaintiff rests."

Judge Adams looked at Kit. "Have you any witnesses to call, Miss Shannon?"

"Yes, Your Honor. I call Kathleen Shannon to the stand."

More voices murmuring, and a few of the press boys laughed and scribbled vigorous notes.

Kit walked to the clerk, placed her left hand on the Holy Bible, raised her right hand, and was sworn in. She took the witness stand and looked directly at the jurors. They were looking back at her like she was the new exhibit at the zoo.

"Gentlemen," she said, "I have just sworn an oath to tell you the truth, the whole truth, and nothing but the truth. I figured you should get that from at least one of the witnesses here today."

Laughter arose in the courtroom, and from a few of the jurors.

"Objection!" Barker Wesley said. "This is a speech, not an examination."

"Your Honor," Kit said, "if Mr. Wesley would like me to jump up and down off this chair, I can oblige. But I think we should not waste the court's time. If I may be allowed to give my testimony in my own way, we can expedite matters considerably."

Judge Adams looked like he had no idea what to do. His lower lip quivered for a moment, and then he looked at Wesley.

The lawyer responded. "Your Honor, if you please. Miss Shannon is merely going to try to inflame this jury."

"No, Your Honor, I intend to put out the flame of lies ignited by Mr. Wesley's client."

"All right," Adams said. "That will be enough. Miss Shannon, I am not going to allow you to make speeches. You will limit your testimony to the facts, if any, that you have personal knowledge of. Nothing more. Is that understood?"

"Yes, Your Honor."

"Continue."

Kit thought for a moment, then looked once more at the jury.

"Miss Wynn has told you about the great love she says was professed to her by Ted Fox. Unfortunately, Mr. Fox is not here to refute this. You must decide, between the two of us, who is the more credible. I ask you to look into my eyes, gentlemen, as I tell you my side of this tale."

The jurors did as she requested. Kit also felt every other eye in the courtroom watching her.

"At no time did I attempt to misdirect the affections of Ted Fox. To the contrary, I respected his engagement to Miss Wynn. When the engagement was broken, and after the trial in which I was his lawyer, I did have some social engagements with him. I will say to you honestly that I was attracted to him. But there was something between us that prevented me from giving him my heart, even though he was completely free."

Kit paused as some of the jurors leaned forward. "Gentlemen, I am a Christian, and my faith is the most important aspect of my life. Mr. Fox did not share that faith, and thus I could not consent that our courtship continue. I thought that—"

"Objection," Barker Wesley said. "Miss Shannon's testimony about religion is irrelevant."

"Sustained."

"Exception, Your Honor!" Kit said. This was patently unfair.

"And," the judge added, "I am going to have your statements stricken from the record."

Kit was speechless with anger.

To the jurors, Adams said, "Gentlemen, I instruct you to disregard the testimony of Miss Shannon. It is to have no bearing on your deliberations."

The courtroom was growing loud with voices as Kit looked at the judge in disbelief. She was vaguely aware the courtroom door was opening. A deputy sheriff moved to prevent anyone else from entering the crowded chamber.

"Your Honor," Kit said, "how can I—"

"You may step down, Miss Shannon," Adams said. Then he began to pound his gavel. "Order!"

"Let me pass!" a voice cried out. Kit looked to the door, as did everyone else in the courtroom. And she was not the only one who gasped.

There in the doorway stood Ted Fox.

Time seemed to stand motionless, and Kit thought she was lost in a dream.

But then he spoke again, and Kit knew Ted Fox was as real as the courtroom. "Am I too late for this circus?" he said.

# Chapter 12

AUNT FREDDY SAT ON her terrace as the afternoon sun began descending on the Pacific horizon. Soon another day would be past, and she could not shake the feeling that had been coming to her more and more often now—that the number of days she had left on this earth were few.

That feeling was precisely why she had summoned Professor Stillwater to her home, why she was having her palm read for the fourth time in a month. "The lines become clearer each time," the professor told her. His fee of fifty dollars per reading was eminently reasonable. Many of the wealthy women of Los Angeles felt the same way.

"You are trembling," Stillwater said softly. Sometimes his appearance was like that of a Russian prince—thin black mustache, angular features, and a cultured voice that was a symphony for her ears. With so much coarseness in the city, it was ever so pleasant to be around a learned and courtly man.

"I suppose I am," Freddy said. "My nerves are always fluttering these days. Or so it seems."

"I have noticed, of course."

"Oh, of course. I cannot hide anything from you, can I?"

"This is part of my gift, no?"

"How silly of me."

"Have I been a comfort to you?"

Face flushing slightly, Freddy said, "Yes, yes. But I must confess I am fearful of the future. Do you see anything about my well-being?"

Stillwater smiled and looked at Freddy's palm. With his right index finger he traced a pattern on her skin. "I see good health for you in the foreseeable future."

"Truly?"

"And something else, of monumental importance. The chance to help many others like yourself."

"Do tell!" Freddy was beginning to forget her physical ailments in light of the professor's predictions.

"I see here a great legacy. The name of Frederica Fairbank upon many lips, forever."

"Forever?"

"Possibly."

"Only possibly?"

"There is a cloudiness here. A decision you must make."

She shuddered. "What is it?"

"As yet I cannot tell."

"Look harder."

Stillwater smiled and patted her hand. "My dear Mrs. Fairbank, my gift cannot be forced by my will. This will require more time. If you would like, I will return in the coming days to study further."

"Oh yes!"

"But I hesitate. I do not wish to . . ."

"Speak plainly."

"Thank you. I do not wish to take money from you. Perhaps in a month—"

"No! I cannot wait that long. Professor, you are too modest. Let me decide how I shall spend my own money."

Stillwater smiled. "I would not have it any other way, Mrs. Fairbank."

———

Elinor Wynn fainted into Barker Wesley's arms.

Amid the roar of voices in the courtroom, the pounding of Judge Adams' gavel was almost lost, and Wesley's howls of protest were muffled by the feathers of Elinor Wynn's hat fluffing into his mouth.

Kit herself felt she might fall right out of the witness chair. Ted Fox was standing in the middle of a throng looking directly at her, smiling.

Finally order was restored, and Judge Adams bellowed, "What is the meaning of this intrusion?"

"My name is Theodore Fox," Ted said. "I believe I have been mentioned in this charade."

Judge Adams' face turned instantly pale. Barker Wesley, who by this time had lowered his client to the floor, seemed torn between Elinor's well-being and the shock of seeing Ted standing on crutches a few feet away.

Kit stood and walked down from the witness chair. "I have one more witness to call," she said. "Theodore Fox."

Not even Judge Adams would be able to stop this. There was no objection possible from Barker Wesley that would be grounded in law. Ted Fox came forward to be sworn. "Nice to see you again, Miss Shannon," he whispered as he walked by.

"Your Honor," Wesley said weakly, "in view of the condition of Miss Wynn, I would request a recess and a conference in chambers."

"Granted," Adams said quickly, and just as quickly he left the bench.

In the judge's chambers, Barker Wesley looked like Robert E. Lee at Appomattox. "In view of this development," he told the judge, "I believe it would be in the best interest of my client if Your Honor dismissed the action forthwith."

"Yes," said Adams, "it would seem to be so."

"Not so fast," Kit said.

Both men looked at her as if she were holding a gun to them.

"I can well understand Mr. Wesley's concern that Mr. Fox would tell the whole truth to the jury in a public forum. I can well understand his concern that Miss Wynn might expire under the strain. I can also understand his reticence to have any further testimony come out, as it would no doubt result in enough fodder for a counter suit against his client."

The judge and lawyer were silent.

"I will not oppose the motion to dismiss," Kit said, "provided Mr. Wesley agree that my legal fee will be taken care of by his side of the dispute."

Wesley opened his mouth to protest, but Adams quickly interrupted. "Pay the woman, Barker. You're licked."

———

Gus was waiting for them in a motorized carriage that was sputtering on the street. Kit was amazed Ted could take the stairs so quickly on his crutches. With a horde of newspapermen and curiosity seekers trailing them from the courtroom, the two managed to hop into the carriage just ahead of the pack.

Issuing a loud bang, the conveyance lurched forward. The

reporters back at the courthouse were wildly hailing horse-drawn cabs. A chase was on.

"Now tell me," Ted said over the auto's racket, "were you surprised to see me?"

"Ted Fox, what on earth?" Kit could hardly believe he was here, though she had to admit his timing was exquisite.

He took her arm. "I got here as quickly as I could."

"But how—"

"I have a story to tell you."

The noise from the car, mixed with the dust that was flying, would not make for a tranquil tale. Kit tied the sash of her hat more securely under her chin, not only so it would stay on her head, but to keep the dirt out of her hair.

They were speeding toward the ocean, the road becoming bumpier until it turned into little more than a rutted path. Kit saw no sign of the pursuing mob behind them. Gus drove with a placid attitude past orchards and fields, toward the sun.

Finally, Gus pulled the car to a stop at the edge of an unplowed field. As soon as the car's engine shut down, Kit could hear the cry of sea gulls in the near distance. The smell of something like wild onion wafted through the air—not an unpleasant odor at all but rather hinting at unregulated nature and purity. Part of God's untouched creation.

Alighting on his right leg, Ted helped Kit out of the auto as Gus sat with his arms folded. Ted got his crutches and helped Kit down.

"Walk with me," he said.

They went several yards away from the auto until Ted stopped and turned toward her. She saw his face then in the unforgiving light of the sun. It shocked her. He seemed to have aged far beyond the mere months he had been gone. More, there was an etched sadness there, as if some sculptor had endeavored to convey a permanent sense of melancholy in his subject.

Kit wanted to take that face in her hands and comfort it, caress it until it came back to her as it was before—young and hopeful, unafraid and upturned toward the future. But she did not know if he wanted that, and so she held back.

"You hit the Chicago papers, you know," he said. "When I read about Elinor's suit, I had to come back. I could not allow her to get away with such a fraud, especially at your expense."

"I must say you made quite an entrance," Kit said with a lilt. There was no similar jovial tone reflected in Ted's eyes.

"I did not intend to return," Ted said. "I was living in a flop-house in Chicago, trying to make a decision."

"What decision?"

"Whether to live or die."

The matter-of-fact way he said those words made Kit tremble. How close he must have been to choosing death. She could see it in his expression.

"There is a side of life that is almost like death," he said. "I lived it. I was one of the people without faces. The ones who cannot work except for paltry wages because they are sick or injured or simply too old. Most are without homes. At night they can't sleep in the parks. The cops won't let them. So they walk. Walk around at night looking for food. They finally find places in alleys and old boxcars to sleep, until rousted by railroad bulls or police. They are driven out of sight in the daytime so the wealthy and respectable don't have to look upon them."

A flare of remembrance lit Kit's mind. She had seen and known such people when she lived on the lower east side of New York.

"One night I stood on the shore of the great lake," Ted said. "The wind was so cold it turned my bones to ice. I looked up into the sky and saw the stars. That night they were bright, like millions of candles in windows. I asked myself if there was anyone behind those windows. And then I looked at the blackness of the water. If

I should disappear under that water, would anyone take notice? Or would I just be like one of those candles, going out?"

"There would have been one who noticed," Kit said. "The One who watches over all, even the apparently unseen."

Ted smiled, though hesitantly. "I wondered about that, and that is what kept me from jumping. I'm a curious sort. I wanted to give myself one more chance to find out if there is really a purpose to all of this."

Kit knew he meant life itself. "And what have you found?"

"You." He paused briefly before continuing. "The very next day I snatched a Chicago paper, and what did I see on the front page?"

"The very front?" Kit said, placing her hand on her chest.

"Scandal knows no boundaries," Ted said.

Kit wondered in amazement at the speed of modern news reporting. In just days a story in Los Angeles could be picked up in other cities with the use of a telegraph. But why did it have to be her story?

"So," Ted said, "I gathered up all the money I had—I was working in a slaughterhouse—and caught a train. I had not planned such a theatrical entrance. I just got here as fast as I could."

"And now you are here," Kit said, and without giving it a thought, she put out her hand and grasped his. She looked into his eyes, willing him comfort. He seemed for a moment to receive it, then gently removed his hand.

Looking at the ground, Ted said, "You have been a great friend to me, and I'm sorry that you must have worried about my condition."

"I did for a time," Kit said.

"Only a time?"

"I placed you in God's hands through my many prayers. Have you thought that it might have been God's own hand that kept you from jumping that night? That it was God's hand that lit those candles?"

When he gazed at her quizzically, Kit reached out for his hand again. This time she held it firmly. "We shall not talk of it now. Now it is enough that you are home again. And we shall dine together."

Ted cocked his head. "Isn't it customary for the gentleman to ask the lady?"

Kit smiled. "When have you ever known me to be a slave to custom?"

# Chapter 13

THE MOON ROSE OVER the café on Olvera Street. The air was balmy, so Kit and Ted sat at an outside table, facing the Plaza, a lone candle giving spark to their eyes.

In so many ways this was the Los Angeles Kit had come to love, a part of the city shown to her by Corazón and some of Kit's own clients. Here were good, hardworking people, most of them from families dating back to Spanish rule. And the food—spicy and warm and substantial—was unique and satisfying.

Now, with Ted sitting across from her, it seemed her experience in California had come full circle. Yet there was a gap in that circle, something Kit could not quite identify. Ted, for his part, gave amiable conversation, but he was holding something in reserve.

A jovial waiter served them a plate of warm tortillas and a bowl of fresh salsa. Kit was able to converse with him in Spanish. Corazón had taught her well.

"You speak almost like a native," Ted said.

"Hardly that," Kit said. "I still have some way to go. The other day I tried to tell a friend of Corazón's that I thought she was very elegant, and Corazón burst out laughing. When I finally calmed her down, she told me I had very respectfully called her friend a chair."

Ted laughed a little, seeming to check himself as he did so. As he reached for a tortilla, Kit said, "May I offer a prayer of thanks?"

Ted snatched back his arm. He looked embarrassed as he nodded.

"Thank you," Kit said. She closed her eyes and prayed, thanking God for His provision of daily bread and also for the safe return of Ted to the city he called home. When she looked up Ted was staring at her, emptily. She had no idea if he had joined her in prayer or not.

From the Plaza came the sound of a mariachi band—guitars and violins and the joyous music of old Mexico. It broke the silence that hung between Ted and Kit. It was hopeful music, which is why Kit had warmed to it the first time she'd heard it.

"Are your affairs in order upon your return?" Kit said.

"What do you mean by that?" said Ted.

"If there are legal matters that need your attention, I shall be happy to help."

"Don't think so. There's some money, not much. I can get by."

Kit knew that Ted's mother had not had a substantial estate at the time she died. There were other dealings that Kit did not fully know about, but she thought there were some underhanded events in the past.

"I have my mother's house," Ted said. "I'll put up there for a while."

"A while?"

"Until I decide what to do."

Kit hesitated, then asked, "Won't you be staying?"

Ted's answer was as if from a distance. "How can I know that? The future is anything but certain. I found that out."

His words offered an opening—Kit felt it, as she often did when interviewing a client. To get to the heart of a case you had to first get to the heart of the client. It would often take a lot of prodding, but then a moment would come when the door, however slightly, was opened. That moment was here.

"There are different certainties," Kit said. "I don't know what tomorrow may hold, but I am certain there is One who holds me."

"I always admired your easy faith," Ted said.

"It is not always so easy. But it is always certain."

"Well, there is a goodness to the Christian religion one cannot deny. There are rules that would make us better people."

"I don't believe it is a religion of rules."

"I know you don't." His directness startled her, and Kit wanted him to continue. But he stopped. Kit, suddenly uncomfortable, lifted her cup of water and sipped. The mariachi music had stopped.

When she couldn't stand the silence any longer, Kit said, "What about the plane?"

It was then that something seemed to burst inside Ted, like the waters of a dam. He tried to hold them back, but it was clearly a struggle. "Why did you bring that up?"

"I only thought—"

"Don't think. About that. About flying." He looked away.

Kit thought she should let the matter go. But another part of her reasoned that if she did not say something now, she would never get the chance again.

"Flying is your life," she said.

"*Was* my life."

"But why can it not be so again?"

"Where is that waiter?" Ted said, turning his head toward the doors of the café. "Can't we get some real food around here?"

"Ted." She waited for him to look at her. "There is no reason you can't—"

"Isn't there?"

She did not know what he meant, and the confusion must have been apparent in her face, for Ted said, "If you are so certain about things, Kit, then tell me why God did this to me."

"Did this to you?"

"Yes. You once told me the voice of God was telling me to fly. Why, then, did He take me down? Why did He take my leg?"

As if to provide what the theater called comic relief, the mariachi band struck up another song, even more sprightly than the last. Yet the situation was anything but comic—Ted's gaze bore in on her, willing her to answer.

"That's not something I can answer," she said.

Ted sat back, issuing a heavy breath. "I thought not."

"Did you, now?" The sharpness in her voice surprised her. But she was not going to stop. "You think that little of me?"

"No, Kit."

"The answer has to come from God himself, and only to you."

"And where do I get this answer?"

"You ask for it. You search for it. And it may surprise you."

"I've been surprised enough."

"God is not finished with you."

He stared at her for a long moment, then said, "I believe there is a force that made the world. Those starry candles . . . someone had to make them. But does this creator care what happens down here?"

"Yes."

"And that is your belief. Leave me to my own."

"I will not."

Ted looked as if he'd been poked by a stick. "And just what do you mean by that?"

"I cannot leave you to your own beliefs."

"How can you—"

"Ted, listen to me."

Ted leaned back, arms folded. "Do I have a choice, Miss Shannon?"

"Tonight you do not. You are my guest here, remember?"

"And now you add the indignity of reminding me that a woman is buying my dinner."

Kit did not know if he was joking or not. His demeanor had not changed. But neither had her intention. "I want you to make me one promise. Will you do it?"

"You ask me for a pledge before I hear the terms?"

"You can trust me."

His smile was wry. "Oh, can I now? You are an Irish charmer, aren't you?"

"I want to give you something."

"A gift, is it? A bribe?"

"No, Ted. Something better." She reached for her briefcase, which was her constant companion now, and set the familiar leather-bound book on the table.

Ted looked at it. "Your Bible?"

"It was my father's. It is the dearest possession I own. I want to lend it to you. I want you to promise that you will read it."

Ted tenderly placed his hand on it. He rubbed the leather gently. "I've not read the Book, except for familiar passages on special occasions."

"Begin with the Gospels," Kit said. "I have found that the life of the Savior is the best place to start."

He nodded, but without commitment.

Ted was still engulfed in the torment that had taken him away from the city in the first place. It was a torment that kept the gulf between them wide and precarious, and Kit wondered, with a sinking heart, if it could ever be crossed.

# Chapter 14

A NIGHT'S SLEEP did not dissipate the unease Kit felt about Ted. Nor did the walk from the Westminster Hotel for Women to her office.

And it increased when she found the note, written on expensive stationery, slipped under her office door.

Signed by William Randolph Hearst, it requested—no, demanded, if one read carefully—that Kit meet him in the dining hall of the Nadeau Hotel promptly at noon. Undoubtedly his summons was related to the Hanratty case, but why? All sorts of possible answers came to mind, none of them making quite enough sense.

Perhaps, unwittingly, Mr. Hearst would give her information that would help her client. Would a *mea culpa* be too much to hope for from the titan of yellow journalism?

Kit would not be holding her breath. But she did find it increasingly difficult to concentrate as she went about her morning work. She was out the door of her office at exactly 11:45.

When she got to the Nadeau Hotel, she noticed several police-men milling about the street. Inside, she walked to the desk and asked if Mr. Hearst was in for Kathleen Shannon. The formal man behind the desk immediately walked her through the lobby—under the hotel's magnificent chandelier—and into the formal din-ing room. It was empty, save for a solitary man sipping from a china cup and reading a newspaper.

"Mr. Hearst," the clerk announced.

The man looked up, scanned Kit for a moment, then stood. "Miss Shannon, I presume?"

"How do you do?" Kit said tentatively.

"Please." Hearst motioned for her to sit. He nodded to the clerk, who poured a cup of tea for Kit from the pot on the table.

"I have secured this room for our meeting," Hearst said. He had an educated voice and manner about him, though in his casual suit he appeared to be trying to look like an ordinary businessman.

Kit knew, however, that he was anything but ordinary. His face was not remarkable and his hair, parted in the middle, was rather thin. But he had the look of massive wealth and power about the eyes. A man who knew what he had and how to use it.

"I value privacy," Hearst added.

He said it as if to indicate that anything he valued would be his. A man used to getting what he wants. She had seen his kind before—Heath Sloate came to mind—but never with the power Hearst wielded. Both financially and in influence, William Ran-dolph Hearst was a man to be reckoned with. Elected to Congress in New York, he had nearly won the nomination as the Democrats' candidate for the presidency, for a fall campaign against Teddy Roosevelt.

"They tell me you are a woman of faith," Hearst said.

"Who are 'they'?"

"My minions," Hearst said with a lilt. "In the newspaper business, information is everything."

"Have you been investigating me?"

"I investigate everyone of importance." Hearst did not say this defensively, but with an openness that suggested he had nothing to hide. "And you, Miss Shannon, are of some note in this community."

Kit took a sip of tea, waiting for him to reach his point.

Hearst continued, "I admire strong convictions. I have a few myself. Justice for the common man, for instance. You share that sentiment."

"Yes," Kit said. "That is why I am in the practice of law."

"And is your passion for justice tied to your faith?"

"It is the natural outcome of it."

"Well said. To the point, then. Your desire to see justice for the man on the street, which I share, cannot be viewed in isolation. There are institutions in our society that work against these interests. My papers take on these institutions, and that is why the man on the street values what we say."

Kit anticipated where he was leading. "Because you are taking on the Los Angeles police?"

Hearst narrowed his gaze. "Quite so."

"I agree with that cause. Our police force must be law abiding. But a cause cannot ever be allowed to compromise the rights of individual citizens."

"Sometimes it must, for the greater good."

"Here we part company, Mr. Hearst. My client has proclaimed that he is innocent."

"Do you really believe him?"

"At this point, I must. He has the presumption of innocence."

"And the certainty of the gallows." Hearst issued an impatient sigh. "Hanratty is as guilty as sin, and the *Examiner* has proved it."

"The *Examiner* is not a judge or jury."

"No, it is better. It can go where the evidence leads without worrying about lawyers muddying up the water."

"Mr. Hearst, I don't think you called me here to formally debate the merits of our justice system."

An impish smile came to Hearst's lips. "I have no desire to see your client hang, but he will. If necessary, I will make it my mission to see that he does. I won't let anyone stand in my way."

Kit waited, wondering just what methods he was prepared to use.

"That would put me in a position to fight you," Hearst said. "And I don't want to do that. You are too good a lawyer, and a remarkable woman. I think you are someone I can use."

"How so?"

"The *Examiner* needs a general counsel. I think you are the person for it."

"Lawyer for your newspaper?"

"For a start. If I like the results, a national position might be arranged. At top salary, of course."

William Randolph Hearst offering her top salary? No matter what it was, it would be more money than she could ever garner defending criminals.

"Clarence Darrow serves in this capacity for my Chicago paper," Hearst added. "You and he are old friends, I believe."

"We've met," Kit said.

"The great debate, yes. I understand you acquitted yourself admirably."

"Your paper said as much."

Hearst smiled. "I always believe what I read in my papers. I am prepared to pay you a bonus here and now. Would ten thousand dollars do the trick?"

Some trick indeed. "A generous offer, Mr. Hearst."

"Then we have a deal?"

"I will have to think about it. It's so sudden."

"Of course, it will require that you withdraw as Mr. Hanratty's lawyer."

Hearst drummed his fingers on the table. It was the first sign of nervousness Kit had observed in him. Had he been a witness in court, she would have taken this as an indication of weakness in the testimony—or that the witness had something to hide.

"That I cannot do," Kit said.

"For twenty thousand dollars?"

"I'm sorry, I thought you offered ten."

"It is doubled. That's how badly I want you on my team."

"Is that it, Mr. Hearst? Or is it that you want me off Mr. Hanratty's?"

Anger quickly flashed over Hearst's face. "Young woman, how can you turn your back on certain success, for a cause that is certain failure?"

Behind her a voice all but shouted, "Willie!"

Kit turned around. A stout man was walking rapidly toward them.

"Mr. President," Hearst said. "May I offer you some tea?"

The singularity of the circumstance hammered at Kit's mind, as if to remind her this was not a dream. She was sipping tea with Theodore Roosevelt, President of the United States, and William Randolph Hearst, who might someday occupy that office.

And all she had done was consent to defend a man sitting in a lonely jail cell. America was indeed a grand place.

"Willie and I are old adversaries," Roosevelt said to Kit, "and I daresay I'd better watch my backside in aught eight, eh, Willie?"

Hearst barely smiled. "Teddy, we can only hope."

"Willie told me about you," Roosevelt said to Kit. "You have a policeman for a client." He had keen, probing eyes behind thick glasses, and a bushy mustache that was more whisk broom than whiskers. Every part of him seemed charged with energy. He looked strong as a bull.

Kit stammered, "I do, sir."

Roosevelt nodded. "I was police commissioner of New York City not long ago."

"I remember."

The president's eyes widened. "How so?"

"I lived in a rooming house on the lower East Side."

Roosevelt slapped his thigh. "Small world. And do you have any recollection of the police department?"

"A tough bunch. I saw several take money from local merchants in exchange for protection."

"Precisely. That's what I wanted to clean up. And we did it, by jingo. Now you face the same problem here in Los Angeles. Willie and I have our political differences, but in this we are agreed—a clean police force is a necessity for our way of life."

Swallowing, Kit said, "I believe this as well."

"Splendid," Roosevelt said. "Now, it is my experience that the best course of action would be for you to settle this thing quietly. Willie has briefed me on the matter, and I am sure that would be in the best interest of all. A quiet plea of guilty might give this client of yours some hope of rehabilitation."

Kit felt the pressure of the two men as they looked for her agreement. "Mr. President," she said, "if I may be so bold?"

"Certainly."

"The president of the United States is sworn to uphold the Constitution, is he not?"

"Indeed."

"The Constitution protects the right of every citizen to confront the witnesses against him in any criminal proceeding."

Roosevelt nodded. Hearst's face remained impassive. "I represent a man who only wants what the Constitution grants to him. I believe that right is greater even than the desire of a president."

"Young woman," said Hearst. "Don't you realize to whom you are speaking?"

Roosevelt stared at Kit through his thick glasses, waiting.

"Yes, I do, Mr. Hearst," Kit said. "And I find nothing objectionable in what I said."

After an uncomfortable silence, Roosevelt slapped his knees and stood up. "I tried, Willie, but it appears our young lawyer has made up her mind."

"Principles can be foolhardy," Hearst said, looking at Kit.

"I don't agree, sir," said Kit.

Hearst declared, "You may do your best, Miss Shannon. But rest assured, the *Examiner* will not let this scoundrel go unpunished."

"If you will excuse me," Kit said.

"I want Los Angeles to be a clean city," Roosevelt said.

Kit could not help looking at Hearst as she replied, "So do I, sir." She left without another word.

# Chapter 15

KIT WALKED INTO the Braxton Arms nearly breathless from her extraordinary meeting. All this because of one policeman. Hearst had been so concerned that he had called on the president of the United States to try and sway her. Why the heavy artillery?

Could it be that he knew, somehow, the case his paper had been building against Hanratty was rotten at the core?

Kit had to find out. And she had less than three weeks to do it.

The man behind the desk gave her a large smile. He had his hair slicked back with pomade in the latest fashion to hit the States, that of the Italian lover. For some reason Kit could not fathom, Los Angeles society was imbued with a Mediterranean fixation. Perhaps because it was still a city in search of its own identity.

"Hel-lo," he said with ladled charm.

"My name is Kathleen Shannon and I am—"

"Welcome, little lady. They sure grow 'em pretty out here. My, my. I'm from Maryland originally, they call me Maryland Slim. That's on account of I'm slim."

"Yes, I wonder if I might—"

"Quite the dancer, too. You dance, miss?"

"Sir, would you mind if—"

"Slim. Just call me Slim."

"Sir, I am here on a matter of some importance."

The man put his elbows on the desk and leaned forward. "What could be more important than getting to know a new friend?"

Kit masked her impatience. This was not the first masher she had ever encountered, but this was certainly not the best timing. "I wish to speak to some of the residents on the second floor. Do you have a register?"

Slim drew back slightly. "Now, what would your business be, little lady?"

"A legal matter."

He studied her a moment. "What was your name again?"

"Shannon."

"The lawyer?"

"Yes."

A smile slid back onto his face. "My, my, I've only read about you. You are prettier than a picture."

"Sir, I wish—"

"Slim."

"Have you a register?" Kit asked.

"Supposing I do?"

"May I see it, please?"

"For nothing?"

"Whatever do you mean?"

"The register is private property. But I might be willing to share it with you for a small price."

Kit shook her head. "I am not going to pay you money for the information."

"Who said anything about money? Supposing you and I were to have dinner tonight and trip the light fantastic?" Slim put his right hand on his stomach, extended his left as if holding a dance partner. He swayed behind the counter and winked at her.

"Sir," Kit said, "would you like me to return with a subpoena? We can do this the easy or hard way, but let me assure you that if I have to use the force of law against you, it will not feel anything like the light fantastic."

The would-be lothario stiffened, his smile melting like ice on a hot sidewalk. "Women lawyers," he said. "It's not natural." He reached under the counter and produced a book, slamming it on the surface. Then he stared at her.

Kit ignored him and opened the register. She noted the rooms and names on the second floor, then closed the book. "Is Room 202 vacant?" she asked.

"It is, if it's any of your business."

"Did Mrs. Chausser leave a forwarding address?"

Slim's smile was smug. "Not that I know of."

"I should like to see Room 202, if you please," Kit said.

Slim turned without a word and took a key from a hook. He tossed it on the counter. "Won't find anything."

"Just having a look."

"The district attorney know you're here?" he said.

"No, sir."

"Maybe I should ring him on our telephone."

"I am sure Mr. Davenport will be happy to inform you about my legal remedies against you." She turned and headed for the stairs, feeling Maryland Slim watching her all the way.

As she started up the steps she encountered a stout man in a light blue suit coming down. He gave her a cursory nod, then passed her by. Kit paused long enough to hear Slim say, "Good morning, Mr. Hervey."

Hervey was one of the names she had seen on the register, under room 204. She studied his face for a moment, then continued up the stairs.

She examined the door to Room 202. It was obviously new, having replaced the one broken by Hanratty. She unlocked the door and entered. She knew the crime scene had been thoroughly analyzed by the detectives and the district attorney, and even Tom Phelps of the *Examiner*. The room had been put back into order. But Kit wanted to see how the room was laid out so she could picture the events—Hanratty's version of them at least—in her mind.

It was a simple room with a sofa, chairs, and a wall bed. The bed was up now, but when brought down it would have taken up a good portion of the space. To the right was a doorway to a small kitchen area.

According to her client, Jay Chausser was lying on the bed, alone, when he entered. His son, Robert, was standing. The two had been arguing just before he broke down the door. The wife, Edna, had been in the kitchen.

Hanratty said he told Jay Chausser not to move and for everyone to stay calm. But, suddenly, Chausser had pulled a gun from under a blanket and fired. The bullet missed, and Hanratty fired in return. Chausser was hit and fell off the bed.

As Hanratty stepped forward to check on him, Edna appeared in the kitchen doorway and screamed. When he looked at her Robert hit him, knocking him to the floor. Then Robert fled. Hanratty struggled to his feet and shouted "Call the police!" then gave chase to Robert, losing him two blocks away.

"Hey!" a voice said behind Kit.

Kit turned in the open doorway and saw a man there, hands

on his hips. "What are you meddling around in there for?"

He had the tough look of a policeman but was not wearing a uniform. "My name is Kathleen Shannon. I am a lawyer."

The man eyed her suspiciously. "You on the killer-cop case?"

"May I inquire as to your interest?"

"You may not," the man said. "I have given my statement to the district attorney."

"Then you are a witness."

"What of it?"

"I would like to know what you saw."

He scowled. "I will say this and no more. I heard everything. The voice of the cop, the broken door. Shouting. And two shots. I saw the cop chase the Chausser boy out of the hotel. I live directly across the hall, and that's the way it was."

Kit's mind scanned the names she had noted. "You must be Mr. Seldon, then."

His perplexed look told her she had connected him to the right name.

"You're a smart one, ain't you? Well, let me tell you, missy, you'll get no help around here. Jay Chausser was liked. I hope they string that cop up."

"Did you actually see the shooting, Mr. Seldon?"

"I told you, I ain't saying no more. I know how you lawyers try to twist what good people say. You'll hear me in court."

Kit was about to speak when she heard footsteps rushing up the stairs. Turning, she saw Maryland Slim in the company of a uniformed policeman.

"There she is," Slim said. "Trespasser."

She faced the cop, who said, "Come along, ma'am."

"I have a right to be here," she said.

"Not if he don't say so." The cop cocked his thumb at Slim.

"I don't say so," Slim said.

It would be no use arguing. This was not a court, and Kit had no judge to appeal to. The cop was the only law around.

Kit tossed the key to Room 202 to Slim and walked toward the stairs.

"Don't come back," Slim warned.

———

As arranged, Corazón was waiting for Kit in the Plaza. Corazón had cooked up tamales for a picnic dinner, at Kit's request. They sat on the grass in the fading sunlight as Kit recounted her extraordinary afternoon.

"The president?" Corazón said in wonderment. "You sit with the president?"

"Indeed," Kit said.

"I cannot think."

"Funny, that's what Aunt Freddy says about Mr. Roosevelt."

Corazón laughed and handed Kit one of the corn-husked tamales. Kit offered a prayer of thanksgiving for the meal, then unwrapped what had become her favorite California food. She bit into the warm cornmeal and beef, savoring the ripe olives and raisins and chile sauce that would have burned her untrained eastern palate a few months before. But she was becoming a real southern Californian now, able to eat whatever Corazón chose to cook.

"Now that Señor Fox is home, will you be to see him?" Corazón said.

"I expect so," Kit said. Then, smiling, added, "I hope so."

"He is much changed, yes?"

"Much."

"All the time we pray for him, it helps, yes?"

"Yes."

"Then I will pray for the marriage."

Kit wondered at her syntax. "Whose marriage?"

"You and Señor Fox, of course."

The warmth that came to Kit's face was not from the tamale. And she didn't mind it a bit. Was marriage truly on her mind? Was Ted, even converted, the man for her? She would need time to find out.

"Now you must tell me of your case," Corazón said.

Her interest was curious to Kit. Her friend's brother had been through a terrible ordeal, and Corazón had shared every bit of his arrest and trial. Though he was acquitted, Corazón expressed her fear of the law on several occasions. Kit tried to explain the difference between the law and the people who sometimes abuse it, but her words had seemed to make little difference.

"Do you really wish to hear about it?" Kit said.

"I am your friend, no?"

"Yes."

"Then tell."

Kit recounted her decision to represent Hanratty the cop and her visit to the hotel. She found herself thinking out loud. "There is something strange about the way people will not speak to me. It is as if all of the witnesses have been tied up in a package and presented to the district attorney. There has to be someone who will open up."

"There is no one?"

"No one I have been able to find. And time is going to run out."

Corazón squinted in thoughtfulness. "Tell to me more."

"My, but you are the anxious one."

Corazón smiled shyly, nodded, and waited for Kit to continue.

"The man who lived across the hall from the Chaussers," Kit said, "a man named Seldon, says he heard two shots and then saw Hanratty chase the son out of the hotel."

"How he see?"

Kit nodded at Corazón. "Good question. He didn't say. He would have had to have his door open at that point."

"Yes, and why would he open if there is the shooting?"

"Why indeed. And where is Mrs. Chausser? And the son? Davenport no doubt has them holed up somewhere until the preliminary hearing. There is probably no way I will get to question either of them before that."

"What about the others who live at the hotel?"

"Probably all of them have given their stories to both the *Examiner* and the D.A. I have a list of names but can't get into the hotel."

"But you are the lawyer."

"Unless I get a judge's order of some kind, they can keep me out. I can't even depose them until after the preliminary hearing. It is disgraceful."

Corazón shook her head. *"Cómo?"*

"Disgraceful," Kit said. "Full of disgrace. It is a word you use for something that is very bad, that brings shame. They are bringing shame on justice."

The two ate in silence for a few minutes. The sound of a train whistle issued in the distance, sounding like a fleeing bird. Kit looked up to the sky and said to herself, "Now, have I left anything out?"

"I think," Corazón said.

Kit had not expected an answer from her friend. She looked at her quizzically.

Corazón nodded. "There is one who should know what is going on. This is a hotel, yes?"

"Yes."

"The maid."

Of course. A maid is always a good witness to what goes on in a residence. She sees and hears things most people miss.

"Corazón," Kit said admiringly, "you are brilliant."

"Bril...?"

*"Muy inteligente."*

Corazón smiled shyly. "I would like to help you."

"You already have."

"No, help. I will find this maid. She is like me, I think. I will find her."

It made perfect sense. Corazón would be able to speak to the maid in her native tongue, assuming she was also a Mexican domestic, for that was what most of the hotels in Los Angeles employed. And Kit, being *persona non grata* at the Braxton Arms, would not have to show her face there.

"But be careful," Kit said. "There are people who don't want us to have the information we're looking for. We have to be clever about it."

"No worry," Corazón said. "I am muy inteligente, yes?"

# Chapter 16

"DON'T TALK TO ME about flying," Ted Fox said.

"Yer just bein' stubborn," Gus answered.

"Then that's what I'll be." Ted was plowing down Broadway as rapidly as his crutches could carry him. Which was not very fast, and that only made him angry.

"What are you afraid of?" Gus said.

"I'm afraid I'll go nuts if I keep listening to you."

The late afternoon bustle on Broadway was a swarm of people, which parted politely for Ted when they saw him moving with such a determined gait. He observed their actions with some degree of awe, for he had no idea where he was going. All he knew was that he was propelled by an inner restlessness, as if something just beyond his grasp awaited him if only he would move fast enough.

Gus kept up with him every step. He was a good friend, always had been, but now Ted wanted to be alone. Having Gus at his side was a reminder of all that they had once been together—partners in the enterprise of building a flying machine. For a quick moment Ted felt a wave of forgotten excitement, the feeling of being in the sky, floating on the wind. That only made him more determined to stop all this talk Gus was flapping his lips with.

Ted stopped and faced him. "If you're looking for a flyboy, you're going to have to look somewhere else. If God wanted me up there, He wouldn't have let me crash. He wouldn't have left me a . . ."

"Cripple?" Gus said. "You think God did this to you?"

It was the question Kit could not answer that night. Nor could Ted. He had heard some Bible teaching growing up, about God's power and love, about how not even a sparrow falls to earth without God knowing about it.

So why had He allowed Ted to fall to earth? Why did He snatch away his dream?

Ted continued walking, turning at the corner of Sixth Street, heading west toward the river. Was something drawing him there? When his family had first come to Los Angeles, the waters of the river that ran down the western edge of the city had been a hospitable place for some fishing, for gentle summer days spent in solitude. That's what he was after, he realized. Time alone. He had Kit's Bible in the army knapsack he used to carry his things when he went about on crutches.

"Go home, Gus," he said over his shoulder.

"No, sir," Gus said. "I ain't gonna let you get away again. You have to go back up. I know one thing, too. That young lady of yours wants you to try."

Ted did not stop. "She is not my young lady."

"Don't feed me that load of mackerel. You're stuck on her."

That compelled Ted to stop once again. He looked at Gus directly, willing his friend to understand. "I don't want her stuck with me."

Gus chewed for a moment, then spit his wad of chewing tobacco onto the street. "Any fool can see she has her lamps set on you."

"Maybe," Ted said. "And maybe for a minute or two I thought there might be a chance. . . ."

"There is, boy, if I can see anything."

"That's just it, Gus. Kit's feelings for me might be pity. I don't want that from anyone."

"Just what do you want, boy?"

Ted breathed in as he felt the warmth of the setting sun on his back. "I don't know. Go home."

With a grumble and dismissive wave of the hand, Gus turned and walked away. Ted made for the river.

At the river's edge he found a grassy spot near a magnolia tree, white flowers dotting the branches like snowy doves. He sat down and listened to the water. The sound was calming, but the churning of the waters mirrored his soul.

Maybe he should go back into banking. It was a decent way to make a living. But having once tasted the sky through flight, such an earthbound pursuit seemed somehow empty.

Yet there was the cursed irony. He was not going to fly again. That was clear. A wooden-legged pilot? Might as well be a peg-legged mountain climber. Too many risks, too many people watching to see if you'll fall.

Kit, for instance.

Ted put his head in his hand as he reclined, watching the river run. Kit would always be watching him, should they ever be married. He couldn't stand that thought. She was on her way to a brilliant legal career. He would only be holding her back as a husband. He would need care, special attention.

No, he could not put that on her. And the thought caused his heart to ache. He knew he loved her more than he would love anyone. But that was lost to him now, too.

His inner turmoil bore through him, and he realized he had grabbed handfuls of grass. He looked down at his tight fists, then threw the blades away with all his might. They scattered in the wind, like old dreams.

With near desperation Ted reached in his knapsack and grabbed Kit's Bible. Answers were in here. They had to be. Besides, he had promised Kit he would search for them.

He began to read.

---

The office of the Los Angeles County coroner was at the corner of Sixth and Main—far enough away from the central district so the specter of dead bodies wouldn't drive business away from local merchants. Housed in what was a former armory building, it was the domain of Raymond Smith, a former medic during the Spanish-American War, now the chief of medical examinations for the county of Los Angeles.

Kit had seen him testify once in a murder case Earl Rogers had won. Rogers, by knowing as much medical science as Smith, was able to cross-examine him with scalpel-like precision. Kit had gone out and bought her own copy of Gray's *Anatomy* that very afternoon.

Now it looked as if she would be cross-examining Smith during the preliminary hearing. She had come to his office hoping he wouldn't mind sharing the facts, no matter where they led, so she might prepare her questioning. She also wondered, with trepidation, if the facts might lead her to an informed opinion about her client's innocence. Or guilt.

"I don't like lawyers," the coroner said after Kit had been announced by a confused-looking assistant. Smith was at a table

measuring a skull with calipers. Kit wondered if Smith was referring to her or the skull.

"Yorick?" Kit said.

"Eh?"

"The skull," Kit said. " 'Alas, poor Yorick.' "

"Are you a raving loon?"

Apparently references to Shakespeare weren't going to have any
effect. "Mr. Smith—"

"*Doctor* Smith." He was a short man with a mustache that
drooped almost down past his chin. A little more length there and
he might have had the look of a Chinese mandarin.

"I'm sorry. Doctor, if you will share your report with me at this
time, perhaps we might save time at the hearing."

He shook his head. "Lawyers. Always meddling. Can't wait. You
used to work for that Earl Rogers, didn't you?"

"Yes."

"Don't like him. Thinks he's better than anybody. Wanted to
tell me my job, too."

"I work alone now, Mr. . . . . Doctor."

"But you're still a lawyer. And a woman. That's two meddlers
in one package."

Kit held her anger in check. "Then you refuse to speak to me?"

The coroner looked at her knowingly. "Oh, I get it. You want
me to clam up so you can go telling a judge or a jury that I
wouldn't talk. Then everybody is going to think good old Dr.
Smith is not interested in the truth, is that your game?"

Kit merely raised her eyebrows.

"Meddler," he grumbled. "All right, listen then. Jay Chausser
was killed by a bullet to the heart. Death was practically instanta-
neous."

"You performed the autopsy yourself?"

"Always do."

"So Jay Chausser was shot once, and that's what killed him?"

"Not what I said."

"But—"

"You didn't listen. I said he was killed by a bullet. I didn't say there was only one in him."

Kit flinched and the coroner smiled at her. "You see," he said, "you don't know my job. There were two bullets in Mr. Chausser. The one that hit his heart, and one that got him in the right shoulder."

He opened a small drawer in his desk and pulled out a linen handkerchief tied with a string. He untied the string and opened the handkerchief on the desk.

In the middle of the linen were two bullets.

"There they are, Miss Lawyer," Smith said. "You might say this case is tied up in a neat little package."

Kit felt color draining from her face.

"Not even Mr. Earl Rogers could talk himself around that," Smith said. "Now, will there be anything else today?"

————

"You are not telling me the truth," Kit said, balling her hands into fists.

"I am, I swear it," Ed Hanratty said.

"You should never lie to your doctor or your lawyer," Kit said. "In either case it may prove fatal."

"I am not lying." His face, at least, seemed sincere.

"The witnesses say they heard two shots. Two. And Jay Chausser had two bullets in him."

Hanratty ran his hands through his hair. "I can't explain it. He fired at me, I fired at him. Boom, boom. That was all. Then the boy knocked me down and ran for the door, and I went after him."

"Then how do you explain the other bullet lodged in Mr. Chausser?"

Hanratty shook his head vigorously. "I can't explain it."

"Let us consider the possibilities," Kit said. "One is that Chausser was shot by someone else after you left the scene."

"Yes, yes." Hanratty looked anxiously hopeful.

"But the neighbors heard only two shots, one right after the other. That is what the reports have been."

Hanratty's face fell.

"Second, perhaps the other bullet in Mr. Chausser was there from an old wound."

Again, the cop appeared relieved. "That is possible. It happens. War wounds and the like."

"I will ask the coroner about this," Kit said. "But if he answers that it was a fresh wound, we are back to the first possibility."

Hanratty sat heavily on his stool. "It keeps going round and round."

Kit felt pulled, once more, in opposite directions. Part of her wanted to believe her client so she could give him a vigorous defense. The other part possessed a chord of deep discomfort at how his story differed from that of the witnesses and, perhaps, the coroner.

And if the latter should be the case, what would she do? Press forward with a client who did not tell the truth? How could she possibly allow herself to do so?

These were questions that would have to wait until after the preliminary hearing. Much would become clearer in the cold light of testimony and cross-examination.

"There is a third possibility," Kit said. She watched his eyes carefully as she said, "And that is that you are not telling me the whole truth."

She expected him to yell again in protest. But he did not.

Instead he looked crestfallen. His head hung down on his chest. It was not the look of a liar. At least that is what her heart told her.

"Edward," Kit said, using his given name for the first time since she had become his lawyer, "if there is more to this story than you have told me, now is the time."

"No, Miss Shannon," he said quietly. "I am not hiding anything. He shot first, I fired, and then gave chase to his son."

Kit thought a moment. "If he fired at you, where is the bullet?"

Hanratty frowned. "Yes, where?"

"Tell me, where were you standing when he fired at you? Show me."

Hanratty stood up in his cell and traced a frame in the air with his finger. "I was standing at the door. Or what was left of the door." A wry smile came to his mouth. "I'm sorry," he said quickly, erasing the grin. "And he was right in front of me, on the bed. We had some words, but quick as a wink he drew a gun and fired."

"So the trajectory of the bullet was upward?"

"I suppose."

"Please don't suppose," Kit said. "Think about it and tell me."

Hanratty nodded and mulled it over. "Yes, it had to be that way."

"Did you sense where the bullet missed you, to the right or the left?"

"No."

"Did you hear it lodge in the doorjamb?"

Hanratty shook his head.

"Then it is logical to assume it went into the opposite wall, in the hallway."

At that, Hanratty's eyes opened wide. "Yes," he said. "That must be it."

In her own mind, Kit thought the very same thing. And what if a bullet wasn't there? She turned to leave.

"Stay a moment," Hanratty said. His voice was hollow. "Tell me the truth, Miss Shannon. Are we going to lose?"

She had not expected the question. She had no easy answer. The case was troubling to her because she was not completely convinced of Hanratty's innocence. And the preliminary hearing was not often the time when a case got thrown out. Yet even if he was telling the truth, Kit was not certain she could find a way to win. That was the nature of the law. Sometimes the innocent did not walk away.

"I will do everything I can," Kit said.

As she walked back to her office, Kit mulled over possible questions for the coroner, trying to imagine what the preliminary hearing would sound like. She was so engrossed in her thoughts she barely noticed the horse-drawn fire brigade, loudly clanging its bell, racing down First Street.

She found Corazón waiting for her at the office, looking dejected. "I no find her," Corazón said.

"The maid?"

"*Sí.* She is gone."

"Gone?"

"From the hotel. I ask another maid for where she is. She tell me she is no there no more, and I ask for where, and she no know."

Kit put a hand on Corazón's shoulder. "Calm yourself. It's all right. Did you get a name?"

"Sí, she tell me her name. Maria Espinoza. But the other maid, she say Maria went quickly away after the shooting."

Kit thought about that a moment. There might have been a good reason for her to leave. Perhaps she was just upset at what happened. But might there be another reason, one more suspect?

Patting Corazón's shoulder, Kit said, "You have done well."

"Truly?"

"Detective work is a series of steps. You got the name. Now we will take the next step. We will try to find her."

"How we do that?"

"We apply a little pressure."

# Chapter 17

AT THE END OF THE DAY Tom Phelps liked the comfort of a corner booth in Jakob Schneider's saloon. A German immigrant, Schneider was the purveyor of fine beers and an outspoken opponent of the budding temperance movement. Reporters from both of the big newspapers, the *Times* and the *Examiner*, gathered here to swap stories and perhaps steal a few for their own use.

When not bantering with his colleagues, Phelps would sometimes scrawl odd lines of verse. At one time during his misspent youth he had entertained notions of becoming a poet. That was until he found out that the only writers who made less than newspapermen were poets.

Tonight, though, was a poetry night. In a reflective mood, Phelps sipped a beer and set a few lines in pencil on a sheet of paper. He decided they sounded too much like bad Longfellow when he heard a voice say, "Deathless prose?"

It was Kit Shannon, and Phelps almost knocked over his drink. In this den of male fellowship, the last person he expected to see was a woman—Kit Shannon least of all.

"May I?" Kit said, sliding into the booth opposite Phelps.

Phelps's gaze darted between Kit and the bar. "You can't sit here."

"This is a public establishment, isn't it?"

"How did you . . ."

"I entered through the rear."

"Slide in further." He waved her deeper into the booth so she would become obscured to the rest of the crowd. "If anyone sees you they'll be here like bees on honey."

"Am I the honey?"

"Quit being coy. Get in there."

Kit slid in. "Better?"

"What are you doing here?"

"I came to see you."

"I gathered that." He lowered his voice. "Why couldn't you come to my office?"

"Nervous, Tom?"

He bit his lower lip. "What makes you say that?"

"Your eyes haven't remained steady since I got here."

"State your business, won't you?"

"Did you know you were the first Angeleno I ever met?"

His mind rotated upon itself. He did indeed remember meeting the Irish rose on the train from the east and the way his feelings for her had always been a muddle. Grudging respect was the latest incarnation of his emotions for her. But he also knew that his employer would not fancy his clandestine meeting with the lawyer for their villain, Ed Hanratty.

"Of course I remember," Phelps said. "We were on the train."

"Destined for the same place, the same events."

"You here to talk about Hanratty?"

"I'm here to get some fair treatment, which is more than the *Examiner* is willing to give."

Phelps frowned. "You'll get nothing from me. I'm a reporter, that's all."

"You were the first one on the scene, weren't you? Reporter, I mean."

"So what if I was?"

"The story didn't come out in the *Examiner* until well after the shooting."

"I had to piece it together," Tom said, squirming in his booth. Why did she have this effect on him?

"It seems to me you shifted gears. It wasn't much more than a criminal being shot by a policeman. Then you come out with a big series about a renegade cop. Why the switch?"

"Sometimes it takes a while to get all the facts."

"Or else someone decides to create a few facts. Someone who owns a newspaper, perhaps."

"If you are insinuating that the *Examiner* is behind all this . . ."

"If it is just about the facts, Tom, why don't you share them with me?"

"It wouldn't be right, that's all."

"I'm a lawyer in a murder trial. Is it right to withhold information?"

"I've got my . . ."

"Orders?" she speculated.

"Kit, you're a good lawyer—everybody knows that. But you get into these things too deep."

"It's never too deep when a man's life is on the line."

They paused as, at the bar, some men erupted into uproarious laughter.

"Just a start, Tom. Believe me, I won't let anyone know. I need a location. The maid, Maria Espinoza. Where is she?"

Phelps felt his mouth go dry. "I have no idea," he said.

Kit smiled at him. "You were never a good liar, Tom."

"I can't tell you anything." He looked again toward the bar. So far no one seemed to be paying him any mind. "Slip out the way you came in."

"It's not that you can't—it's that you won't."

"Right."

"This is a rather sociable place, isn't it?" Kit's eyes danced as she leaned over and gave a look toward the bar.

"Sit back!" Phelps said.

Leisurely, Kit returned to an upright position. "What would happen, I wonder, if I were to stand and give the place a few stanzas of 'Rock of Ages'?"

Phelps's mouth opened, but nothing came out.

"That's right," Kit said. "Everyone would see me with you and, being reporters, might wonder what the *Examiner*'s star scribbler is doing meeting with Ed Hanratty's defense attorney. I wonder if that story would get back to Mr. Hearst."

"You wouldn't dare."

"Papa always said I sang like an angel. Want to hear?"

She actually started to slide out. Phelps shot his hand out to her arm. "You extortionist!"

"Extortion requires the corrupt taking of a fee, Tom. All I want is information."

Phelps clenched his jaw and knew Kit Shannon's methods of persuasion stretched well beyond courtroom walls.

"You'll find her at the Arcadia Hotel," Phelps said. "But don't you breathe a word of how you found out."

"Don't worry, Tom. I may be a singer, but I'm no canary."

# Chapter 18

ON SUNDAY KIT and Corazón took the Main Street trolley all the way to 23rd Street for church.

The simple white building looked like it had been transplanted from a midwestern town square—clapboard exterior, an arched oak door, a steeple with a modest bell tower. Kit had discovered it one day on her way to visit a client. Something about the simplicity of the place called out to her, as did the name—Los Angeles Bible Church. No denomination, she would come to find out, but an independent house of worship pastored by the Reverend Miller Macauley.

He was a man who reminded her very much of her father. Genial eyes—though Macauley's were of Scottish hue—and a warm, inviting voice. Mostly, though, she sensed his love of God and the Word. He had started a little Bible institute he hoped would one day become a leading venue for the training of ministers. It was rough going, however, as it seemed always short of funds.

The people at the church were also a reason Kit kept returning. They were not like the wealthy strata who attended the uptown churches, but working class people, and even some people of Mexican descent. You would not find such a mix in the Protestant churches in the city. But here both Kit and Corazón felt at home.

They were in the midst of singing the third hymn, "A Mighty Fortress is Our God"—one of Kit's favorites—when, from the corner of her eye, she saw someone moving.

Ted was entering the pew.

He moved in with his crutches, as the people made way for him. By the end of verse three he was standing—smiling—next to Kit. "Sorry I'm late," he whispered.

Kit held her hymnal up so they could finish together. Ted did not make an attempt to sing, but rather simply read the words. In truth, Kit could hardly continue. She was ablaze with joy to see Ted here. She wanted to embrace him and shout, but decorum kept her in check.

The hymn ended, and as they sat down Ted whispered again. "I had a little trouble finding the place. I thought you said it was—"

A few heads in the vicinity turned around. Kit put a finger to her lips.

"But I've got to—"

Kit tapped her lips for quiet. Reverend Macauley was at the pulpit. He seemed aware of the slight disturbance, for he was looking directly at Kit and Ted when he spoke. "Welcome, one and all, to the house of our Lord."

Macauley stepped down from his podium and folded his hands in front of him. "I will not be bringing you the message this morning, for we have with us a very special visitor. I have asked if he would not mind preaching for us today, and he has graciously consented. He is a good friend to the Bible institute. Indeed, he is donating half of his lecture proceeds to us, that we may finally gain a foothold in this city. In fact, he is a good friend to all who preach the Word of God. It is my privilege to introduce to you Dr. G. Campbell Morgan."

A man stood up in the first row and assumed the pulpit. Kit recognized him at once as the man who had congratulated her after her debate with Darrow and Lazarus. He had seemed rather unassuming then, unremarkable in speech and bearing, though certainly very much a gentleman. But now, standing in the pulpit, holding a Bible in his hands, he had the aura of greatness about him.

Ted whispered, "I was reading by the river, and—"

"Listen!" Kit whispered back, with a bit more verve. She wanted Ted to hear all of the message to come.

"I thank you for your warm welcome," Morgan said. "Your city is quite hospitable, though I must say you have a rather robust and curious group of newspapermen prowling about."

Kit nodded, wondering what sort of angle they wanted to get on an English preacher in their midst.

"One gentleman from the *Examiner* rode with me to Glendale the other day, where I had a date for golf with three other clergymen. Let me say at once that I beg you to judge my stay by what I bring to you from the Word of God, and not how I handle a niblick."

Titters of laughter rose from the assembly. Kit noticed that this got Ted's attention.

Morgan continued. "After the round of golf, this reporter had a rather gloomy look about him, and I asked him what the matter might be. He said, 'Dr. Morgan, I was sure I could catch you four doing something, but I wasn't able to do it. This is the first round of golf I've ever witnessed where not one curse word was uttered all day!' "

Now the laughter was pronounced, and Ted was part of it. His eyes were focused unwaveringly on Morgan.

"While I am gratified the behavior of four men of God upheld the good name of our calling, I cannot help but comment upon the fundamental misunderstanding of the Gospel as it is commonly spoken about today. This is why I have come to your country to lecture, for I feel it is my sacred duty to proclaim what I believe to be the truth.

"You will find no argument today for the claim that the teachings of the founder of our faith have given the world the most perfect ethical code that has ever been handed to man. Nor will you have much quarrel for the proposition that Jesus lived a life of unparalleled perfection. The problem arises, however, when the message stops there. Nay, it is more than a problem—it is the Great Lie."

Kit sensed every person in the church connecting with Morgan. She had observed juries and courtrooms responding in the same manner when Earl Rogers was making a case. This felt much the same way, but with the added weight of eternal truth.

Ted, for his part, was leaning forward, rapt.

"This is not the Great Lie merely because no man can hope to live the life that Christ lived. If Jesus has done no more for men than to give them a pattern of living, He has only succeeded in revealing the depth of human degradation and the impossibility of man's ever attaining the highest or best. If Jesus has done no more than illuminate the ideal, He has made me the most helpless and despairing of men, for I cannot reproduce it in my own life.

"But even more, my friends, the Great Lie is that Christ is no more than a teacher of the principles of life. It is not fashionable to speak the truth, a truth that has not changed one whit over the centuries: That Jesus Christ is not merely an ideal presented, but the very atoning sacrifice that brings us new life *imparted*. He is the way, the truth, and the life. That is what we must come to believe again."

*Yes*, Kit thought, remembering her confrontations with Dr. Edward Lazarus. That was his message—the life of Christ as ideal, without the call to be born again, or even any basis to believe that Jesus rose from the dead.

For the next half hour Morgan lectured, read Scripture, and expounded upon the Bible in the clearest, boldest, and most majestic of terms. It was one of the greatest sermons Kit had ever heard, and she knew all who listened could not help but benefit. She even knew that Morgan had made sense to Ted. At least she thought so, judging from the number of times Ted nodded during the talk.

But Kit was not prepared for what happened next.

Morgan drew to a close. "Oh, the grand mystery of the Spirit! I do not know how the change was wrought in me, how the fleshly life I lived was transformed into one that sees something of His love and beauty. I just know when He did it. He did it when I believed on Jesus and was born again. From that moment on I began a life as different from the old as noonday is different from midnight.

"Oh, begin this life if you have not already. Turn in obedience to the redeemer of men. There will be no newspaper paragraph; there are some things the newspapers cannot describe. But it will be recorded in heaven, and you will pass from death to life, from the slavery of this world to the freedom of God. This is the greatest truth of all."

And then Morgan led the congregation in prayer, a prayer for souls. He prayed that the message he had preached would go forth in the hearts of the listeners, to be spread like seed in the fields around them.

When the prayer ended, Kit looked up. Ted was not beside her.

Then she saw him, on his crutches, moving toward G. Campbell Morgan.

---

"How am I supposed to feel?" Ted asked as the three of them—Kit, Ted, and Corazón—rode the trolley back toward downtown.

"How do you feel now?" Kit asked.

"As if I've made a decision. The right decision. But . . ."

"What is it?"

"I don't know, exactly."

There was a look of concern in his eyes. Was it related to his newfound faith? Or did it have something to do with her? She wanted to reach out to him, to cry and laugh all at the same time. He'd given his heart to Christ. He'd broken through the barriers of sin and disbelief. The chasm between them had closed now. But why did she feel it was not?

As if rising to her own defense, Kit said, "Feelings are not the crucial issue, Ted."

"But you rely on feelings all the time," Ted countered. "You've told me before of having gut feelings for clients and their situations."

"That kind of feeling is more intuition. Reading people and their words—their actions." She laced and unlaced her fingers. "I suppose what I'm trying to say is that I've known too many people who were waiting for the right feeling from God before they made decisions."

"Doesn't that make perfect sense?" Ted replied.

Kit bit her lower lip for a moment. The trolley slowed and Corazón stood. "This is my stop. I go see my family."

Kit forced her gaze from Ted and turned a smile on Corazón. "Please send everyone my love."

Corazón nodded and hurried down the aisle to exit the trolley.

Her absence made Kit feel even more vulnerable.

"You were saying?" Ted said.

He was anxious to talk, but about what? There was something under the surface. Was it about her? She wished he would come right out and say it—they belonged together now! But she was not going to be the one to bring it up.

"I suppose," Ted added, "I'm confused about why things happened the way they did."

Kit wanted to take his hand but held back. "God is always God, even in the bad times. Even when things feel wrong or we don't understand them. We may not always have a feeling about God, but we always have God's promise."

"What promise is that?"

"To never leave us or forsake us," Kit replied.

"So if God is there when the bad things happen . . . life changing things . . ." Ted said softly. "Did He mean it to happen?"

Kit found she had no ready answer. She was troubled by this and by Ted's expression as she stepped off the trolley at her stop. What should have been a day of joy, of Ted's salvation, was heavy with uncertainty. He tried to force a smile and a wave as the trolley moved on, but it did not lift her spirits.

As she walked back to the Westminster, Kit wondered if she would have any life with Ted Fox. Her deepest wish had come true, by God's grace. Ted was a believer. There was nothing to stand in the way of their marriage. Her love for Ted had never died, not even in the wake of Jeffrey Kenton's whirlwind romance. They should be together now.

But somehow, Ted was still distant.

"Lord," she whispered, "I don't know what's happening. I don't know where to go from here. What should I do?"

She decided to leave the matter with God. Meanwhile, she had a case to think about. Perhaps if she concentrated on that, God's answer would come through at an unexpected moment. A sign. She would wait. And pray.

# Chapter 19

THE ARCADIA HOTEL in Santa Monica sat on the beach between the gum trees on Ocean Avenue. Majestic in its solitude, it was a favorite spot of well-heeled visitors to Los Angeles. The combination of surf and sun made it nearly irresistible to travelers from the East and Midwest. Completed during the population boom of the 1880s, it had three stories and two wings reaching out toward the sea, as if to embrace it.

Until now, Kit had only seen it from afar, from the bluffs where Ted had his hangar. Up close it was imposing, a rich man's beach resort, a taste of European elegance. But opulence was not on Kit's mind as she and Corazón approached the front desk.

The desk clerk was a young man with shiny black hair, a smart uniform, and a smile as authentic as a three-dollar bill.

"May I help you?" he said.

"Perhaps," Kit said. "I wish to speak to one of your employees."

His expression turned from service to suspicion. "And who would that be?"

"Maria Espinoza. She is a maid, I believe."

"Espinoza? I am not familiar . . ."

"She would be relatively new. Who does your hiring?"

"That would be—" He stopped himself. "What is the nature of your request?"

"Official business. I won't take up too much of her time."

"Well, I . . ." Any semblance of a smile was long gone. "I am not at liberty to divulge—"

"Direct me to the person who is, please."

With a barely audible *hmph* the clerk turned and strode to a door with frosted glass at the far end of the desk. He rapped on it quickly and entered.

"He is no helpful," Corazón said.

"I am not surprised," Kit replied. "We don't seem to be getting much help anywhere."

Corazón was scanning the interior of the Arcadia. The smell of salt air and fresh laurel filled the foyer. Presently the young man returned, followed by a gray gentleman whose stomach strained against a dark, vested suit. He looked displeased. "Miss?" he said.

"Shannon."

"You wish to speak to someone in our employ?"

"Miss Espinoza."

"Are you an acquaintance?"

"No, sir. I am a lawyer."

The older man's eyebrows danced upward. "Shannon, you say?"

"That is correct."

"Well, I'll be." He turned to the younger man. "Curtis, this is Miss Kit Shannon, the lawyer."

Curtis seemed unimpressed.

"I have a law degree myself," said the older man. "Made more money in the hotel business, though. Do you know why? I'll tell you in one word. Family. I treat my employees like family. Curtis here will tell you that, won't you, Curtis?"

Curtis's face said one thing while his mouth said, "Oh yes."

"Right. I am the father, you might say, and I don't like to see my family disturbed. And as you and I well know, a lawyer coming around to my place of business to ask questions is bound to be a disturbance."

"Mr. . . ?"

"Hawthorne. Basil J."

"I appreciate your concern. I would not be making this request in order to create any sort of disturbance. If there is a more convenient time when I might return?"

Hawthorne, Basil J., said, "Why don't we simply leave things as they are? But allow me to buy you a drink before you go."

How many ways was she going to be pushed before someone would cooperate with her? Was the whole city becoming like the tar pits at Rancho La Brea? She felt that the more she struggled the deeper into muck she sank. It had to stop somewhere.

"I am afraid I must insist," Kit said.

Hawthorne stood erect. "You have no legal right to insist upon anything, Miss Shannon. Unless I see a judicial order you will get no information from me."

She knew he had the right to deny her access, at least on his property. But she was not about to move. "I am not leaving yet. If need be, I shall walk the premises myself."

"No," Hawthorne said. "I am afraid you won't." He slapped the desk bell so hard his own hand muffled the ring. With his other hand he motioned to a strong-looking man in a derby who had been standing by a large potted palm. As he made his way toward them Kit thought he looked familiar.

"My house detective, Miss Shannon," Hawthorne said.

The light of recognition went off. Terrence O'Toole, the man in the derby, said, "Well, I'll be a monkey's landlord."

"You two know each other?" Hawthorne said.

"Miss Shannon and I are old friends."

Terrence O'Toole was one of the cops drummed out of the force after the Ted Fox trial. He'd been part of the corrupt team under the former chief, Orel Hoover, a fact uncovered by Kit and Earl Rogers at the trial.

"Yes, I know the former Officer O'Toole," Kit said.

"Well, that's just grand," said Hawthorne. "You two will have much to talk about as he escorts you out."

O'Toole flashed a phony smile as he motioned for Kit to move to the door. No use fighting a battle here. This was the wrong ground for it.

She turned to Corazón but discovered that Corazón was not there.

"Shall we go?" O'Toole said.

———

The beach at Santa Monica was cooler than the city center. Soft breezes kept the air a comfortable temperature, and men, women, and children splashed about in the gentle waves.

Kit, hoping Corazón knew what she was doing, decided to wait within sight of the hotel. She did not care that O'Toole conspicuously watched her for a long time. He would not dare to do anything to her in public. But his malevolent gaze made her wonder if he might approach her in a more secluded place.

Taking off her shoes and stockings, an action she was glad Aunt Freddy could not observe, Kit stepped over the sand and found a spot with wild grass where she might sit. She reposed and observed the happy multitudes in the water.

As a child, she'd been to the ocean only once. Papa and Mama had taken her to Coney Island during a preaching tour outside of New York. What she remembered most about it was the frenetic activity of the place. All sorts of vendors hawked goods and food of all kinds, New Yorkers of every size and shape moved and yelled and seemed generally displeased with everyone else. A fight broke out between two men over, as near as Kit could make out, a two-cent hot dog.

All of that was in keeping with her memories of the East. Crowded and hurried.

Here, on the other hand, the people in the water looked as if they were concerned only with each other's enjoyment. And then Kit thought about what might be under the water, where the naked eye could not see. All sorts of hidden dangers might repose there—jagged rocks, vengeful tides, perhaps even a shark—and yet one would not know it from looking at the surface.

That seemed an apt picture of Los Angeles. For in her time here Kit had seen under the surface—of social custom, of courts of law, of justice as practiced by police—and the sight had not been pretty.

She continued to watch the bathers for a long time until she felt a gentle tap on her shoulder.

"I find her," Corazón said.

"Maria Espinoza?"

"Sí."

"And?"

"She is very afraid."

"Of what?"

"You."

Corazón sat on the grassy place next to Kit. "She has heard your name and was told to no speak to you."

"Did you find out who warned her?"

Corazón shook her head. "I no think she know. She only know

a man told her to get this better job, and that she would no work at Braxton."

"Did she describe this man?"

"She say she no see him before or after."

"Not a resident of the hotel, then," Kit said. "What else?"

"I ask her about the Chaussers. She know them. She see them before and after the shooting."

"All of them?"

"No, the son she no see."

Kit thought about all this, trying to place the pieces in some sort of order. "She may be a witness for us."

"I do not think. She is so afraid."

"Did you find out where she lives?"

"Sí, I know the place where."

"Anything else?"

"Only one thing. She say she is no the one to talk. Rachel Travers she say."

"Rachel Travers? Who is that?"

"Maria only say she hear the name at the Braxton. She hear it from the man Seldon."

*It could be something, it could be nothing,* Kit thought. But her investigation had revealed little helpful information. She made a mental note to try to find out about Rachel Travers. Any witness favorable to her side would be welcome, if indeed any existed.

"You have done well," Kit said. "You may be looking at a new profession."

"Profession?"

"As my investigator."

Corazón did not react at first, then a beautiful smile appeared. "Sí, I think I like to."

"I will pay you, of course."

"No."

"Yes. I insist."

"But my work at the hotel?"

"You can do a little of both, to start. When would you like to begin?"

"Now!"

"Seems as good a time as any."

Corazón clapped her hands, like a little girl getting a pony. "What do I do?"

"Get in touch with the Indianapolis police. Find out anything you can about Jay Chausser."

"I will do."

"And I'm going to send you back to the Braxton Arms."

"For why?"

"I want you to find a bullet."

# Chapter 20

KIT WATCHED TED with the same scrutiny she used to watch witnesses on the stand. He had agreed to come to her office, where she had hoped they might talk uninterrupted. Now that he was here, she found the office much too stuffy and formal.

"Perhaps we should take a cab to my Aunt Freddy's," Kit suggested. "She won't mind me dropping by, and I know she'd prefer my entertaining you there as to entertaining you here."

Ted's flashed a hint of a smile. "Is that what you're doing?"

Kit wished she knew. She couldn't explain her thoughts or her feelings these days. Not a good thing for a lawyer with a preliminary hearing coming up.

"I just felt it would be good for us," she replied.

Ted shifted in his seat and stared past her to the window. "I've been reading your father's Bible. There's a great deal to consider."

"Tell me what you've read," Kit said.

"The Gospels, at least three times each," he began. "I suppose what I see there gives me peace as well as cause for concern."

"Concern?"

Ted looked at Kit directly. "Jesus is baptized and then He goes into the desert. He's there for a long time."

Kit nodded. "Forty days and forty nights."

"Yes. He fasted during that time, and I'm of a mind to believe He prayed during that time, as well."

"That would seem reasonable."

"The entire matter seems reasonable."

Kit leaned across her desk. "What are you suggesting?"

Ted shrugged. "I feel God is calling me for a purpose—that much is clear. But I don't know what. So when I read those passages about Jesus in the desert, I wondered if it was something to consider for myself."

"To go into the desert for forty days and nights?" Kit asked. This conversation wasn't going the way she'd hoped. She had thought they would talk about the past and the present, all with the purpose of pointing them toward the future.

"Time away," Ted said. "I don't know where yet."

Kit felt a sinking sensation in the pit of her stomach. She had just gotten him back. How could she tell him goodbye—again? She didn't like the desperate way she was beginning to feel. She didn't want to lose Ted, but neither did she want to keep him from doing what God wanted him to do. She got up from her chair and paced behind her desk as she was wont to do when something disturbed her.

"What do you hope it would accomplish?" she asked, trying to help Ted reason this through.

"I suppose it would accomplish a time alone with God," Ted replied rather matter-of-factly. "I don't know how this works— what I should do or not do for that matter." Ted leaned forward, his gaze following Kit's every move. "Is it possible God would call me away from Los Angeles?"

Kit stopped in mid-step. "All things are possible with God. The Bible says that much. I suppose there is an aspect of what you're suggesting that frightens me."

"I need time to figure out what God wants of me," Ted said, rising.

Hearing him move, Kit turned and went to where he stood. "You come here and talk about leaving again. I suppose I'm just as stunned as when you appeared in the courtroom, and then at church."

Ted reached out and touched her cheek. Kit refused to even breathe for fear he'd take it wrong and remove his hand. "And that is a problem, Kit. I'm unpredictable and unreliable. I don't know who I am or what I'm supposed to do. Up until a few weeks ago, I wouldn't have given you two cents for my life."

"And now?"

Ted shook his head. "I don't know. I just don't know."

He stepped away and the absence of his hand upon her cheek left Kit feeling empty. She wanted to be strong. She wanted to say the right thing. This was almost more than she could bear.

Ted picked up his hat and crutches and headed to the door. Kit followed after him. She barely kept herself from embracing him. "Confusion doesn't come from God," Kit whispered. "He'll show you the right way to go."

Ted slowly nodded. "I hope so." He opened the door.

Kit wanted to call him back. It felt like losing him again. But he had to come to his own conclusions. She knew that now.

When the room became silent with his departure, Kit slowly returned to her desk. The notes she'd made on the Ed Hanratty case caught her attention. She had no clearer understanding of that situation than she did of Ted's.

Kit ran her fingers through her hair as it fell to her shoulders. "I need some answers, Lord," she whispered. "I need them soon."

# Chapter 21

*Los Angeles Examiner*
July 2, 1904

### KILLER COP'S VIOLENT PAST
Officer Hanratty Was Known to Beat Suspects
His Strange Association with Kathleen Shannon
by Tom Phelps

*Officer Edward Hanratty sits in the county jail awaiting his preliminary hearing on charges of cold-blooded murder. The facts of the case are clear, as given to this newspaper by various witnesses. In addition, the arrestee's own past has come into the picture for all to see.*

*Other questions about this case are being raised. Primary among them is why Kathleen Shannon, the noted attorney, has agreed to represent him. Hanratty played a dark role in the case of Juan Chavez, acquitted of rape charges through the brilliant defense of Miss Shannon. It was Hanratty who beat a* "confession" out of Chavez when the man was innocent all along.

What could have caused the change in heart of Miss Shannon toward Edward Hanratty? Some might suppose that the lawyer is convinced of her client's innocence. Others ask if the motive is money. This would not be the first time an attorney-at-law in criminal court has taken a case based upon financial remuneration.

Either way, the city watches to see if justice will be done.

---

*Los Angeles Daily Times*
July 2, 1904

### YELLOW JOURNAL SEEKS SCANDAL
### Case of Officer Hanratty a Matter of Circulation
### Rumors That Witnesses Have Been Bought

*Ever since the unfortunate slaying of Jay Chausser at the Braxton Arms Hotel, the yellow newspapers, whose aim is to vilify and belittle a competent and honest police officer, have been making every effort to incite the public to the belief that the officer who shot Chausser did so with deliberation and malice, and that his act was nothing short of cold-blooded murder. The term "murderer" has been freely used in referring to the unwilling slayer of Jay Chausser, shot and killed while resisting a legal inquiry.*

*Those of a more objective bent who have been covering this story, which the yellow journals have sought to turn into a "scandal" of monumental proportions, report not only that much has been created that is at odds with accuracy on the factual level, but also that rumors abound regarding the stories told by various "witnesses" to the events. Only at the preliminary hearing will a full account begin to emerge, and it is on this that hinges the hope of Officer Edward Hanratty for a fair trial.*

*Of further concern to the cause of righteousness in our courts is the portrait painted of Hanratty's lawyer, Kathleen Shannon. Enemies of Officer Hanratty are attempting to tar her with the stain of self-interest and feather her with the taint of greed, despite the fact that her reputation as a zealous yet honest attorney continues to solidify. In all things she . . .*

Kit lowered the *Times* and said, "That was not what General Otis thought of me a couple of months ago. Now that I am serving his interests, he sings a different tune."

Aunt Freddy sighed. "Once more you are on the front pages. Whatever is to be done?"

Kit tried to smile. Lunch with Freddy in the Fairbank mansion was welcome, as she had not seen her great-aunt as frequently as she would have liked. But that was partly her choice. It was difficult not to be affected by Aunt Freddy's constant worries about Kit's position in society and life. If there was any acceptance beginning to take hold in Freddy that Kit was who she was and would not be moved, it was of the grudging sort.

"I am afraid I will be constant fodder for the papers," Kit said ruefully. "I suppose there is nothing to be done. They will write what they will write, and I will continue to do what I must."

"At least insist on an acceptable photograph," Freddy said. "The last one in the *Examiner* was less than flattering."

"I have more important things to worry about than how I look in the newspapers."

"Oh dear," Aunt Freddy said. "I can't think what is more important than how one looks to the world. And besides, a photograph tells so much."

Kit did not care to debate the point, but the last thing Freddy said nudged a thought in Kit's mind. The *Examiner* had printed numerous photographs of what they called "the murder scene." Kit had scanned them at the time but was concentrating mostly on

finding testimonial witnesses. Perhaps it was time to study the pho-
tos again. All of the newspapers from the past several weeks were
piled in her office.

Aunt Freddy's butler, Jerrold, entered the dining room and
announced that her other guest had arrived.

"Other guest?" Kit said.

"Someone I wish you to meet," Aunt Freddy said. "Jerrold,
show him in."

It was with some suspicion that Kit observed the entry of the
well-dressed, angular man attired in European fashion, who strode
to Freddy, took her hand, and kissed it.

"My dear Freddy," he said. "How wonderful to see you." Kit
was certain this was another of Aunt Freddy's attempts to find her
a matrimonial match. But she could not flee. The only thing to do
was sit patiently and try to weather the storm of Freddy's inten-
tions.

Kit saw Aunt Freddy's girlish blush as she nodded. "I would
like you to meet my great-niece, Kathleen," Aunt Freddy said.
"Kathleen, may I introduce Professor Benjamin Stillwater?"

The continental gentleman bowed as he took Kit's hand, kissing
it. She preferred the American custom of a firm shake, but she
smiled politely. So this was the psychic Aunt Freddy had told her
about. What was the reason for his visit? Surely, she hoped, not to
read palms.

Stillwater took a chair next to Aunt Freddy, who rang the tiny
bell that sat on the table. Freddy ordered Jerrold to serve lunch.

"Your aunt has told me much about you," Stillwater offered.
The way he looked at her, Kit shuddered to think what Aunt
Freddy might have said. That her niece was young and in need of
rescue? A wayward girl who needed to be diverted away from the
awful profession she was in? She desperately wanted to be alone in
her office doing some real work.

"The professor is the leading seer in the city," Aunt Freddy said excitedly.

"Seer?" Kit said, a gentle tone of derision sounding in spite of herself. "What exactly is it that you see?"

"Various phenomena, Miss Shannon," Stillwater replied. "Especially as occurs in the spirit world."

Kit fought the urge to shout *fraud* but, for the sake of her aunt, merely nodded.

"Do you believe in the spirits?" he asked.

If he was going to examine her, however, she was not going to be reticent. "Yes, I do," Kit said. "I believe in spirits of deceit and in spirits of holiness."

"Interesting."

Kit took a sip of afternoon tea.

"You must excuse my niece—she's young yet," Aunt Freddy said.

As Professor Stillwater grinned a smug pardon, Kit held her tongue. Stillwater pressed forward. "How would one tell the difference, between the spirits, I mean?"

"Holy Scripture tells us to try the spirits, to see whether they are of God. Scripture also tells us . . ." She hesitated. Informing Freddy's guest that God would rather see mediums stoned to death would not likely be viewed by her aunt as the zenith of tact.

"Yes?" Stillwater said.

"Perhaps," Kit said, "it would be best to change the subject."

"But this is a subject nearer and dearer to me than any other," Stillwater said. "And to your aunt as well."

At this Kit tensed. How much of this was Aunt Freddy taking seriously? More than polite conversation was seemingly at stake. "I will say, then, that God views those who traffic in spirits as less than friendly to His cause."

Stillwater's grin faded for a moment, then returned with

studied persistence. "But, Miss Shannon, I believe I can show you that God's view is entirely in the opposite direction."

At that moment the soup was served. Kit observed the steam rising along with her ire. The man wanted a debate, and Freddy seemed an amused onlooker, as if she expected her guest would put Kit firmly into her place.

"I am quite certain that cannot be done," Kit said.

"Be careful, Benjamin," Aunt Freddy chimed in. "My niece is reputed to be quite the debater."

Raising his hand as if to show unconcern, Stillwater said to Kit, "You are a woman who believes strongly in God, then?"

"Yes."

"And in the Bible?"

"Of course."

"And in the power of God for good in our world?"

"All of this is so," Kit said impatiently.

"Then I should tell you that we are on the same side, Miss Shannon. And as you are a lawyer, I shall be happy to provide you with evidence."

Kit was not at all sure what he could offer as evidence, but her curiosity was piqued. "Yes?"

"I have joined forces with a well-respected clergyman to open an institute here in Los Angeles," Stillwater said. "It will be called the Institute of Progressive Religion and Science. How do you like the sound of that?"

"Who is this respected clergyman?"

"You know him, I think. Dr. Edward Lazarus."

Kit closed her eyes for a moment, then opened them and looked at Aunt Freddy. She had an expression of such sweet innocence that Kit almost said nothing. But that same look compelled her to speak. "Professor, I do not seek to offend, but I must tell you that I do not believe in charlatanism, especially when it comes to the matter of religion."

"Oh dear," Freddy said.

"What you are proposing is, in my opinion, nothing less than snake oil for the gullible."

The professor seemed unflappable. "If you are referring to your great-aunt, I am sure she might have something to say on that."

"Kit, dear," Aunt Freddy said, "you have not given the professor a chance."

"I am sorry," Kit said, "but there are things that do not deserve a chance."

The air grew still. Even the sound of the birds outside the window, normally at a frenetic pitch this time of day, was absent. Aunt Freddy's face began to flush as she took a kerchief and waved it furiously in front of her face.

"I am used to skepticism," Stillwater said. "But I said I would offer proof. How would it be if I were to solve your current case?"

Kit shook her head. "I am sure I don't know what you mean."

"I keep abreast of the goings-on in my community. You have taken upon yourself, if the newspapers are any indication, a rather difficult case."

"Kit is always getting into difficulties," Aunt Freddy chimed.

"I would be very happy to lend you my services to find out what really happened at the Braxton Arms," Stillwater said.

"You cannot expect me to seriously—"

"Kit!" Aunt Freddy said. "This man is offering to help you."

"I cannot accept such help," Kit said. This was her cue to rise. "Aunt Freddy, I cannot deny you your companions, but my advice is that you not give this man another dollar or moment of your time."

"You cannot speak to me that way in my own house!"

Kit looked at her aunt, feeling protective and distant at the same time. She had a feeling this was not the last time she would be clashing with Professor Stillwater and whatever twaddle he was professor of. But this was not the time or place.

"I am sorry if I have offended you," Kit said.

"Oh, but you have," said Stillwater, his voice like ice. "You have indeed."

Had she really? Yes. The expression on Aunt Freddy's face was confirmation enough.

As Kit walked to the front door, past a confused-looking Jerrold, she began to wonder if this might be the last time she would be invited here.

# Chapter 22

THE CARRIAGE RIDE down the hill from Aunt Freddy's mansion, usually so restful and lovely to Kit, was now lacking its usual charm. In Kit's experience, Los Angeles could be a city of light or darkness, with very little of the spectrum in between. When the sun was shining and a breeze was in the air, it seemed an open, friendly city, welcoming of visitors and those just passing through. A spirit of optimism prevailed. People seemed to smile.

Then there were the dark times, and not just at night. The period of the Juan Chavez trial was one of those times. A mood of hatred and mistrust seemed to cover the City of Angels like a shroud. Citizen opposed citizen; emotions ran hot. Los Angeles did not feel like a haven of rest then. It was a brooding place where menace lurked in doorways and peril on street corners.

Now, in the rays of the afternoon sun, when her disposition should have been carefree, there was a heaviness in Kit's spirit. She was worried about Aunt Freddy. She hadn't looked well. There was a pastiness to her complexion and dark circles under her eyes. The presence of this psychic fraud was equally worrisome. There was no telling what this Stillwater character had told Aunt Freddy. No doubt he could very well be part of her ill health. Her aunt had always had a fascination for spiritual things—except Christianity. Countless conversations had not moved her toward the truth. Yet she would fret and stew for days on end about something a psychic had revealed.

How should she stop this man from preying on Aunt Freddy and the other easy marks he no doubt sought like a hungry snake? Aunt Freddy was, after all, an adult. Kit could not force her to do anything. But they had quarreled, and now Kit was again on the outside of her aunt's good graces.

Poor Freddy. She wanted so much to control the various elements that surrounded her life. She wanted to see Kit married with children. She wanted to restore her somewhat tarnished throne at the pinnacle of Los Angeles's social elite. In fact, Kit had no doubt that should Aunt Freddy figure out how to arrange the surge of the ocean's tides, she would want to control that as well.

Yet for all the strength and control Aunt Freddy loved to purport, she was very vulnerable—perhaps even fragile.

As Kit directed her rented carriage toward the office of the district attorney, she turned to the other matters weighing on her mind. Concerns about Aunt Freddy's health and her own confusion over her feelings for Ted Fox rivaled for position in Kit's mind. But most persistent of all was her concern about the case she had gotten herself into.

She did not need a psychic, but she certainly needed the guidance of God on this. She could find no witnesses to confirm her client's story. And yet something in Hanratty, when he spoke, made her believe him. She would not be satisfied with only a partial story.

At the intersection of Main and Temple, Kit paused to observe workers decorating a building with red, white, and blue bunting. The Fourth of July was just around the corner. Soon the streets would be filled with celebrants, many with too much liquor in them. Kit wanted nothing more than a quiet evening at the hotel—unless Ted were to call upon her. And that uncertain hope, she knew, was a large measure of her melancholy. She did not know what he would do. He'd talked about going away again, and Kit was overwhelmed with concern that he might do exactly that.

Should she be the one to break the silence between them? Society might frown upon it. Aunt Freddy would surely succumb to a state of apoplexy if she found out. But Kit had learned early on that if she waited for other people to act, she often missed out on what was needed. Yes, she decided as she approached the D.A.'s office. Forget about social niceties. She wanted to see Ted, to determine how her heart felt toward him. She would need to settle that account, and soon.

Now, however, she needed information.

The same bloodless secretary sat in front of Davenport's door. She did not bother to say a word to Kit this time. She merely opened the door and announced Kit's presence, leaving it open when Davenport told Kit to enter.

At least this was some progress.

"Good afternoon, Miss Shannon." Davenport was in his shirtsleeves and held a drink in his hand. "May I offer you a sherry?"

"No, thank you," Kit said. "May we talk about Mr. Hanratty?"

"My dear girl, what is there to talk about?"

*Dear girl?* When would she be treated as an equal? Perhaps never. But she would act as if she deserved it. "I want to know why you are keeping witnesses from me."

The dapper D.A. looked at her coldly, then sat in his large swivel chair. "Whatever can you mean by that?"

"I have tried to interview witnesses, as any good lawyer should. But it is as if the word has gone out from this office not to co-operate with me."

Davenport raised his hands in the air, as if to signal helplessness. The hint of a half-smile appeared on his face. Kit knew he was under no obligation to help her, but if he were to be actively engaging in a scheme to keep evidence away from her, she might be able to argue to an appellate court that her client's conviction—should it happen—was due to fundamental unfairness.

She did not expect Davenport to admit wrongdoing. She only hoped her message would be heard and any active opposition would stop.

"Am I to understand," Kit said, "that you are professing no knowledge of such a scheme?"

"What you understand, or don't understand, is of no concern to me. This case will be conducted in court, and I shall win. Officer Hanratty must pay the penalty for his crime."

In a burst, Kit said, "Have you met with William Randolph Hearst within the last week?"

The tone of the question, if not the question itself, must have stunned John Davenport. His face tightened. "How dare you," he said, standing up.

His reaction was more than she expected and difficult to read. But he was, somehow, vulnerable. And he was using outrage to protect himself. He would expect Kit to back down.

She did not. "There is nothing untoward about my asking."

"There most certainly is. You are questioning my ethics. You are insinuating that I am in league on this case with a yellow journal. Who do you think you are? I have been a lawyer thirty years. You come here wet behind the ears and question *me?*"

"Sir, you have not answered my question." Kit felt her heels digging into the floor.

"I will not."

"Then I shall take it to the judge."

"You are a fool."

"And to the Court of Appeals if I must."

Regaining composure, Davenport shook his head. "Such a waste of talent. You might have given all of this energy to teaching children to obey their betters."

"I demand that you stop obstructing justice in this matter."

Calmly, Davenport said, "You may demand all you wish. It will not move me, it will not move the judges. What you are supposing is a fantasy. You are desperate, Miss Shannon. Desperate lawyers do not serve their clients well. Now if you will excuse me." He motioned her toward the door.

A deep anger boiled within Kit, but she could do nothing now. She had failed to coerce his professional respect with the threat of legal action. And she knew deep within her that no such respect would ever be forthcoming from this office. The only alternative she had was to win her case. That prospect was beginning to look even bleaker than when she first walked in his door.

As Kit passed through that same door to leave, she almost hit a man entering. She opened her mouth to voice an apology, but then saw the face. Her breath left her, and her body jolted as if exploding from within.

"Well, if it isn't the infamous Kathleen Shannon," Heath Sloate said.

---

"My heart," Freddy said. "Oh dear."

"Are you feeling ill?" Professor Stillwater said. He took her hand and patted it.

"Just a flutter," she said. She did not want to alarm him. He had just completed a reading for her—using his odd cards and her palms—and she was still thinking about the row with Kit an hour ago. But what his reading had just revealed was no doubt causing her heart to jump as well.

Ever since she had come to Los Angeles those many years ago with her beloved Jasper, Frederica Fairbank had been searching for significance. The social arena was her world, and she could look back on many fine accomplishments—the founding of the Women's Club, the planning of the Festival of the Flowers—now an annual event—and many well-regarded social fetes on behalf of the Los Angeles Booster Club and the Chamber of Commerce.

And on account of how well received all of those were, Freddy was one of several women who could arguably lay claim to the mantle of "city mother." Others, including the haughty Eulalie Pike, had similar designs.

Freddy knew it was prideful, but she had always wished to find a final triumph that would elevate her past all rivals.

And now that time may have come. No wonder her heart jumped inside her.

"Oh, Professor," Freddy said, after the fluttering calmed. "Can you be sure?"

Stillwater smiled and nodded. "I not only see it, I can help to make it happen. In fact, that is what I have been wanting to tell you. Your dreams and mine have come together through a fate that is destiny."

"Yes . . ."

"What you want is some good work to outlive you and hold up your name, and that of your dear departed husband, for all time. What I seek is a way to help more people, to provide a salve to their souls and a bounce to their step."

*He is so poetic,* Freddy thought. *The mind of a great man and the soul of a poet.* "Tell me more," she said.

"My institute will bear another name. It shall be called the Fairbank Institute. Here we will combine the best that science, religion, and spiritualism have to offer. Think of it! What a bold, new world we would open up to the masses. To those who suffer now we would offer hope and a means to realize their deepest desires."

"As you have given me hope," Freddy said.

Stillwater smacked his lips as if tasting something delicious, then squeezed her hand a little harder. "Only doing what I have been led to do. Fate has brought us together, dear Mrs. Fairbank. And fate will see that our work continues."

"The Fairbank Institute?"

"Do you like it?"

"Oh my, yes."

"We will have our own building."

"Will the name be on it?"

"In bold, brass lettering. Something to stand for all time."

Freddy's heart danced again, this time causing a short, sharp pain. But even as she winced, she smiled. Here was comfort of the deepest sort.

"We shall discuss this many times in the months ahead," Stillwater said. "Would you like to help me make plans?"

"Of course! If the institute is to bear Jasper's name, I shall want it to be of the highest order."

"Exactly," said Stillwater. "Just one thing more, if I may ask."

"Anything, Professor."

"A small request. Two, actually. I should like to begin the design plans, initial research, and all of that. Naturally, I will want to consult with you, but the important thing is to get it going."

"I agree. Time is of the essence."

"Indeed. Now, I must secure the initial funding for this project, but I am loathe to admit that at the present moment such capital does not exist. I must therefore seek investors, and I thought—"

"Allow me!" Freddy said.

"To invest? Yourself?"

"But it is to be named after Jasper and me, is it not?"

"Yes, but I wouldn't dream of asking—"

"Stuff and nonsense. How much do you need?"

"Freddy," Stillwater said, raising a hand. "I am grateful, but I must refuse."

"Whatever are you talking about?"

"I cannot take advantage of you this way."

Freddy slapped her knee. "I am doing this of my own free will. It is my money, isn't it? How much do you need?"

"Really, Freddy—"

"How much?"

Stillwater swallowed. "I would think ten thousand dollars would do."

"Is that all?"

"For now."

"Then ten thousand it shall be. I shall arrange to have the amount transferred to your bank."

"You are the kindest woman I have ever known."

Freddy smiled, took out her handkerchief, and began to fan herself. "You said there were two requests."

"Ah yes," Stillwater said. "And this is of the utmost importance."

"Tell me," Freddy said.

"I have rivals in the field, those who do not have the best interests of people at heart."

Nodding, Freddy said, "Charlatans."

"Indeed. So it would be best if we kept all this our secret for the moment. Then, when the foundation is set, we can announce to the whole world that the Fairbank Institute has come for the salvation of all mankind."

"How grand!" Freddy said. "Oh, how grand a vision it is. And for now it will be our secret, yes?"

"Yes," agreed Stillwater.

# Chapter 23

*SLOATE.*

Like the shout of an ugly epithet, the name kept ringing in Kit's mind as she walked through the afternoon crowd on Broadway. Sloate, who had tried to ruin her career and send an innocent man—Ted Fox—to the gallows! That he was back in Los Angeles was bad enough. That he appeared to be assisting the district attorney was like a knife to her ribs.

And how delighted Davenport had been in her discomfort. She had accommodated his delight, too, by becoming immediately flustered. She could still see Sloate's smile as he stood in the doorway, not moving, mouthing polite bromides that hit her like rocks.

This was a declaration of war. Davenport was going to use every weapon he had, even the threat of an old enemy, to keep Kit from interfering with his plans. His political ambitions were well-known. Now Kit knew he would stop at nothing in order to feed those ambitions, even stooping to using Sloate, a man he had once prosecuted! It was shameless.

And then, for a long moment, Kit did not know where she was going.

She was not sure which direction she faced, or if she even had a destination. And though she was surrounded by people, she felt entirely alone.

Lost. She had the sudden sensation of being lost in time and place. Los Angeles was a young city with a young soul. That soul was not yet fully formed, and it could go a number of ways. It could become a place rooted in the values that made the country itself great—industry, civility, and, most important, a goodness that came from good people. For that to happen, the city's churches would have to remain strong and not drift.

Or Los Angeles could go the way of the society in Noah's day. That was a very real possibility, she knew, because of people like Davenport and Sloate, who craved power. But it was also because of people like Edward Lazarus, "having a form of godliness, but denying the power thereof."

Kit finally stopped at the corner of Broadway and Second. A man with a sweeping mustache was on the street corner vending something called "The Electro Belt." A small crowd was listening as this respectable-looking agent held up what looked to be a thick leather belt studded with metallic ornaments.

"I want to help those who are weak," the man said, "who lack the vitality they once enjoyed. To those who are nervous, despondent, and lack self-confidence. Who feel as if old age is coming on too soon because of the dulling of their youthful fire and ambition. I bank on electricity!"

The man showed the belt to the crowd as if displaying a magic talisman. "Electricity is the power that will put more life into anything living. It will restore paralyzed limbs. It is life to weakened organs. It drives away pain. It is doing these things every day—so why not for you? I will pay four hundred dollars in gold to any man or woman who uses my Electro Belt as I direct and takes proper care, and who does not show improvement."

As Kit watched him carry on just like an evangelist, she saw the city dividing at a crossroads. People would always have the choice to buy into either man's nostrums or God's truth. Which way would the people turn? And what could she do to guide them?

She almost began to speak when she got the feeling she was being watched.

She whirled around but saw only the bobbing heads of pedestrians, unaware of her existence. But the sense of menace, small though it was, remained. As Kit proceeded southward on Broadway, she reasoned with herself that her unease was merely a trick of the mind. The forces against her and her client were formidable. It was phantoms that hounded her, surely, but that did not stop her from walking a little more quickly.

One of the swiftly gliding cars of the electric rail passed by, the clang of the bell a signal to pedestrians. Without thinking about it Kit found herself scanning the faces in the car. Was someone on that car looking at her?

She stopped and, again, looked behind her. At that moment she thought she saw another person, a man, stop fifty yards back up the street. As the crowd surged around him, over the heads of passers-by she saw—didn't she?—the dark, rounded hat on this man move toward a building and disappear from view.

*Stop it*, she told herself. *Just keep going on and clear your head.*

Further on she passed the new city hall, a large building patterned after a German town hall of the middle ages. A curious design, Kit had always thought, but in keeping with the emerging personality of the city's architecture, which followed no single style. A Mediterranean project might be found plopped next to a taste of old Spain or modern Chicago. It was like that with the people, too.

Someone bumped her from behind and Kit stumbled, waving wildly with her hands to keep her balance. She fell full force against a telegraph pole, hitting the hard wood with her shoulder.

Then a grip of iron took hold of her arm.

She wanted to cry out as she turned to her attacker, her mind telling her this was broad daylight and surely someone—a policeman, a shopkeeper—would come to her aid.

The man's face was ruddy and contorted in a grimace. A few teeth showed in his mouth.

Kit was so stunned she couldn't speak. The man continued to hold her, hard. And then he shook his head.

"Excuse," he said.

The voice was thick with accent. German?

"Excuse."

He was apologizing. He was also squeezing the life out of her arm. Kit slapped at his hand. "Please let go."

With a sudden realization he released her arm, as if he'd been holding a live bomb. "Oh excuse," he said quickly. "I hit you. From back. You I did not see. Sorry. Sorry."

Kit stroked her throbbing arm. The man was built like a bull. He must have been a blacksmith or a tanner.

"It is all right," Kit said.

The man bowed three or four times as he backed away, and Kit felt how fast her heart was racing. She leaned against the pole for a moment, then continued on her way. She passed the post office, the armory hall, and the central marketplace, racing past them as if on a bicycle.

Finally she came to the little park at Sixth Street, across from Hazard's Pavilion with its horticultural splendor. She sat on a park bench under a shade tree and took stock.

She had God's promises, and the faithfulness of His past

actions. Hadn't He brought her through all of her trials—both in court and out?

The peace of God, which passed all of her understanding, began to take hold again.

She watched as wayfarers stepped into the park from the city street, and how the placid scene seemed to take them into another world. They strolled instead of hurried. They found comfort.

Kit was silently thanking God for the day when across the park she saw him—the man in the rounded hat.

This time he made no attempt to hide the fact that he was staring directly at her. Smiling.

It was Terrence O'Toole.

Her blood ran cold, but she could not avert her eyes. He was leaning casually against a tree, his arms folded.

Kit did not move. She had no idea what to do. A beat cop strolled nearby, but what could she say? There was no law against a man staring at someone.

Should she try to make it back to her office or the hotel? What if he followed her there, as well?

And then another thought seemed to come out of nowhere. *Face him. Go up to him and ask him what his business is.* The only thing commending this course of action was the element of surprise. He was clearly trying to intimidate her. As were half the men in Los Angeles. What if she did not act intimidated?

It would indeed be acting, because she was already trembling. But Kit stood and with a determination she did not feel, walked across the grass, praying for protection all the way.

O'Toole's smile faded as she approached, which told her the surprise had some effect. And though he did not move from the tree, his arms unfolded.

"Good day, Miss Shannon," he said.

"What are you doing here?" she said.

"This is a public park, ain't it?" O'Toole said.

"Why are you following me?"

"I am just out for a stroll."

"You want something from me? You have a message to deliver?"

O'Toole said nothing. His smile returned.

"Who sent you?" Kit said, as though she were questioning an unexpected deliveryman.

"I ain't no messenger boy."

"I think you are. You wouldn't be here on your own time. Is it Hawthorne, Basil J.?"

"I told you—"

"No," Kit said, "he isn't interested in this, just his hotel. Someone else."

O'Toole made a tiny sucking sound, like he was trying to expel some particle of food from his teeth. She had clearly set him on edge. She searched her mind for the right words—the words that would not only back him up against the ledge but also send him plummeting over the edge.

"Well, who is it?" Kit said, emboldened by his silence.

His hands balled into fists. "Don't push your luck, Miss Shannon."

The reality of the situation came home to her then. She was no match for him physically, of course, though she knew a few holds from her orphanage days. One didn't survive long without them. But he was big, strong, and a former cop. If he wanted to hurt her, he would have no problem.

But she could not stop herself. She realized she felt as Ted once described flying—once you are in the air and launched, you have no choice but to ride it out.

"Luck has nothing to do with this," Kit said. "But I want you to stop following me or *your* luck will change."

He looked unconcerned. "And how might that be?"

She wasn't entirely sure. But thinking on her feet was an ability she'd had to develop as a lawyer. "Assault."

"You're dreaming. I'm not assaulting anybody. I'm here to enjoy the view. Can I help it if you're the view?"

"You're attempting to put fear into me. And to a large degree you are succeeding. But I will not be intimidated. I will bring an action for assault against you."

"But I ain't done nothing." He seemed a little less sure of himself.

"Mr. O'Toole, in 1872 the Commonwealth of Massachusetts prosecuted a man for pointing an unloaded weapon at another man. The victim dove under a table and was injured. There was no intention to injure, but an action for assault—for the intention to cause apprehension—was upheld. If you want to try me in court, then by all means continue this game. But understand I am in dead earnest."

As if by itself, O'Toole's arm rose. At the end of it was a fist.

"Do you wish to add battery?" Kit said quickly.

He held his arm in the air for a moment, then lowered it slowly. "You can't stop him this time," O'Toole said. "That's the message."

"Stop whom?"

O'Toole turned and walked toward the street. Kit wanted to shout at him, demand that he answer. But then her mind suggested one, and it was the same thought she'd had earlier, the one that had sent her charging through the city in the first place.

*Sloate.*

# Chapter 24

NEVER HAD HE FELT such an emptiness.

Though he had spent many wonderful years here, Ted was now a stranger in his mother's house, his house. No voices filled its rooms. No warmth of companionship was shared beneath its roof. He had been alone before, but now hollowness came to him in its fullest force, cold and uncompromising.

Things he'd once taken pleasure in meant nothing now. Nothing but a swirl of memories, none of which offered him any comfort. If anything, they only served to emphasize his loneliness.

And he knew the only person who could remove the feeling, but it was the one person he could not have.

It was a dull morning, and the light that came through the windows was not cheery in the least. Ted bumbled his way into the kitchen, managing to light the stove and heat water, into which he would dump the last of his coffee beans. He was no domestic. He wanted a wife.

He wanted Kit.

Yes, her feelings toward him seemed warm. But could he allow himself to even hope that she would consent to a life of caring for him? Oh, he would manage something—banking, perhaps—but he would always be aware of his need. So would Kit.

When the water boiled he poured a healthy dose of ground coffee into it and stirred. He waited until it grew black and then ladled himself a mug full.

He sat on a hard chair in the kitchen and took a sip. He felt as if he were drinking hot oil. Coffee, apparently, was not going to lighten his outlook.

*What do I do, God?*

He heard himself say it and realized he was praying. Why hadn't he thought of that before? He was a believer now, and Christians believed in prayer, right?

So Ted prayed. It spilled out of him, like rain from a dark cloud.

He wanted Kit. Yet he loved her too much to saddle her with a cripple. *God, direct me. Give me a sign, anything.*

He waited, listened for a voice. Isn't that how God answered prayer? But Ted heard nothing except the sound of his own breathing.

A knock at the front door snapped him to attention. Ted grabbed his crutches and went to answer. A well-dressed man, holding a whip in a gloved hand, stood there.

"Would I be addressing Mr. Fox?" he said.

"Yes. Who—"

"The lady would like a word with you." The man turned and indicated a carriage, drawn by a single horse, waiting on the street.

Ted could not see into the cab, but his heart picked up its pace.

"She's a pretty one, too," the driver said.

Ted's spirits lifted higher than the trees lining the street. So this was how God answered prayer, by bringing Kit directly to him. What a mighty and loving God.

With a laugh, Ted bounded forward, taking the steps, racing faster than he could ever remember going on crutches before. In his mind he knew what he would say. Even before Kit would speak, he was going to kiss her, then demand they be married. Today, if possible. They would go directly to find Reverend Macauley and then they'd . . .

The cab door opened, and Ted stopped short when he saw her face.

"Hello, Ted."

Elinor Wynn's voice fairly purred. She smiled rather smugly, as if she'd somehow accomplished a great victory in bringing him to her side.

Ted backed up a step. It would not have been any different if he had been aloft in a plane and had come crashing to earth.

Elinor patted her gloved hand on the seat beside her. "Get in," she said. "We have much to discuss."

---

Corazón did not like the way the man looked at her. His smile had intent behind it. Bad intent.

Kit had warned her about him, this clerk at the Braxton Arms who called himself Slim. It was a public place, Corazón had said, so she would not be afraid. But now that she was here it was different. Now he could reach out and touch her.

"Good morning to you," Slim said, stretching out the *you*.

"I would like," Corazón stammered, "to see a room."

Slim's smile remained unchanged. His eyes roamed her body. "You're a Mex, is that it?"

Corazón did not answer. She knew he didn't seek one.

"I always said Mexican women are pretty if you give 'em half a chance. Looks like you took the whole chance."

"Do you have a room?"

"I got a room." He leaned forward on his elbows. "But it costs money."

"Sí," Corazón said, then, embarrassed, quickly said, "Yes."

"American money."

"Yes."

"You got American money? I don't take tortillas or goats or anything like that."

Swallowing, Corazón said, "Please, if you show me."

"Yes, that's what I always said about Mexican women."

Now what should she do? Nothing was stopping her from turning and walking out. But she had come with a purpose, and she was going to see it through.

Then Slim stepped around the desk and said, "Come on along with me."

He escorted her, as she had hoped he would, to the second floor.

"I got one room down here at the end," he said. Then he leaned toward her and added, "Very private."

As he walked down the hall, Corazón noted the door to room 202. She slowed so she could look at the opposite wall carefully. It was painted a pale light green. She saw no hole.

"Come on, now," Slim said.

She caught up with him. He led her to the last door on the right, unlocked it, and opened it up.

"Yes, private," he said, waiting for her to go in. She did not.

"Go on in," he said.

Corazón shook her head.

"Well, how are you going to know if you want it?" Slim said. He sounded exasperated.

"I can see," she answered.

The sound of a bell came from down the stairs. Then another. "The new phone," Slim said. "You wait right here." He ran, in an absurd-looking fashion, down the corridor. The moment he disappeared down the stairs Corazón raced back to the wall opposite 202.

In Kit's office they had estimated the height the bullet should be—if there was a bullet. Corazón could tell from Kit's voice and expression that she was unsure, but that she wanted a hole to be there.

But the wall was without a mark. In fact, it looked freshly painted.

Corazón could hear Slim at the desk, talking loudly into his telephone. She ran her hand over the wall, covering as large an area as possible.

No hole.

It had to be here. In her heart Corazón believed Hanratty was innocent. She had been with Kit once to see him, and though she feared him because of what he did to her brother, her instincts told her Hanratty spoke the truth.

What if the bullet hit something—a nail, perhaps—and ricocheted off in another direction?

Slim was still talking on the phone, and no one else was in the hallway. Corazón began searching a wider area. She noticed that just to the left of the area where she had thought the bullet would be, the wall seemed different. Older somehow. The plaster was slightly rougher, the paint a little lighter.

But there was still no hole.

Corazón turned and studied the opposite wall. If the bullet had indeed zipped in another direction, it could have landed anywhere. But the opposite wall was as pristine as the other.

Then she saw a mark.

It was small and close to the floor. And it was in the wall next to the door to 202. Corazón got to her knees and examined it closely. She ran her finger over it. It was not a bullet hole but simply a dimple in the plaster.

She realized then the hotel was silent.

Quickly she got to her feet and turned, but it was too late. Slim was standing at the top of the stairs, his face reddening.

"I don't like being made a fool," he said.

# Chapter 25

THE RICH BURGUNDY and amber tones of The Imperial seemed foreign to Ted. Though he had dined here often among the cream of Los Angeles society at one time, he now felt more like the proverbial fish out of water. Had such things really been important to him once?

They were obviously still important to Elinor Wynn, who had ordered the cab to bring them here. Her visit had caught him completely off guard, but more surprising was her veiled threat. He had better come with her to lunch and hear what she had to say. Or things might go very badly for a certain Kathleen Shannon.

She had played the game of not addressing the subject unless he dined with her, but he knew Elinor well enough to know that her games could be brutal. Her lawsuit against Kit was a game she had lost, but that did not mean she didn't have more up her sleeve.

"Isn't this just like old times?" Elinor said. They were seated at an elegant table in the rear. Elinor had told the maître d' she wanted privacy. She pressed her advantage, leaning forward as she removed the light, wispy wrap that she'd worn around her shoulders to expose the deep V of her neckline.

"This is not old times," Ted said. He felt the chill of her look even as she batted her eyes coquettishly. He had seen this look before. He pressed back against the chair, having little desire to appear even the slightest bit interested. His look of ennui apparently had its effect.

"Let us try to be kind," Elinor said. "After all, we were almost married. And I've been so alone of late. Mama is in Europe, you know. I have the house all to myself." She looked at him with suggestive eyes, beautiful in their way yet ugly at the same time. The ice blue color was only a reminder of her frozen heart.

A waiter appeared at the table and bowed slightly. Elinor smiled at him. "Marcel, would you be so kind as to bring us a bottle of your finest champagne?"

"Not for me," Ted said.

Elinor laughed. "Oh, don't worry, dear. I will pay for the meal."

Ted looked at the waiter, who tried to hide an embarrassed expression. "This was not a good idea," Ted said and began to rise.

Elinor caressed his hand with her gloved fingers. Ted pulled back as though he'd been touched by a flame. Elinor appeared unconcerned. She touched her hand to the center of her neckline and drew her index finger along the lace edging. "Stay here, dear. Miss Shannon would surely want you to."

At the mention of Kit's name, Ted lowered himself back into his chair.

"Bring the champagne, Marcel," Elinor said. "If I have to drink it myself, well, *c'est la vie.*"

The waiter seemed relieved to have a way out. He backed away from the table.

"Tell me what this is about," Ted said. He had battled his disappointment and anger all the way to the restaurant. Now he had little patience left.

"Dear, at least let us pretend to like each other."

"I don't like you, Elinor. I am sorry to say it."

She tossed her head back slightly, the amused look leaving her face. "When did you become so cruel, Ted?"

Was he being too harsh? Elinor Wynn, whose life always revolved around money and position, had been through the social equivalent of hell over the last year. She had brought it upon herself, of course. She had lied once in criminal court—against him, no less—and recently in an ill-begotten civil action. Like a petulant child, her choices had brought her certain rebuke. But at one time, indeed, she had been the woman who might have been his wife. She'd had her good qualities. Once.

"Elinor, I know how circumstances can arise over which we have no control. Look at me. I thought I was going to be flying aeroplanes by this time, but as you can see . . ." He paused, trying to discern if he had any connection with her. "I don't know what the future holds for me, but I can tell you that I have been changed."

"Changed? In what way?"

A bit of peace washed over him. It gave him courage to go on. "Inside. I have become a Christian."

Elinor issued a small laugh. "But of course you are a Christian, dear. So am I."

Ted shook his head. "No, not in that sense. Not because of how we were brought up. Every man has to make a decision for himself."

"What sort of decision are you talking about?"

"To give his life fully to God. To no longer live for himself or herself. That's what I've done."

"Ted, dear, everyone lives for himself. It's only natural."

"But the natural man is an enemy of God. You know, Jesus said some very strange things. At least I thought they were strange once. He said we must lose our lives in order to gain them. I think I am beginning to know what He meant."

"Oh, piddle! Jesus said a good many things, but that does not mean we have to go around doing them all the time."

"This is not an idle romp," Ted said.

"People don't change. Inside they remain who they are."

"Haven't you changed, Elinor?"

She paused at that, scanning his face. For a moment a look that resembled regret touched her porcelain features. Then just as quickly as it had come, it was gone. "I have always been one to get exactly what I want. No, dear, I have not changed."

"Then perhaps you had better tell me why I am here."

Her casual smile returned as Elinor spoke. "Ted, despite everything, I have remained fond of you."

Ted found that difficult to believe but listened anyway. No doubt there was something specific that Elinor was after. There always was.

"Would it surprise you to know that I have had dreams?" Elinor said.

"Of what?"

"Of you, Ted. You and me."

Before Ted could reply the waiter returned, rather sheepishly, with the champagne and two crystal flutes. He appeared hesitant about showing the bottle to the woman for approval, but when Ted shook his head the waiter held the bottle for Elinor. Then he pulled the cork, which came out with a dull pop, and poured some of the bubbly into Elinor's flute. She tasted and nodded. But when the waiter went to pour for Ted, he refused it.

"Please, Ted," Elinor said.

"No, thank you," he said.

With a sigh, Elinor waved the waiter away. "Has God changed your taste in wine as well as women?" she asked.

"Elinor, I can't imagine why you would be thinking of me in that way. A lot of water has passed under the bridge."

"I'm still standing on that bridge, Ted. I have been ever since you left me."

"You almost got me hanged, if you'll recall."

"That was Sloate's doing. He had me so confused I didn't know what to do. I was hurt, Ted. Out of my head. You must believe me. My feelings for you have never changed."

"Frankly, I don't believe you. You have never, for even one minute in your life, been out of control. You ran your parents' household. You run your social circles. But you won't run me as well. I have no romantic feelings for you whatsoever."

"But those feelings could be rekindled," Elinor said, seeming quite sure of herself.

Ted slowly shook his head. "I'm sorry, Elinor. If there ever was any chance for such a thing, it passed long ago."

Elinor took a long, lingering sip of sparkling wine, her gaze never leaving Ted's face. Then she said, "Our chance may have just arrived."

"No."

"Oh yes. For you see, any thoughts you may have about Miss Shannon in this regard are to be left here at this table."

Ted was stunned, as much by the solemn look in her eyes as by her tone of voice. "I am sure I don't know what you mean."

"How plain must I make this? You are not going to see her anymore, dear. That is what is over."

Her tone was clipped, authoritative. Ted could scarcely believe she was serious. "I will see whom I please," he said.

"Does she know?"

"Know?"

"About you."

"What are you getting at?"

Putting her gloved hands under her chin, Elinor leaned forward. "There was a certain woman, in France I believe it was, a woman of rather dubious reputation. And another man, who worked for the French government, who was shot through the neck. An ugly business."

Ted went cold.

"Oh yes," Elinor continued, "and a certain American was asked to leave the country."

"How could you possibly know?"

"Mama insisted on it. If I was to marry you, your social background had to be pristine. Her detective found the facts, but I insisted they remain quiet." She toyed with the silverware, then offered Ted a demure smile. "I wouldn't have wanted to start my married life under such a cloud. The stigma on our union—on our children—well, let's just say, we decided it was better to keep it to ourselves."

Ted struggled to say, "You never told me you knew."

"Oh, I thought perhaps someday I would share the information with you. The only question now is whether I shall share it with Miss Shannon."

The waiter approached once again. "Get out of here," Ted snapped. Marcel quickly withdrew. Ted turned back to Elinor. "Why are you doing this?"

"I can only wonder," Elinor continued. "What would Saint Shannon think of her man after this information comes to light? Could she ever look at him the same? Would the light still shine in her eyes?"

"You would stoop to that?" Ted's teeth were clamped as he spoke.

"That and more, dear. What would it do to Miss Shannon's

sterling reputation if she were to become involved in yet another social scandal?"

Ted looked down at his hands. They were shaking.

"Besides," Elinor added, "you don't want pity. That's what it would be, after all. You would never know if her affection for you was out of her duty to care for you or whether it was true love. You would never know if you could be a real husband to her. But with me, you would never have that concern. My cards are on the table, so to speak."

"Why, Elinor? Why such hatred?"

"Because I still love you."

He examined her face and noticed then how much powder she used. Strange how he had never noticed before, or simply chose not to. Now it seemed like a mask. He looked into her eyes and searched for an ounce of true feeling. He saw only lifelessness there, as if her soul had withdrawn and left nothing behind her expression.

"No," he said suddenly. "That's not it."

"Not what, dear?"

"You don't want me."

A flush appeared under Elinor's powdered cheeks. "Whatever can you mean?"

"It's Kit you're after. You won't stop until she's ruined. Kit's the one person you came up against and couldn't control. My, but how that must have grieved you."

Elinor picked up her champagne flute. It shook slightly in her hand as she drank.

"Tell me, Elinor," Ted said.

"Keep your voice down, dear." A hardness came to Elinor's face. "There is more to this than you can possibly know. And I am not lying when I say I still care for you. But I am issuing you a warning. Stay away from that Shannon woman. If you don't, disaster will fall on both of you."

After a rush of anger, an unexpected feeling of pity fell over Ted. It surprised him.

"Don't do this," Ted said, rising. He took up his crutches. ""I don't know what unholy alliance you have struck, but it might just as well be with the devil. I urge you to turn away from it."

"Sit down, Ted."

There was a warning edge in her voice that Ted knew he could not ignore. He slowly dropped back into his chair.

"It is too late for any turning back," Elinor said. "For me, for you. And for Kit Shannon."

# Chapter 26

KIT WAITED AT the corner of Fifth and Main, feeling like a spy. Which is what she was, at the moment. Unseen but seeing, watching for the enemy.

Rhodes Hervey, the tenant she had seen briefly on the stairs at the Braxton Arms, worked at the Provost Building. That much Kit had managed to find out. The only way she was going to get any information from Hervey before the preliminary hearing was to talk to him away from the hotel. And maybe not even then. But she had to try.

She had been watching the door for almost an hour with no sign of him, and she began to wonder if she was being foolish. But there was no other choice. She had no money to hire a detective, and this was no duty for Corazón. She wondered if she should just forget the whole thing.

Then she saw Hervey, stepping out into the light, putting on his hat. He took a fresh cigar from his coat and bit off the end, spitting it onto the sidewalk. He lit the cigar with a match, gave a quick glance up and down the street, then started to stroll south.

Kit followed on the opposite side. At least his walking was leisurely and she had no trouble keeping him in sight.

At Seventh Street he turned right and entered an establishment with swinging doors. The painted sign above the doors simply said, *Bar and Grille.*

Kit paused a moment before crossing the street. Taking a deep breath, she went inside.

Hervey was sitting at a table in the middle of the place. The lighting was dim, provided mostly by the sun through yellow windows. The sawdust on the floor crackled as Kit approached the table. "Mr. Hervey?"

The man looked up. "Yes?"

"My name is Kathleen Shannon."

Hervey's face tensed. Before he could say anything Kit pulled a chair out from the table and sat.

Snatching the cigar from his mouth Hervey said, "See here!"

"I won't be a moment, Mr. Hervey."

"I don't wish to—"

"Please."

Her plea stopped his protest short. He looked around as if to see if anyone was listening. "I know who you are," he said in a low voice. "You're the lawyer."

"Yes."

"I am not supposed . . . I cannot . . ."

"Who has told you not to talk to me?"

His eyes darted back and forth. "Please, miss, I don't want to get into any trouble."

"What sort of trouble?"

"Miss, they are very serious about this case."

"Who are *they*?"

"You must know. The district attorney, for one."

"Has he spoken to you personally?"

Hervey's demeanor darkened further. "That's all. Please go away. I do not wish you ill, miss, but I have a wife and daughter to consider."

The thought that this man might have been threatened astounded, then angered, Kit. He was obviously frightened and would have to be handled with great care. Yet something told Kit he wished he could speak to her.

"Mr. Hervey," Kit said, "I will make a pledge to you. I will not tell anyone of our conversation. All I desire is the truth. And that is all you owe to Mr. Davenport."

"The truth will come out. In time."

"Will it?"

Hervey did not look convinced that it would.

"What is your daughter's name?" Kit asked.

Rhodes Hervey blinked. "Allegra."

"Ah, from the Longfellow poem."

"Yes! You know it?"

" 'The Children's Hour.' I loved it as a little girl. 'Between the dark and the daylight, When the light is beginning to lower, Comes a pause in the day's occupations, That is known as the Children's Hour.' "

Hervey smiled, nodding.

Kit continued. " 'From my study I see in the lamplight, Descending the broad hall stair, Grave Alice and laughing Allegra, And Edith with golden hair.' "

Hervey eyes danced with delight. "I read that to her sometimes at night. She is only seven. She is a joy to me."

"Mr. Hervey, my client, Edward Hanratty, has young daughters, very near that age. He is sitting in a jail cell right now, forced apart from his family, facing the hangman's noose."

With his right hand, Hervey began to rub the table nervously.

Kit said, "If I don't find out what really happened at the Braxton Arms, I will have failed not only my client, but his wife and his children. Won't you help me?"

A waiter with a large, curling mustache appeared at the table. "What will it be?" he said.

Flustered, Hervey stammered, managing to order the fifteen-cent luncheon.

"And for the missus?" the waiter said.

"She is not my wife," Hervey said. "She will not be staying."

The waiter paused, shrugged, then walked away.

Kit nodded slowly. "I am sorry to have troubled you, Mr. Hervey." As she rose, she felt like a weary explorer leaving an island after discovering it had no water. *Where do I turn now, Lord God? You will have to tell me, for I am without any idea.*

She must have paused then, for the world stood still for a moment. She saw Edward Hanratty's face behind bars, and she wondered what she was going to tell him. The preliminary hearing was but three days away.

Then the immediate world came back to her, and she took a step toward the door. Hervey grabbed her wrist. Startled, Kit almost cried out.

"Not here," Hervey said. He paused a moment, looking around. "Do you know the Quarter?"

"Yes."

"I will be there at eight o'clock."

Kit put her hand on his. "Thank you, Mr. Hervey."

———

"Lousy Mex," Slim said.

Corazón took a step backward and hit the wall.

"What's your business here?"

Was he going to hurt her? No one else was within sight. What if she screamed? Would this man end it with his hands on her throat?

She didn't know. She only knew she was frightened, and Slim was not going to let her go until he was satisfied.

Slim leaned toward her until she could feel his hot breath on her face. He reeked of tobacco and the burnt orange smell of cheap pomade.

"Answer me!"

Corazón felt shivers in her limbs, as if she were blasted by a cold, biting air. *What would Kit do?* she suddenly thought. *What would she say?* And then a word popped into her mind.

"Disgrace," Corazón said.

Slim's chin dropped. For a second the man's menace dissipated. "What did you say?"

Corazón put as much authority into her voice as she could. "Full of the disgrace."

Slim's lip twitched, as if unable to formulate a word.

"I mean, disgraceful," said Corazón.

Slim did not move away. "You better tell me what you're talkin' about, and you better tell me now."

His desperation was showing. Corazón had him confused, and that took away some of his menace. She began to feel he would not do her harm, that he was like an animal who tried to scare its enemy rather than kill it. Or a bully who cannot stand the prospect of being stood up to.

"How it looks, the hotel," Corazón said.

"Looks? What in the—"

"Yes, you have not the beauty."

With a shake of his head, Slim finally stood up straight and leaned away from her. "Who *are* you?"

"Look at these, the walls." Corazón stepped away from her

interrogator and he did not try to stop her. His face was an odd mixture of anger and befuddlement. Corazón began to feel a confidence in herself that had never been there before, especially when dealing with those who considered themselves better than "her kind."

"Not even the same," Corazón said, with a wave of her hand.

Slim shook his head, bewilderment completely taking over his expression now.

"See?" said Corazón. "The color. No same."

"You some kind of decorator?"

"You know the name Fairbank?"

Slim squinted. "Old Freddy Fairbank?"

"She would no like you to call that name."

"Wait a minute here. You don't work for her, do you?"

"Many years. She would no like this."

Swallowing, Slim asked, "What's her interest in this hotel?"

"Oh, she can be very, how do you say, like to talk. Much talk if she find something is of the disgrace."

"Will you stop saying that word!"

"Your boss, he no like it if Mrs. Fairbank no like this hotel."

"Now hold your horses there, who you going to—"

"Who is the one who paint these walls?"

"Freshly painted. Ambrose and Sons, and they just happen to be the finest—"

"No good. You are the one who hire these men?"

Slim put his hand to his bow tie and fiddled with it, making it more crooked than it had been. "It's just paint!"

"No," Corazón said with as much conviction as she could muster in her voice. "It is what you show to the, how you say, public. Mrs. Fairbank, she will no—"

"You're not gonna bring her into this now, are you?" Slim's forehead was beginning to break out in sweat drops. "If the boss gets the word that old, I mean Mrs. Fairbank ... listen now, I'm sorry about what I ... that little ... I didn't mean anything by it. I need this job. ..."

It was everything she could do not to break out into a smile. "I know what it is to have work. I no say anything to Mrs. Fairbank."

Slim's eyes showed sudden relief.

"If you will promise," she added.

"Promise?"

"To think more about these things. This city is home, no? We would like it for our visitors to feel good about our home."

"Yes. Certainly. Good."

"Now, if you do no mind?" Corazón waited for Slim to step aside, which he did, quickly. He stood there as she went to the stairs and did not move to go down with her. As she descended, the smile came to her face. This time she didn't try to stop it.

# Chapter 27

KIT ARRIVED AT the Quarter at seven forty-five. The Quarter was a block of land on the southwest corner of the city rectangle, as folks sometimes called the developed portion of downtown. At one time it had been owned by Abbot Kinney, who had grandiose plans to develop the property into a shopping district. But he had abandoned the plan, and the Quarter had fallen into disuse. Kinney had gone on to put his fortunes into a visionary housing development—named after its inspiration, Venice—which was more fantastic than any in the entire country. Kinney now planned to re-create the European city here on the Pacific Shore, canals and all.

The man who had bought the Quarter, one Phineas Haynes, shortly thereafter lost most of his fortune in a misguided venture involving British shipping. Thus this piece of land, once so promising, lay covered with shrub and neglect. The only evidence of development was the unfinished boardwalk that encircled the parcel.

Night was just covering the city with a cloudy gloom. No moon shone and the sounds of the street—trolley clangs, shouts of merchants—were fading into silence.

Kit did not like being alone in this section of town. But at least she could begin to see the glow of city lights and hear something of the sounds of the evening.

A carriage approached from the east side, looking like any other that might have emerged from the city's nightlife. Then it stopped, the driver pulling at the reins. Rhodes Hervey stepped out.

"Thank you for coming," Kit said.

"I told you I would," replied Hervey.

"Shall we sit?"

"I'd rather not. I'd rather this be short."

"Of course." She sensed his nervousness, even in the cover of darkness.

"Tell me," Kit said, "about the facts, as you know them, on the night of June 7."

Hervey cleared his throat. "I live in 204. I was alone that night. Mrs. Hervey was on a holiday with our daughter—Allegra—in San Diego. That's where my mother-in-law lives, you see."

Kit nodded.

"Well, I was in my room, having just completed a warm bath, when I heard shouting. Arguing. Two voices."

"Did you recognize the voices?"

"Only one. Young Chausser. There is no mistaking his voice. Young tough, that's what I'd call him."

"He was arguing with his father?"

"I suppose."

"It is important that you don't suppose anything. When you

testify, you must state only those facts of which you are absolutely certain."

"But it had to be."

"What happened next?"

"There was a crashing noise, like a door broken down. The papers say your client did that. Anyway, a voice shouted again, I don't know who it was. And then two gunshots."

"Two only? Please, you must be absolutely sure."

Hervey nodded in the darkness, his head a shadow. "That's all. Two gunshots. One right after the other."

"How far apart in time?"

"Like I said, one after the other. No pause."

"What did you hear next, if anything?"

"I heard another shout, something like 'Stop you!' and then feet running."

Kit paused, trying to fit all this into a consistent narrative. Hanratty said he chased young Chausser after the exchange of shots.

"And then what, Mr. Hervey?"

"Here it gets a little confusing. I think I heard a door slamming."

"Were you able to sense what door that was?"

"I thought it was Chausser's door. I know it was broke and all, but it still sounded like it."

"Anything else?"

"Yes, ma'am. I heard a loud thump."

"What sort of thump?"

"It was like something heavy hitting the floor."

"Like a body?"

"Yes. I suppose now it was Mr. Chausser's body."

Kit was about to remind Hervey not to suppose anything, but she let it go. This was consistent with both Hanratty's and the D.A.'s accounts. Two shots and a dead body. But Hervey had corroborated Hanratty on one very important point, the argument between two men inside Room 202, one of them being young Chausser and the other most certainly his father.

Still, that was not enough to cast any doubt upon the theory of the prosecution's case—that Hanratty had fired two shots into the body of Jay Chausser after breaking in.

Where did that leave her? In exactly the same place as before. She had managed to find one witness to speak to her, and he did not give her anything that would aid Ed Hanratty.

"Mr. Hervey," Kit said. "Does the name Rachel Travers mean anything to you?"

"No, ma'am."

"You have never heard that name?"

"Can't say that I have."

The sound of a distant gunshot cracked the night. This was not an uncommon sound in Los Angeles during the dark hours. It did not mean murder, necessarily. It could be roisters kicking up their bootheels after having a little too much to drink. Or maybe somebody was shooting a coyote that had wandered down from the hills.

Or, perhaps, a homicide. But it was impossible to tell from the sound alone what had happened. It was the same, Kit mused, with the testimony of Rhodes Hervey.

"May I go now?" Hervey said.

"Of course," Kit said. "Thank you for coming. You've been the one person who has had the decency to talk to me. Before you go, can you tell me why you changed your mind?"

Hervey paused a moment. "I teach my daughter to always tell the truth. I guess I just figured I couldn't do that if I did not do the same."

With that, Rhodes Hervey turned back to his carriage. "I would offer to drop you," he said, "but you understand . . ."

"Yes," Kit said. This was intimidation of a witness, pure and simple. But unless Hervey himself would swear to it, she would not be able to make any headway. She watched Hervey's carriage until it disappeared into the inky night.

The Quarter was now fully enclosed in darkness and silence. To Kit it was more than the absence of light. There was a heaviness in the air, an oppressive weight. She thought then she should pray, but something stopped her, from inside. A kind of fear.

When she lost her father at the age of eleven, she had that same feeling. He was gone, and no amount of prayer was going to bring him back. She was angry and hurt then at God, who had allowed a good man to be gunned down and ripped from her life. But mostly what she felt was fear. Knowing that never again could she run into his big, strong arms and have her tears dried by the soft brush of his hands. She regained her reverence later, knowing that is what Papa would have wanted from her most of all. But it had been a struggle, one of the worst seasons of her life.

It felt that way now. She was representing a client who might very well be guilty as charged, and that possibility rubbed raw against her principles. Yet she could not turn away from him, not at this hour. She had to go forward with the hearing, at the very least. It was part professional obligation, part inner need to know the truth.

But here, in the weighty darkness, the fear was rising. For through all her efforts, Kit had not found a single person to help her or a single piece of evidence that would suggest her client was innocent.

She longed for Papa's touch then, and her tears began to fall.

*Part Two*

# Chapter 28

THE MORNING OF THE Fourth of July brought Los Angeles to its feet with the sound of firecrackers just outside Kit's window at the Westminster. She heard the laughter of children, too. The celebration was starting early.

And why not? The guest of honor at the big parade was none other than Teddy Roosevelt himself.

Kit and Corazón had made plans to be at the Plaza with just about everyone else in town. The president would be giving a speech, a rouser no doubt, and the city would, for one day at least, put aside its currents of disquiet and enjoy the camaraderie of being one—Americans all.

Or so Kit hoped. She was still not sure about Roosevelt after her meeting with him. Was this a man of principle, as was the popular belief, or was there something behind those glasses that the public did not see? Kit did not like the fact that she would think such things about the president of the United States. But hard experience was telling her to suspend judgment just now.

After breakfast at the hotel, Kit and Corazón walked arm in arm across town, drinking in the sights. The city planners had done a splendid job. Red, white, and blue was everywhere, in the shape of fans, flags, swirls, and banners. There seemed to be a light step in the feet of the citizens, many of them dressed as if going to church. Of course, much of the finery had to do with the president in their midst.

The women, including Kit and Corazón, wore hats with wide brims, some plain, others strewn with faux floral design or grand ribbons. All seemed to have a tasteful bavolet attached, the frill necessary to protect fair necks from what was sure to be a harsh sun.

The men wore high silk hats or bowlers, most eschewing the less formal fedora, though a few men in cowboy hats served as a reminder that Teddy Roosevelt was, at least according to the press, still a Roughrider at heart.

The crowd grew thicker as Kit and Corazón approached the Plaza. Starting at Sixth, the parade would come down Main Street and end where a rostrum was erected for the president to speak.

Corazón seemed like a little girl, entranced with all of the gaiety.

"It is a *fiesta!*" Corazón said. "I have seen many things in my city, but to have the president, that is making this more, how you say, *excitante.*"

"Exciting."

"Sí."

Kit wondered if Ted was in the crowd somewhere. She had not seen him in days. Not even a note. If only he were here. She wanted so much to share the day with him, as well as with her dearest friend, Corazón.

As they approached Main Street, Kit heard the sound of a distant band of brass, drums, and fifes playing a grand marching song. Perhaps it was one of the marches by that composer Sousa, who seemed to be taking the country, and the world, by storm.

The crowd on Main was in a celebratory mood. Every now and again a cheer would go up from the southern distance, where the parade was making its way toward the Plaza.

Kit took a look at the faces on the street and allowed herself a moment of enjoyment. Soon enough she would be facing the hostility of a courtroom. Today, she merely wanted—

She stopped. She was not prepared to meet his gaze, nor, apparently, was he ready to see her. But there they were, but ten yards from each other, and there was no turning away.

Edward Lazarus nodded at Kit, formally, without a smile. Kit nodded in return. *Leave it at that,* she told herself, but she knew she could not. She walked up to him and said, "Good day."

"Yes, good day," Lazarus replied with something less than sublime enthusiasm. He was wearing a clerical collar and looked hot under it.

"If you don't mind my asking," Kit said, "I should like to inquire about your planned institute and partnership with this man Stillwater."

"The institute? It is a project that has occupied my thoughts for some considerable time. If you are truly interested I would be happy to tell you about it."

"Be assured that I am interested, Dr. Lazarus."

"Quite. We are in the most exciting time in the history of man, Miss Shannon. This is the age of progress in many areas and soon, if we are wise about it, we will arrive at a utopian shore where, finally, we can dwell as one."

Kit got the odd feeling that Lazarus was repeating part of a Sunday sermon. That, or he loved to bathe in the heady waters of his own verbiage.

"That is why," Lazarus continued, "I have taken you to task on your view of the old-time religion. That is the very term that describes the problem. We do not live in the old times. We are different people, Miss Shannon. We can learn from the past, but we dare not repeat its mistakes."

"Some of us believe the mistakes of the past are precisely what mankind fails to understand."

"I know, I know. I get them, the little old ladies who corner me after services to inquire into the state of my soul. That is why I have found it troubling that you, a young woman of obvious intellect, should align yourself with such as they."

"I try only to align myself with the truth."

"Ah, but what is the truth? Religion, as practiced the old-fashioned way, has brought us more bloodshed and suffering than comfort and hope. I do not blame the church as much as some. Ignorance is its own form of oppression. But we have no excuse for ignorance now. We know so much. Science is the great hope of our world, for its methods are rooted firmly on the ground. What we need is a ground sown with equal parts science and metaphysics, for the good of the whole man."

"Is that where this Stillwater comes in?"

"Professor Stillwater is a man of science first and always. He has merely applied his scientific method to the life of the soul and a world we cannot fully see. For my part, the principles of practical living will give our institute a usefulness that will sweep the world."

"You have rather large plans."

Lazarus's eyes shone now, gleaming in the sunlight. "Can't you see the possibilities? War, for example, is a thing of the past. We will never fight another war in this country. That business in Cuba settled the account on that score. Our warlike energies will be turned to a better use, to wipe out suffering here on our own shores. We will learn to get along with one another."

The sound of the marching band was growing louder. Kit got the impression Lazarus would speak over the music, no matter how resounding it was.

"When has mankind ever gotten along?" Kit asked. "What makes you think man's nature will change so drastically?"

"Because man can think," Lazarus said.

" 'The heart is deceitful above all things, and desperately wicked.' "

"Quoting the Book again?"

"Man's hope is in the Gospel, not science or metaphysics."

Shaking his head, Lazarus said, "That is why this institute must be built. To prove to people like you that our methods will work."

She came now to the crux of it. "Who is going to pay for all this?"

With a look of suspicion, Lazarus said, "We have those who believe in our work."

"Is my aunt one of them?"

"Just what are you insinuating?"

"I am being very direct, sir. Have you asked my great-aunt for money?" Kit felt like she was examining a lying witness, which Lazarus could very well be. She did not trust the man.

"It seems that resentment is always going to be my reaction to you," Lazarus said. "Even if I had made such a request, I would not tell you. You are not your aunt's guardian, so far as I know."

True, and Freddy had made it plain she would not want it so. But Kit was going to look after her no matter what.

Just then a loud blast from the band, which was almost upon them, caused Kit to look up. Lazarus looked toward the music, a cue that he was finished with this conversation.

Kit rejoined Corazón as the first of the horse brigade strutted by. Horsemen in grand red uniforms and plumed hats kept in a seemingly perfect line. The marching band came next, the musicians looking particularly proud.

Cheers rose from the assembled crowd and confetti was tossed in the air. And then he came—Teddy Roosevelt himself, seated in an open-air carriage pulled by two beautiful white horses. The carriage, wheels and all, was covered with an array of flowers—roses, magnolias, daisies, and azaleas. The stout President doffed his top hat vigorously to the crowd, his large white teeth gleaming under his walrus mustache.

Men, women, and children burst forth with applause and whoops.

Along with the crowd, Kit and Corazón followed behind the carriage as the president was driven to the Plaza.

The scene reminded Kit of her days in New York, when anything public was packed with people. She had learned how to get to the front of a crowd then, and she now pulled Corazón along with her until they were within arm's reach of the platform that had been erected.

Up on the rostrum Kit saw various city dignitaries, including Eulalie Pike. *Aunt Freddy should be up there,* she thought. The fact that she wasn't caused Kit concern. Freddy was not an admirer of this "cowboy President," but this was a social event of momentous importance.

She also noticed that two sworn enemies were, for the time being, putting on a show of mutual affability. General Harrison Gray Otis and William Randolph Hearst sat together on the platform, though separated by a tasteful, and no doubt scrupulously planned, span of ten feet.

Finally, all of the players were seated. The band ceased, and Mayor Fitch spoke entirely too long in introducing the leader of the nation. But when Teddy Roosevelt rose to speak, the cheers were long and loud.

Roosevelt began. "Mayor Fitch, assembled guests, good citizens of Los Angeles. I am gratified by your warm welcome, made warmer, I should add, by your California sun."

Laughter from the people rose like waves of heat.

"I feel, however, that you cannot but be invigorated by that star, for this land is indeed a fertile soil for the American spirit. I see that spirit everywhere about me."

When he said that, Roosevelt looked around at the faces nearest him. Kit was flabbergasted when he paused on her own face, hesitated a moment, and blinked at her. He had recognized her, but she did not know if she was pleased with that or not.

"As I say, everywhere," Roosevelt said, pulling himself up to his full height. He looked rather like a bulldog at that moment.

He delivered his speech in clipped, vigorous tones, using his fists to punch the air for emphasis. It was uplifting and inspiring, with his talk of American industry and the exaltation of the "strenuous life."

"Americanism means the virtues of courage, honor, justice, truth, sincerity, and hardihood—the virtues that made this country. The things that will destroy America are prosperity-at-any-price, peace-at-any-time, the love of soft living, and the get-rich-quick theory of life."

He leaned forward as he spoke, as if to crash his head through some invisible wall.

"Far better it is to dare mighty things, to win glorious triumphs, even though checkered by failure, than to take rank with those poor spirits who neither enjoy much nor suffer much, because they live in the gray twilight that knows not victory or defeat."

He was interrupted by cheers many times. Even Kit felt a sense of energy rush through her.

Then the president said, "Do not let the darkness of lost souls dampen your civic spirit. You have, indeed, some who would seek to harm this fair city. They occupy corners or bawdy houses, some of them sit in jail cells"—he looked at Kit—"and these must be rooted out."

Roosevelt paused and Kit, expecting a cheer, heard herself saying, more loudly than she wished, "No!"

Everyone on the rostrum heard her. She saw heads turn. Otis, Pike, Hearst, police officers, dignitaries, and, more important, Theodore Roosevelt himself. It was as if she had shouted an epithet at a saint's funeral.

Corazón looked at her, mouth slightly agape. Then she smiled like a mischievous girl.

Roosevelt cleared his throat, raised his arms, and finished his speech. As the applause arose and the band started playing, Kit tried to get away from the platform as quickly as possible. She wanted to melt into the sea of humanity. But it was thick, and she moved hardly at all.

Then she felt a hand on her shoulder. A policeman, large and looming, said, "He wants to see you."

She knew who he meant. And she could not refuse to go. She only wished for a convenient rock to crawl under. Resigned, Kit followed the officer as he led her up the wooden stairs. They creaked with a portent of bad things to come.

Theodore Roosevelt was at the top of the stairs, waiting for her. He had his hands on his hips. "So we meet again," he said.

"I . . ." She could not find the words.

"Did you like the speech?"

Over the president's shoulder Kit could see William Randolph Hearst, his imperial face glaring at her. "Yes," she said. "For the most part."

Roosevelt cleared his throat. "I seem to remember a bit of it on which you commented. You know, I like spirit in a woman. I just don't always agree with its expression."

"Sir," she said, keeping her tone respectful. "I have a client who is in jail. He is considered innocent until proven guilty. That was the intent of my comment, and no more."

Roosevelt stuck his chin out, almost in the pose of a fighter. For a moment he sized her up, as a boxer might examine his opponent in the center of the ring. "I shall keep an eye on you," he said. Then, pivoting swiftly, he was gone to receive congratulations.

Gratefully, Kit slipped back down the stairs, where Corazón was waiting.

"You talk to the president again!" Corazón said. "He like you, I think."

"Think again, Corazón."

"You no think he like you?"

Kit forced a smile. "Let's just say I don't believe I will be asked to the White House for tea anytime soon. Come along." Kit put out her arm, and she and Corazón made their way through the crowd.

# Chapter 29

TED BLINKED AWAKE and hesitated a moment before sitting up in the bed. Leaning against the high oak headboard, he tried to pull together his thoughts. His senses were confused by the aroma of coffee and bacon. Someone was cooking. But he lived alone and hadn't even bothered to hire a housekeeper.

He reached for his crutches, the full impact of the morning smells still not permeating his sleep-fogged mind. Someone was actually in his house—cooking!

Ted struggled into his trousers, then cautiously opened the bedroom door. He peered into the hall and then down toward the staircase. There was no sign of anyone. He moved the crutches forward as quietly as possible, not worrying to close the door behind him. He neared the top of the stairs and paused. The aroma was even stronger here, and it smelled wonderful.

Whoever it was, Ted figured himself to be safe enough. How many burglars broke in, only to prepare their victim's breakfast?

He tucked the crutches under one arm and held onto the banister with his right hand. Rather than battle with the crutches on the stairs, he'd gotten much better results by merely hopping down in this manner. A couple of times he'd contemplated sliding down the banister as he had when he was a boy. Somehow, he figured, even from heaven his mother would disapprove.

The crutches made a thudding sound as he landed on the first floor. He quickly tucked the wooden supports back under his arms and moved toward the kitchen, past rooms filled with canvas-covered furniture. The lack of life in this house saddened Ted, but he could hardly worry about it. He tried not to think of what had once been, but images sprang to mind much too easily. Even the furniture served as a reminder. Those silent, shapeless ghosts sleeping in the memories of the past. This house once held grand parties. This house once knew the laughter and joy of happy people.

Ted shook the thoughts from his mind and pushed the servants' door open and gazed into the kitchen.

"I thought this might wake ya up," Gus said as he turned from the stove to pour coffee into an elegant china cup.

Ted thought it rather odd that his mother's Haviland china should appear in the hands of a man such as Gus. "What are you doing here? How did you get in?"

Gus grinned, lighting his eyes with a devilish twinkle. "I learned me a few tricks when I was a boy. As for why I'm here, I figured it was time to talk."

Ted took a seat at the servants' kitchen table and stared at Gus as though he had failed to speak English. "You broke into my house to talk?"

Gus laughed and put the cup of coffee in front of Ted. Still chuckling, he turned his attention back to the stove. "I ain't much on cooking eggs any way but scrambled. Guess you'll have to live with it."

Ted thought perhaps the coffee would help him to make sense of things. He took a sip and found it impossibly hot, but the flavor was delicious. Much better than the coffee he'd tried to make for himself.

Gus pushed eggs out of the skillet onto a china plate, then wiped his free hand against his shirt. He forked several pieces of bacon onto the same plate and finally pulled pieces of toasted bread from a plate on the back of the stove.

"Here, you're going to need your strength."

"Why?"

" 'Cause after we talk," Gus said, depositing the plate in front of Ted, "you'll be wantin' to make your way to the courthouse."

"I'm not going," Ted said. Gus eyed him for a moment, but instead of saying anything, he went back to the stove and fixed his own plate.

Joining Ted at the table, he waited for Ted to say something more. Instead, Ted bowed his head. "Thank you, Lord, for this meal. Amen."

"Well, now," Gus said. "You're praying over the meal, but you're refusing to help Miss Shannon."

"Miss Shannon doesn't need my help. There's nothing I can offer her in a courtroom."

"Yeah, but what happened to bein' supportive? You hightailed it back here fast enough when you thought she was in trouble before."

"I didn't even think you liked Kit Shannon," Ted said, reaching for his fork. In spite of his desire to do anything but sit and converse with Gus, the food smelled too good to pass up.

"It don't matter if I like her or not, and I'm not sayin' I do and I'm not sayin' I don't. She seems the decent sort, and since you're so far gone on her, it just makes sense that you'd be supportive of her today. She's going into the lion's den if the stories in the paper are any indication."

"This tastes pretty good, Gus. Where'd you learn to cook?"

"My mother." Gus inhaled a mouthful of eggs and followed it quickly with toast.

Ted hoped it might keep him quiet for a time while Ted tried to figure out what he should do. He really wanted to go to Kit—to show her support. But there was Elinor and her threats to consider. He despised the woman for her interference. He couldn't understand why she should come back into his life at this time.

"If you ain't going to the courthouse, how about we go out to the hangar and start workin' on our next project? I have this idea for—"

"No." Ted should have figured Gus would try to talk him into doing something with the plane and flying. "I've told you before, I'll never fly again."

"Yeah, and I'm never gonna touch another pint."

"Good. You should be much the better for it."

Gus frowned and tossed back the contents of his coffee cup before getting up to refill it. "You know me better." He returned with the filled cup. "I know you better."

"You like to think you know me better, but the truth is, I'm not the same man I used to be."

Gus plopped the cup down, sloshing coffee onto the bare wood of the ancient table. "So you ain't the man you used to be. I'd say that's a benefit instead of a problem."

Ted continued to eat, having no desire to continue the conversation. Perhaps if Gus saw his lack of interest, he'd just drop the matter, as he did the idea of Ted going to the courthouse.

"Still, you probably don't want to talk flying when there's your lady friend to think about."

Ted looked up in dismay. So much for Gus losing the topic of

Kit. "Gus, can't we just eat and forget about everything else?"

"Nope. Figure you've been doing that too long now as it is. I left you alone long enough. I mean, as I hear it, I've probably left you alone too long. I heard it said you up and got religion."

"It's Jesus I found," Ted said.

Gus nodded. "Same thing."

"It's not exactly a simple matter of getting 'religion,' " Ted said, finishing his coffee. "It's a matter of realizing that there was nothing else worth having."

"So what's worthwhile about it?"

Ted thought it strange that here he was so newly born into the family of believers and already he was being called upon to share his faith. He was at a loss as to what he should say. He didn't have any of the Bible memorized. He didn't know what method preachers used to call a person to salvation. All he really had was the testimony of what had happened to him. It seemed inadequate for the task of saving a man's soul.

Gus got up and brought the pot to refill Ted's cup while Ted considered what he should say.

"Kit gave me her father's Bible to read," Ted said. "I saw a lot in there that made sense. It seemed that everything I read spoke of how much God loved the world and wanted to save it. Jesus said He was the only way to be saved and, after a while, it just all seemed right. And since nothing else did seem right—I figured I had nothing to lose."

"So what happens now?"

Ted shrugged. "I'm honestly not sure. I want to do the right thing, and I've prayed to know what that thing is."

"And will God just send you a telegram to let you know?"

"I don't pretend to know how He'll speak, Gus. I just know that making this choice was the best thing I could do. Guess I have to trust that He'll show me what to do next."

"So why couldn't He be showin' you to fly? I mean, I'm here, ain't I? Why else would I be stopping by to break into your house?"

"I thought maybe you were looking for a job as a domestic. If you are, I'll hire you."

"You can't afford me."

"Good point."

"I still have that money you left with me. You know, the money to buy supplies and such. We could start over, Ted. I rescued what I could from the last ship. We can rebuild. The Wright Brothers—"

Ted slammed his open palms on the table. "No! I'm not going to fly, so you might as well drop it here and now. I could more easily grow another leg than I could get back in the cockpit of a plane."

Gus scowled at him. "Thought that all things were possible with God."

The words stopped Ted short. He'd heard Kit say that before. She quoted it from somewhere in the Bible, but for the life of him he couldn't remember where it was located.

"God can do anything," Ted said, grabbing up his crutches. "But I'm not God."

"You got that right," Gus said, laughing. "Glad you finally realized it."

"Just what's that supposed to mean?"

"It means you gotta stop trying to be in charge of everything. Stop limiting yourself to what you suppose a cripple ought and ought not to do. Stop being so bullheaded and go help Miss Shannon."

Ted no longer wanted to hear what else Gus might have to say. He hobbled down the hall in a rush of emotions and confusion.

———

"This is a preliminary hearing," Judge Andrew Cartwright said.

"All I have to find is enough cause to believe that this case should be referred to a jury. Are you aware of that, Miss Shannon?"

"Yes, of course, Your Honor," Kit said, wondering why the judge had asked her such an elementary question. She was seated in his chambers along with Davenport. Judge Cartwright had requested to see them both before the hearing began. That was unusual, but then, Judge Cartwright was an unusual man.

He had come to Los Angeles in 1871, a penniless drifter from the east who rode the rails to get here. On his arrival, a railroad yard bull gave him a beating that left Cartwright partially deaf in one ear. He was thrown into jail as a vagrant. Only later was it discovered that Andrew Cartwright was from a prominent family of which he was the proverbial black sheep. He had been thrown out of both Yale and Harvard before setting out on his journeys.

Cartwright pulled himself up by his bootstraps and began to study the law. Without a completed college education, armed only with a sterling intellect, Cartwright found a position as a clerk for a former United States senator from California, Harlan Green. Under Green's tutelage, Cartwright became a first-rate legal mind. He was admitted to the bar in 1876 and practiced law for ten years. Green championed him for a judicial appointment, which came in 1887.

The word on Judge Cartwright, which Kit picked up from Earl Rogers, was that he was still something of a drifter at heart, prone to go his own way. And he never lost a dislike for railroad bulls or the police. Rogers warned her that Cartwright was not going to be sympathetic to her client in the least. She would have her work cut out for her.

"I do not want this turned into a prolonged spectacle," Judge Cartwright said. His bushy sideburns were flecked with gray. "That depends entirely upon you, Miss Shannon."

Kit glanced at Davenport, who had his fingers entwined and

resting on his stomach. He was looking at the judge.

"I am afraid I don't understand, Your Honor," said Kit.

"Let us be practical, shall we?" Judge Cartwright reached to a small onyx box on his desk, opened it, and pulled out a slug of tobacco. He bit off a piece, worked it into his cheek, and replaced the lid. "This case is going to trial. John here has at least enough evidence to go that far. Why waste the court's time?"

"I do not see it that way."

Judge Cartwright stopped mid-chew. "What way do you see it, Miss Shannon?"

"I do not believe a decision should be made before testimony is taken."

"Do you think that I . . ." The judge did not finish and looked for a moment as if he knew the answer to his own unspoken question—the implication was that he had made up his mind. "Look here," he added quickly, "you are entitled to put the prosecution to its burden. I am just telling you that the burden is low, and I don't see how you can . . . oh, hang it all, do what you will. But I am not going to let this get out of hand."

"I intend to put on a case," Kit said.

Davenport did not react. The judge, however, shook his head. "You are going to put up an affirmative defense?"

"Yes, Your Honor."

Judge Cartwright masticated his plug of tobacco for a good minute before speaking again. "I am going to hold you to relevant evidence."

"That is all I intend to offer."

"I will be the judge of that. I trust you will not forget that, Miss Shannon. I am the judge."

"Of course, sir."

Cartwright paused. "I don't mind telling you that this idea of a woman in a courtroom does not sit well with me. But I have no say in the matter. That's the legislature's decision. Now that you're here, I just want you to know I'm not going to treat you any different. I have a soft spot in my heart for my mother, but not for women lawyers. You follow?"

Ever so slightly, Kit nodded.

Judge Cartwright leaned over and spat his wad into a silver spittoon. "All right, then. Let's get this thing started."

# Chapter 30

GUS FOLLOWED TED into the library. "You should be at that courthouse!" he yelled.

All Ted wanted was for him to leave, but instead Gus followed him around like a boy with a pup. "You my nursemaid now?"

"Looks like you need one."

*True*, Ted thought. He was unkempt, unshaven, unwashed, and didn't care who knew it. He thought he would be alone this morning. He had no plans to leave the house, and then he'd awakened to coffee and bacon.

"What's eating at you anyway?" Gus said.

"I just want to be left alone," Ted said. "Haven't you got some machine to fix?"

"Doing hub work for the trolleys, but that's not what I want to do. I'm ready to work on the monoplane."

Ted shook his head as he sat down at the highly polished library table. A book he'd forgotten about sat there. *Principles of Psychology*, by William James. Kit had commented once that she was studying it to better understand the human mind. That had been all it had taken to promote it to Ted. He'd gone out that very afternoon and purchased his own copy. Now it only served to torment him. He shoved it aside.

"You realize," Gus said, "the Wrights are figuring on going five minutes in the air? Five! Do you hear that? And what are you doing? Sulking."

"Then let a man sulk, will you?"

"And all the while your lady is down there fighting old Davenport, and you're not there."

Now it was Ted's turn to pound the table. "Don't talk to me about her again, do you hear? We're through."

"Through? Why, I never heard such a—"

"I mean it, Gus. I don't want you to mention her name. If you do, so help me, I'll come after you, even on one leg."

Gus paused for a long moment, the hurt apparent in his eyes. Ted's gut twisted inside him, but he said nothing.

"I just never thought you'd quit on me," Gus said.

"Things change."

"I guess maybe I won't be coming around anymore."

Another twist. Ted could not look his friend in the eye. "I guess maybe you shouldn't."

Gus stood up. "Don't worry. I know my way out." He put his cap on—it was stained with the grease of machines—and stormed from the library.

*So this is what the new life is all about,* Ted thought. *This is the gift of God. Lose your friends. Lose the one woman you love. Lose your chance at happiness.*

Bitterness swelled within him. He let it. At least with bitterness came relief from the pain of lost hope.

Ted knew it was dangerous to be this way. Was his faith so

fragile? He had embraced it in the heat of emotion. Maybe that's all it was. Maybe he'd been a fool. Just like he'd been a fool to believe his past could stay buried.

He saw Elinor's face, distorted, in his mind's eye. It seemed to dance in front of him, reflected in the polished shine of the library table. It was twisted into laughter and for a moment he thought he could hear that laughter—a distant, mocking echo.

Ted grabbed a handful of his hair, pulling it until his eyes watered. "What am I supposed to do?" He looked around the room as if to ascertain the answer. Frustration overwhelmed him. When he became a believer he'd hoped to leave his troubles behind. Instead, his troubles trailed him like bloodhounds to the scent. They hounded his every step.

There was no other choice. He'd have to leave again. Leave for good. He'd write Kit a letter, though he would not mention Elinor. He would merely say it was God's will. That's how it was shaping up, wasn't it? Kit would just have to understand.

Opening the library desk drawer, he reached in for some paper. That's when he saw it. The cold, nickled steel of a Colt .45.

---

There were no empty seats in Cartwright's courtroom. By now Kit was accustomed to the attention. Like it or not, she was a Los Angeles attraction, a curiosity, like the Angels Flight observation tower or the elevated Echo Mountain trolley. She was also used to the full row of press that sat just behind the rail. Tom Phelps was there, as usual, and Kit had the distinct impression he knew more about this story than he was willing to write.

Notably absent, at least for now, were the two most important witnesses in the entire matter—Edna and Robert Chausser. The widow and son were no doubt sitting in a secret room somewhere or in the office of the district attorney himself. They would not be called, Kit was sure, unless the prosecution needed them. Otherwise, Davenport would want to save their testimony for the trial.

Nor was Corazón present. Kit had expected her to be here, sitting at the table as her official investigator. She hoped she was only late and not unalterably detained.

Then Kit saw Hanratty's wife in the gallery, looking haggard. Kit tried to offer her a smile, but she seemed to look right through Kit. This was also a familiar sight now—the suffering of wives, which was often worse than that of their accused husbands.

But when Edward Hanratty was marched in, Kit knew he'd had the worst of it. She had seen him two days before, but in that span he looked as if he'd aged years. This was the look of lost hope.

A deputy sheriff sat Hanratty down in a chair next to Kit, and all she could do was pat him on the arm. It felt stiff, lifeless.

*Oh, God, help me do what is right,* she prayed silently. *May justice be done.* Kit felt a momentary loss at the realization that her father's Bible was still in Ted's possession. It would be the first time she'd gone into a court proceeding without it. But she knew God was faithful. And ever since she was a young girl with Papa reading to her, she had hidden God's Word in her heart.

Judge Cartwright entered the courtroom as his clerk ordered all to rise. After he gaveled the proceedings to order he looked into the gallery. "This is a judicial proceeding," he said. "I will expect nothing but perfect decorum in this courtroom at all times."

Kit noticed that the judge's cheek was filled with a fresh chaw. Decorum, it seemed, had its limits.

"This is a preliminary hearing in the case of the People of the State of California versus Edward Hanratty. Prosecution ready?"

Davenport, dressed in an elegant blue suit, said, "Ready for the People."

"Call your first witness."

"We call Detective Michael McGinty."

The detective came forward to be sworn. Kit thought he looked out of place without a cheap cigar in his mouth. But she knew he was anything but a stranger to courtrooms. He was a seasoned police witness, and an honest one.

"Detective McGinty," Davenport said, "did you examine the crime scene at the Braxton Arms on the night of June seventh?"

"Yes, sir."

"What time did you get there?"

"Must have been around eight-thirty in the P.M."

"And according to witnesses, what time did the shooting take place?"

"Around eight."

"What did you do upon arriving?"

"First thing I did was tell everybody to keep out of the room. There were a lot of folks on the second floor standing around. But nobody was inside."

"What did you do next?"

"I asked Mrs. Chausser what happened. She was distraught, but I managed to get most of it. Then I talked to the hotel clerk and Mr. Seldon, and everything started to make sense."

"What do you mean by that, Detective?"

McGinty looked down. "I mean, sorry as I am to say it, that a shooting like this was bound to happen."

"Please explain that to the court, sir."

Without looking up, McGinty, with obvious reluctance, said, "I mean Ed Hanratty was bound to shoot somebody sooner or later."

"Objection!" Kit said. "This is mere speculation. What Detective McGinty thought might have happened has absolutely no relevance."

"All right," Judge Cartwright said. "I'll sustain that. Detective, stick to what you actually saw and heard at the scene."

McGinty nodded.

"What did you see upon first entering Room 202?" Davenport asked.

"I saw Jay Chausser on the floor. There was blood on the floor. I went to the body, keeping clear of the blood of course, and checked the man's pulse. He was dead."

"What did you do next?"

"Took my coat off."

A few laughed in the gallery.

"Why did you do that?" Davenport asked.

"It was hot in there. So I opened a window and started to make an inventory."

"Of what?"

"Everything. I write down a description of the scene as I find it, all the items that are in a location, that sort of thing. First rule of detective work is to get a full picture of the crime scene before anything is moved."

"Was that solely a written inventory?"

"Usually it is, but this time I had some help. Doesn't seem like you can have a decent murder these days without the *Examiner* showing up."

Laughter from the audience. Cartwright banged the gavel.

Davenport said, "Who was it that arrived?"

"A reporter and his one-eye. The one-eye wanted to take a photograph. I told him I'd let him only on the condition he make two prints and give one to me. That was the deal."

"So, Detective McGinty, you made not only a written inventory of Room 202, but you also received a photograph of the scene, is that correct?"

"Yes, sir."

"And in either case, Detective McGinty, did you find, at any time then or afterward, a gun in the room?"

"No, sir."

"The Braxton is one of those hotels with kitchen areas in the rooms, isn't that correct?"

"Yes, sir."

"Did you examine and inventory the kitchen?"

"Yes, sir."

"Did you find a gun in there?"

"No."

Davenport made a theatrical gesture toward Kit. "Take the witness."

Kit knew she had to be careful. McGinty was not going to break under questioning. He was honest and shrewd. In fact, she respected him. That meant she would have to interrogate him narrowly, finding out just exactly what he was contending, searching for a fact that might prove helpful.

"Detective McGinty," she said, "how did you know there was no one inside Room 202 when you got there?"

"I found Mrs. Chausser out in the hall. The clerk identified her for me. She told me what happened. Seldon, the neighbor who saw the whole thing, was also helpful. He told me he'd seen to Mrs. Chausser and brought her out of the room and watched it so no one went in."

"So your knowledge of who was in or out of the crime scene was based solely on what you were told?"

"That's right."

"You say you made a written inventory of the room, correct?"

"It's what I do."

"Do you have that with you?"

"Yes." McGinty reached into his coat and pulled out a small jotting book with a leather cover.

Kit took it from the detective, who was somewhat surprised, and immediately set it in front of Judge Cartwright. "I would like to move this into evidence as defense exhibit one," she said.

"I must object," Davenport said. "This is a prosecution witness."

"I call the judge's attention to section 1855 of the evidence rules. There can be no evidence of the contents of a writing, other than the writing itself. Mr. Davenport has brought forth testimony from Detective McGinty, based upon his written inventory. Unless Your Honor is going to strike all of that out of the record, the writing itself must be entered into evidence."

Working his chaw like an angry cow, Judge Cartwright pondered for a moment. "The booklet will be admitted into evidence."

"Thank you," Kit said. "May I see it, please?"

The judge waved his hand over the book. "Be my guest."

Kit nodded and took up the writing. She scanned the list for a moment. "Detective, you claim there was no gun in the room."

"No gun was found, that's right."

"But you do not know if a gun was taken out, do you?"

He squinted. "Well, I—"

"You did not arrive until one half hour after the shooting, isn't that correct?"

McGinty nodded. "Yes."

"So you do not know what happened in that room during that period of time, do you?"

He looked like a man being backed into a corner. "I did speak to witnesses."

"That is hearsay. You were not there until eight-thirty, were you?"

"No."

"Thank you. No more questions."

———

The coroner, Raymond Smith, was Davenport's next witness. He looked unconcerned with the pomp of the courtroom. He was a smallish man, but was confident, in his way. He had testified so many times before, Kit had heard from Rogers, that he was "seasoned." But that, Rogers told her, could be an advantage. Seasoned witnesses were often careless. She would watch for an opening.

"For the record," Davenport said, "how long have you been coroner for the county of Los Angeles?"

"Six years," Smith said.

"And in those six years have you had occasion to perform autopsies?"

"I have. A lot of dead bodies have come my way."

Davenport cleared his throat. "And how many autopsies have you performed?"

"Oh, have to say in the hundreds."

"Did you perform an autopsy on the victim in this case, Mr. Jay Chausser?"

"Yes, sir."

"On what date, sir?"

"That would have been June the ninth. Two days after the murder."

"Objection." Kit was on her feet. "This has not been proven to be a murder, Your Honor."

Judge Cartwright frowned. "The court is well aware of what is at issue."

"I want that comment stricken from the record," Kit said.

"Denied," said the judge. "Go on, Mr. Davenport."

The district attorney smiled at Kit, then turned back to the witness. "Please tell the court what the results of your autopsy were."

"Jay Chausser died of a gunshot wound. The bullet penetrated the left ventricle of his heart, resulting in almost immediate death."

"Was it a single bullet that was the cause of death?"

"My opinion? Yes, sir. I found another bullet that had penetrated the shoulder, but it did not do any fatal damage."

"So two bullets were fired into Jay Chausser on June the seventh?"

"Yes, sir."

Davenport took a small box from his table and placed it in front of Smith. "Sir, I show you what has been marked as the first exhibit for the People. Do you recognize it?"

"I do. It's the box I put the bullets in, the ones I took out of Jay Chausser's body."

"How can you identify the box?"

"I put my initials on the top, right here." Smith indicated it with his finger.

Davenport opened the box. "Are these the bullets you removed from the victim's body?"

Smith leaned over and peered at them. "Yes, sir. I made a sketch of 'em, and that's what they looked like. The same."

"Your witness," said Davenport.

Kit felt Hanratty's tension as she rose. He knew this was going to be a case fought strictly uphill, against forces well armed and entrenched. No doubt he was waiting in hope, like a weary soldier watching his captain take over the battle. Would she be shot down immediately, or could she find some way to blunt the first volley? All she had now was preparation, the hours spent going over the material she was going to use.

"Mr. Smith," she began, "you are not a medical doctor, is that correct?"

The coroner's face went blank as silence gripped the courtroom. Even Judge Cartwright looked stunned at the question.

"Well, I . . ." Smith started. Then he stopped.

"The question can be answered yes or no, sir."

Anger flashed in Smith's eyes. "I was a medic. I served in Cuba. I was on the front lines, young lady."

"Do you have a degree from any medical college?"

He breathed in. "No." Quickly he added, "What I learned I learned the hard way."

"I will move to strike that last answer, Your Honor. It was not in response to a question."

"Overruled, Miss Shannon. You've made your point and the court notes it."

Kit looked at the witness. "Your medical opinion about the cause of death is not based on your medical expertise then, is it?"

"Yes, it is. I told you I learned in the field."

"You would not wish to offer an opinion that wasn't based on expertise, would you?"

"'Course not."

"Especially in a court of law, under oath?"

"That's right. I would never do such a thing."

The foundation was laid. She had extracted from him a claim that he would not be able to wriggle out of if she asked the next questions correctly.

"By the way, Mr. Smith, do you speak any foreign languages?"

Davenport stood up quickly. "Objection, Your Honor. Incompetent, irrelevant, and immaterial. What can that possibly have to do with this case?"

"Miss Shannon?" the judge said in a warning tone.

"If I may ask this one question, the relevance will appear," Kit said.

"All right," Judge Cartwright said. "I'll allow this one question. The witness may answer."

Smith said, "Spanish, of course."

"Any others?"

"Don't need any others around here."

Kit put her hands behind her back and paced slowly in front of the witness. This was a habit she one day discovered she had acquired. It helped her to think, but Earl Rogers, upon observing it, said it gave the appearance of a shark circling its prey.

"You testified, sir, that two bullets were fired into the body of Jay Chausser on June seventh."

"That's right."

"In fact, isn't it true that you have no basis upon which to reach that conclusion?"

Smith shook his head. "I took the bullets out."

"But how did they get in?"

"They were fired from a gun."

"Which gun?"

"Your client's gun."

"Did you see my client fire the gun?"

"Of course I didn't."

"Then how can you know?"

"Just by looking. I have seen a lot of bullet wounds."

Kit paused, then went to her briefcase and took out a large book, placing it on the table for all to see.

"Mr. Smith, are you an expert in the science of ballistics?"

Clearing his throat, Smith said, "I've heard about it."

"Are you an expert, sir?"

"Maybe."

"You're not sure?"

"I know some things about it."

"Do you read in the field?"

"Sometimes."

"Is it possible to be an expert yourself without reading what the leading experts say about the subject?"

"Of course not."

Tapping the book, Kit said, "Then surely you have read Dr. Schultz's book, which is considered the leading treatise on the subject in the world?"

"I have glanced at it."

"But you are not sure?"

"I'm pretty sure, yes."

Kit took the book to the witness stand and laid it on the rail. "Are you also aware, Mr. Smith, that the treatise is written in German?"

A swell of laughter arose in the courtroom. Judge Cartwright gaveled for order at the same time Davenport was shouting, "Objection!"

"Your Honor," Kit said, "I submit this is highly relevant to the credibility of this witness. He has testified that he would never offer an expert opinion under oath unless he were an expert. Yet he cannot possibly be an expert on ballistics, for he cannot read German. He has undermined his own testimony."

"That is for the court to decide," said the judge. "Are you finished with the witness?"

"I have only a few more questions, Your Honor."

"Be brief," said the judge.

"Mr. Smith, whether you read German or not we can leave for the moment. What I want to know is whether you performed a ballistics test to confirm that these bullets were fired from the same gun."

"I didn't have to. I can see they're the same."

"Are you aware, sir, that when a bullet is fired it travels through the barrel of the gun and picks up marks unique to that gun?"

"That's what I . . . sure."

"And that by firing a test bullet from the alleged murder weapon, you would be able to compare markings?"

"That might be true."

"But you don't know it to be, do you, sir?"

"I know what I saw."

"It's what you didn't see that worries me." Kit turned to the judge. "I have no further questions at this time, Your Honor. But I would like the court's indulgence. I would like to arrange for a ballistics test to be done before proceedings continue."

Judge Cartwright's cheek undulated. "This is a preliminary hearing. I'm not going to pull the reins on it for some wild-eyed experiment."

His words, if not his decision, took her by surprise. If a ballistics test was to be done, she would have to arrange it herself. But the results would not be forthcoming quickly enough to be used here. She could only hope doubt was being sown in the mind of the judge. It was a slim hope at best.

She returned to her chair as Davenport called Julius Seldon to the stand.

# Chapter 31

"MR. SELDON, you reside at the Braxton Arms Hotel?" Davenport began.

"Yes. I live in Room 201, right across from where the murder happened."

"Objection," Kit said. "Once again, whether a murder has occurred is the object of this proceeding. Please instruct the witness to answer only the question that is asked."

"You understand that, Mr. Seldon?" Judge Cartwright said with a tired voice.

"Oh yes," said Seldon, who nevertheless shot a glare at Kit.

Davenport said, "Were you in residence there on the night of June seventh?"

"Yes, I was."

"Did you hear anything unusual that night?"

"Yes. I heard somebody out in the hallway, heavy-footed."

"Can you describe what you mean by heavy-footed?"

"Well, that's what I call somebody who makes a big noise when he walks around. Big men, usually, without the social graces."

Kit, studying Seldon's face as she did any witness, quickly wrote herself a note.

"What did you do in response to this noise?" Davenport asked.

"I looked to see who it was."

"Did you open your door?"

"No, sir. I looked out the transom."

"And what did you see?"

"I saw him"—Seldon pointed at Hanratty—"and he had a gun."

"He had his gun drawn?"

"Yes, sir. Holding it right up in the air when he kicked that door in."

Davenport paused, took a long look at the judge, then returned to the witness. "Did the defendant proceed to fire his gun?"

"Objection," Kit said. "Leading the witness."

"Sustained. John, ask the question again."

Davenport nodded. "What did you see next?"

"I saw the defendant proceed to fire his gun."

Kit gazed to the ceiling and sighed in spite of herself. Davenport was clever, and the judge was certainly giving him soft treatment.

"How many shots did the defendant fire?" said Davenport.

"Two. He fired two times."

Kit felt Hanratty's hand on her arm. "That's a lie!" he said in a loud whisper. Kit patted his hand.

"What, if anything, did you see next?" Davenport said.

"Well, there was something said, and the next thing I know Robert—that's the son—ran right out the door. The defendant, he yelled at him to stop, and I guess he knew he'd already got the old man, because he took off after the boy."

"Objection." Kit said. "The witness is speculating as to what was in my client's head."

"Well, I'll sustain that," said the judge. "I won't take it into account."

"What did you see next?" Davenport asked.

"That was all. As soon as I thought it was safe, I went to look and see if Mrs. Chausser was all right. I opened the door and went across, and I tapped on the door. It was closed. The handle was broken on it. When nobody answered it I pushed it open. That's when I saw Jay Chausser, lying in a pool of blood. Mrs. Chausser was standing over him, and she looked white as a ghost. She looked at me and before I could say a word, she fainted."

"What did you do next?"

"People started coming out then, and Slim, from the front desk, he came up the stairs, and I told him to go get the police but to be careful, because a policeman was on the loose murdering people."

"Objection!" Kit said.

"All right, Miss Shannon," said the judge. "Noted. The witness will refrain from making judgments about murder, is that clear?"

"I apologize, Your Honor," said Seldon. "My manners have left me."

"No harm done, sir," said Judge Cartwright.

"I have no further questions," said Davenport, gesturing for Kit to take the witness.

Kit approached Seldon. "You say you looked through the transom to see all this?"

"Yes."

"That's the small opening over your door?"

"That's right."

"How did you manage to get all the way up there?"

Seldon smiled. "There's an armchair next to the door. I stood on one arm and just managed to see over."

"You do this often, do you, peer through your transom?"

"Objection," said Davenport. "Incompetent, irrelevant, and immaterial."

"Sustained."

"Let me rephrase the question," Kit said. "Was it unusual for you to climb up and look through the transom at what was going on outside your door?"

"I've done it once or twice before."

"And each time you stand on the armchair?"

"Yes, ma'am."

"Does that bring your head to where it can see through the opening?"

"I have to pull myself up just a little, and then I can see."

Kit paused, trying to get a picture in her mind of what his position would have been. "Now, sir, you stated that you saw my client kick in the door, is that correct?"

"Correct."

"And is the door to Room 202 directly across from yours?"

"Yes, ma'am."

"So from your perch at the transom, you must have seen the back of my client as he allegedly went through this act."

"Yes," Seldon said.

"And you heard two shots?"

"Two, yes."

"Nothing said before the shots?"

"No, ma'am."

"Mr. Seldon, with my client's back to you, you could not tell if it was he who fired both shots or not, could you?"

Seldon frowned suddenly. "But I saw him."

"You saw his back. That was your testimony."

"Yes, but . . ." Seldon stopped himself. "I just saw it, the way he moved his arm."

"You saw a movement of the arm and assumed that he was firing shots, isn't that right?"

"But I went in and I saw Jay Chausser dead."

"A single bullet could have killed him, isn't that right?"

"But they said he had two bullets."

Kit pounced. "Who said? When?"

"Objection," Davenport said. "This calls for hearsay."

"No," Kit said. "I am inquiring into what the witness's state of mind was. He has claimed someone told him there were two bullets in Chausser. I want to know when he was told that, and by whom."

The judge thought a long time before looking at the witness. "Mr. Seldon, do you need to think this through?"

"No, Your Honor," Seldon said. "I only meant what I read in the newspaper. I read the *Examiner*."

Titters of laughter in the gallery. Kit was not amused. The judge had allowed Seldon time to think over his answer. If it was a false one, it would now be impossible to prove.

"You testified that Mrs. Chausser fainted when you entered the room, is that correct?" Kit asked.

"Yes," Seldon said.

"Did she fall right there on the floor?"

"Oh yes. Hard."

The courtroom doors opened loudly. Kit looked back and saw Corazón, somewhat meekly, walking toward the rail. All activity seemed suspended as she walked forward.

Then Judge Cartwright slammed his gavel on the bench. "Stop that woman!" he ordered.

For a long time Ted looked at the gun.

The revolver beckoned his touch, the delicate and artistic engraving of the presentation model reminding him of the day his family had been honored by the governor of California. The Colt had been a gift, looking more appropriate for display on the fireplace mantel than hidden away in a drawer.

He picked it up and wrapped his fingers around its grip. He felt the checkered ivory butt with his thumb. It was rough under his hand, like the skin of a lizard. Ted half-cocked the hammer and spun the cylinder. Six bullets were inside.

His body went cold. The flash of a deadly thought coursed through him, with Elinor on the other end. Just as quickly it subsided. He would never resort to that. He was a Christian now, and besides . . .

His mind came back to Elinor, the way she had looked at him at the Imperial. She was not in this thing alone. He had sensed that. Could it be that she herself was under duress?

That's when he knew he would go to Elinor tonight. And take the gun with him, just in case. There was a danger in the air. How it got there he did not know. Who was involved was a mystery.

But tonight he would find out.

# Chapter 32

"I WANT THIS WOMAN taken out immediately," Judge Cartwright said. A sheriff's deputy was already upon Corazón, taking her arm.

"No," Kit said. "This woman works for me."

The courtroom buzzed with voices and Cartwright gaveled for order. "In what capacity?" he said.

"She is my investigator."

"But she's a . . ." The judge stopped and cleared his throat.

"She is the one I have chosen," Kit said. "That is my prerogative. I request the court's permission to have Miss Chavez sit at counsel table with me."

"We have no objection," Davenport said amiably.

"All right, then," said Judge Cartwright. "But I will not have any more interruptions."

Kit motioned for Corazón. She entered through the gate and immediately handed Kit a note. "I see her," Corazón whispered.

"Will you kindly continue?" Judge Cartwright said.

"If I may have just a moment, Your Honor," Kit said, finishing the note. It was written in Corazón's own broken English, God bless her. She was a good student. Kit could read it fine.

"Mr. Seldon," Kit said, facing the witness again. "What was your relationship with the victim, Jay Chausser?"

"Old Jay was a good fellow. We got along."

"Were you friends?"

"Yes, I would say we were friends."

"How long would you say you were friends?"

"Oh, ever since they moved in. About six months, I'd say."

"Did you ever quarrel?"

"With Jay? Heavens no. Like I said, we got along famously."

Kit looked at the note in her hand, then back at the witness. "Isn't it true that on the night of June sixth, the night before the shooting, you had a violent argument with Jay Chausser?"

"Why, no."

"Isn't it true that this argument was over a sum of money?"

Seldon shook his head slowly.

"Please answer out loud," Judge Cartwright said.

"No, sir. I never had an argument with Jay."

Kit held up the note. "Then a witness who would come into this court and swear about hearing such an argument, you would call that witness a liar?"

"Yes, I would," Seldon said, though he was not as forceful as he had appeared earlier.

Kit slipped the note into her pocket. She had Seldon's denial on the record, and if she needed to she would produce the witness that Corazón had spoken to—Maria Espinoza, the maid from the Braxton Arms.

"Your Honor," she said, "I have no further questions at this time. But I would like Mr. Seldon to be subject to recall by the defense."

"So ruled," Judge Cartwright said. "Mr. Seldon, you may step down. But until this proceeding is completed, you will remain available to testify should Miss Shannon call on you. Understood?"

"Yes, sir," Seldon said, looking displeased.

"All right. Mr. Davenport, call your next witness."

Kit wondered who that would be. So far Davenport had carefully placed the initial elements of the crime before the court. The dead body, the means of death, and through Seldon, an eyewitness to the identity of the killer. What was not present, yet, was evidence of Hanratty's state of mind when he fired the fatal shot.

She was sure the next witness would be Davenport's attempt to establish just that—a murderous intent.

"The prosecution calls Otto Balsam," Davenport said.

Kit turned and saw a young, thin man with eyeglasses come forward. He had a bow tie around a skinny neck, looking much like a well-dressed scarecrow. Kit leaned to Hanratty. "Do you know him?"

Hanratty whispered, "He looks a little familiar. But I can't place him."

"Think about it." With the witness sworn, Kit turned back to study him.

"Mr. Balsam," Davenport said, "what is your line of work?"

"I am a taxidermist and furrier."

"You have been in business for how long?"

"I work with my father. We have had a shop on East Third for eight years."

"You have a good reputation in this community, do you?"

"I believe so."

"In all of your time, have you ever had any trouble with the police?"

"Never."

Davenport paused, and Kit thought about the line of questioning. It was clear Davenport was establishing that Balsam's lack of animosity toward the police would make his testimony, whatever it would be, more credible.

"Where do you reside, Mr. Balsam?" Davenport asked.

"The Braxton Arms Hotel," Balsam said, his Adam's apple bobbing above his collar.

"What room?"

"307."

"And were you in residence there on the night of June the seventh of this year?"

"Yes, I was."

"Some time that evening, did you have occasion to leave the premises?"

"Yes, sir. I went out to visit my tobacconist on Hill Street. I had run out of pipe tobacco, you see."

"Continue."

"I left my room and took the stairs down. As I began descending the stairs from the second floor, I heard someone coming up."

"What, exactly, did you hear?"

"Footsteps."

"Were these heavy footsteps?"

"Oh yes. It got my attention immediately."

"Did you see the person?"

"Yes, sir."

"Is that person in the courtroom today?"

"Yes, sir." Otto Balsam pointed at Hanratty.

Davenport said, "Let the record reflect that the witness has identified the defendant."

"The record will so reflect," Judge Cartwright said.

Kit looked at Hanratty and saw his eyes wide and fearful. That sent a shudder through her. He recognized this Balsam and was afraid of what he was going to say. She did not have time to confer with him.

"Was the defendant in uniform?"

"Yes, sir."

"And what was the defendant doing when you first saw him?"

"He was coming up, his head was down, and his gun was drawn."

Voices muttered in the courtroom. Kit gripped the arms of her chair. Here was intent. It was also a little fact that her client had failed to mention to her.

"Did the defendant see you?" Davenport asked.

"Not at first," Balsam said.

"Did you hear the defendant say anything?"

"Yes. He said, 'I'll kill him.' "

Now the voices and gasps rose in volume. Judge Cartwright had to gavel for order.

Davenport, for his part, did not seem in any hurry to ask his next question. The impact of the last answer was only increased by his silence. Finally, with a satisfied look on his face, Davenport asked, "What happened next?"

Nervously, Balsam said, "The defendant, he threatened me."

"With the gun?"

"Yes. He told me to put my hands up."

"And then what?"

"He accused me of sneaking up on him. All I was doing was going out for tobacco."

"How did he accuse you—in what tone of voice?"

"Oh, angry. Very angry. And something more."

"Yes?"

"Well, I could tell he had been drinking. His face was so close, I could smell it on his breath. He had been drinking quite a lot."

"How did you reach this conclusion?"

"I have a very well-developed olfactory sense from working with various chemicals. I can determine volume quite clearly. And that man was drunk and dangerous."

"Objection," Kit said.

Davenport turned with an air of invincibility and said to Kit, "Your witness."

But this was not her witness. This was the witness that had just placed the rope around her client's neck.

Chapter 33

KIT HAD TO WAIT until Hanratty was back in his cell before she could see him. But that was for the best. If she had been with him any sooner she might have wrung his neck.

The first day of the preliminary had ended disastrously. Kit had not even cross-examined Balsam. The only merciful aspect had been Cartwright's decision to end court early.

When Kit got to his cell, Ed had his head bowed on the hard cot. Life seemed to be dripping out of him.

"Officer Hanratty," Kit said, eschewing the friendly use of his first name.

Hanratty did not raise his head. "I am lost," he said.

"Will you do me the courtesy of looking at me, please?" Kit held on to the bars with both hands.

Slowly, Hanratty looked up. His eyes were dark.

"I once advised you never to lie to me," Kit said. "I would like to know why you did not inform me of your drunkenness."

"I wasn't drunk. I can hold my liquor."

"You must have been holding quite a bit for the witness to smell it."

"I suppose."

"And did you say to yourself you were going to kill him, meaning Chausser?"

"I don't remember that."

"Because of the liquor, no doubt."

Hanratty did not answer. He covered his face with his hands. His shoulders began to shake, but Kit could find no sympathy for him in her heart. He had brought all of this on himself.

"I am at a loss as to what to do for you," she said. "You have put our case into a very difficult position. I do not see how I will be able to get a dismissal now. You are going to be bound over for trial and will have to face a jury."

Hanratty's soft weeping filled the cell, echoing off the stone walls. It was the only noise, save for the snoring of a man in another cell.

Kit waited for a response, but Hanratty offered none. She couldn't think of anything else to say. Except, perhaps, to inform him that he should get a new lawyer.

No, that would not do. She had an ethical obligation to see him through the preliminary. She also had, though she wondered at it, a continuing sense that he was not guilty as charged. Whatever happened that night, she was certain it was not murder. Certain because she had looked at him so many times and had not seen a guilty man. Certain, perhaps, because she wanted to be, for the sake of his wife and children.

"Ed," she said, returning to the familiar. "We have to discuss the facts of this case once again. I am soon going to try to put on a defense for you. I haven't much to go on. Will you please, once and for all, tell me exactly what happened on the night you shot Jay Chausser?"

The sobbing ceased, though his head remained in his hands. "Please, Ed."

With a slow resoluteness, Ed Hanratty raised his head. There seemed to be a new resolve in him, as if a chasm had been bridged. He stood and shuffled to the cell bars. "All right," he said.

"Good. Why don't you start with—"

"No. I'll start at the end. I cannot stand to see Carrie suffering anymore."

"She is a good, strong woman."

"It's not right what I'm doing."

"Doing?"

"I have to tell you the truth."

At last. Kit hoped that the truth would be something that would lead her to a witness, or a way of presenting the case that would offer some sort of hope. She waited for him to begin.

"I did it," he said.

"What, exactly?"

"I murdered Jay Chausser. In cold blood."

———

Ted's thoughts were jumbled as he hobbled through the night streets of Los Angeles. He knew this much: He would make Elinor tell him why she was persecuting him. He was sure others were involved.

Would she talk? Perhaps not at first. But Elinor had always been something of a paper tiger. She would put on a bold front, but push hard enough, and that would crumble.

The last time he had been with her, however, she had shown a harder edge than he had ever seen before. She'd clearly thought this through, and for whatever real purpose and motivation, she had the upper hand. He had to be careful, especially for Kit's sake. Elinor was liable to do just about anything.

When he got to the street where the Wynn family had its lovely home, Ted almost turned back. He was so out of place here now. But something drove him on. He had the feeling that if he did not settle this tonight he never would. A desperate man's resolve is not long-lived.

At the gate to the Wynn home Ted paused and noticed a single light in the front window. With curtains drawn, only a sliver of light shone through. The rest of the house was dark. With her mother in Europe, no one else should have been home.

Slowly, quietly, Ted made his way up the walk. As he got closer he saw a shadowy form move in silhouette behind the curtain. Elinor. He could tell from her profile and the way she moved. She had always had the grace of the trained socialite.

He studied the opening in the curtains. He pressed toward the window, softly over the lawn, until he could see a little of what was going on inside.

He heard voices—Elinor's was one, the other belonged to a man. He couldn't make out what they were saying but got the impression it was a quarrel of some kind. A sweeping bougainvillea made it impossible for him to get closer. But the night was calm, and he listened.

At one point he heard Elinor clearly say his name and something like "he will not stand for long."

Who was the man? And should he confront them both?

He had to. He had the gun, after all.

Clumsily Ted turned, his crutches impacting soft dirt, and he almost fell. When he recovered and stood, he found himself staring into a face obscured in the darkness. It was a man, and one thing was certain—he was large.

Ted had no time to react before he was slammed to the ground.

# Chapter 34

OF ALL THE TASKS Kit had performed in her professional life, this had to be the worst.

Kit felt paralyzed as she raised her hand to knock on the door.
She could not do it, yet knew she had to. The sooner the better,
too.

She made herself knock. When she heard the twitter of little
voices, she almost turned and ran. But it was too late. The door
opened.

Two blond-haired girls—about eight and six—with purple ribbons in their hair, smiled up at her.

"Hello," Kit said.

The older of the two curtsied and said, "How do you do?"

"Is your mother at home?"

"Whom may I announce?"

"Miss Shannon."

With that, the younger one turned and ran through the hall

shouting, "Mommy! Miss Shannon is here!"

The first girl said, "Please come in. My name is Julia."

Kit entered the modest but well-appointed home. It was apparent to her that Ed Hanratty had endeavored mightily to provide for his wife and daughters. All the more reason Kit felt such dread at being the bearer of the terrible news.

"Why, Miss Shannon," Carrie Hanratty said as she entered the hallway. She was wiping her hands on the apron tied around her waist. "This is a surprise. Have you been to see Ed?"

Kit breathed in slowly. "May we have a moment alone?"

Carrie Hanratty's face reflected concern, but she tried to sound jaunty when she told the girls to go and clean up in the kitchen. Obediently, they went. Carrie showed Kit into the small parlor near the front door. It held a humble desk and two wooden chairs, where they sat.

"What news?" Carrie said. Her eyes had dark bags under them.

Kit could not find the words. This is what it must be like for a surgeon about to tell a patient he cannot be saved. Does one come right out and say it? Is there any humane way to soften the blow?

"Mrs. Hanratty—"

"Please, call me Carrie."

"You were in court today."

"I will be there every day. My sister takes charge of the girls so I can be there."

A feeling like the grip of a fist hit Kit's heart. "I was with Edward just a while ago. I went to speak with him about the day's events."

"Did he take it well? It seemed to me a bit of a rough go today."

"It was. Some information came out in testimony that I had not been aware of. Edward overlooked telling me about it. The part about Edward drinking on the night in question, that he had his gun drawn as he went up the stairs. These things he did not tell me, and when it came out on the stand it was a shock."

Carrie looked at her hands. They were small but strong, as if she were not a stranger to hard work. "I know that Ed drinks. He has pledged to me to try and stop. But being a policeman and all, it is a temptation. It is his way." She looked at Kit earnestly. "But he never drinks around the house or the children. Never. He's a good man, Miss Shannon."

Kit wanted to leave then and there. But that would be no good. She could not deceive Mrs. Hanratty any longer. "Carrie," she said, "Edward wants to bring this matter to a close. He is concerned about you."

Tiny pools formed in Carrie's eyes and she smiled weakly. "He is always thinking about me and the children."

The fist gripped Kit's heart with greater force. She felt her own tears coming. There would be no easy way out. "Carrie, Edward wishes to change his plea to guilty."

A scream. A child's scream of delight, and then the two little girls came running into the room as if playing a game of tag. When they saw their mother, though, they came to a sudden halt and stood still. Carrie did not even acknowledge their presence. A look of concern came to both the girls' faces.

"Children," Kit said quickly. "Would you go to your room to play for a bit?"

"What's wrong with Mama?" Julia said.

"Your mama and I are having a talk. Please. Show me what good girls you are."

Julia looked back at her mother's face and for a moment did not move. Her little sister looked to her for guidance.

"Please," Kit said.

"Very well," said Julia. Grabbing her sister's hand she exited the room slowly, looking back once before she disappeared.

"Why?"

Kit recognized a deep sense of loss in the saying of that one word, and she reached out to take Carrie Hanratty's hand. It was limp and remained so. "Your husband has admitted to the crime. He wishes to confess and have it over with. I know this is a terrible shock to you, Carrie, but it will keep him from a trial and execution."

Carrie slowly shook her head. "No."

"He wants to end this—"

"No!" Carrie looked at Kit sharply. "He cannot have done this. He would not. I thought you believed in him."

"I—"

"Do you believe he is guilty? Do you?"

"He has told me."

"Do you believe him?"

Kit looked at the floor. "The evidence today was very strong. I don't think he wants to fight this anymore."

"Then we must fight for him."

"Mrs. Hanratty, I cannot keep Edward from changing his plea."

Carrie stood up. She was shaking and tears coursed down her cheeks. "You were our only hope."

"If there is anything I can do . . ."

"Can you prove he is innocent?"

"Not if he himself says that he is not."

"Then there is nothing." She smoothed her apron repeatedly.

"Edward can throw himself on the mercy of the court. I can argue for the least possible sentence."

Carrie shook her head. "Thank you for coming, Miss Shannon."

"Please, if there—"

"Thank you. I must see to the girls now. Can you find your way out?" She did not wait for an answer but turned and walked, ghostlike, out of the room.

---

"You are a fool," Heath Sloate said.

Ted was in no position to argue. He was sprawled in a large chair in Elinor's sitting room, where the huge man had thrown him. The brute, a hired hand on the Wynn estate, stood silent and ready by the door.

Elinor sat demurely across from him. The oil lamp cast a strange glow on Sloate, who was pacing.

"You come here with a gun?" Sloate said. "I should have you arrested. What did you think you could accomplish?"

"I wanted to find out who was involved in this," Ted said as evenly as he could. "And now I know."

"Oh, Ted," said Elinor. "Why did you have to come here?"

"To talk sense into you, Elinor." He looked at Sloate. "I thought you were long gone from these parts."

"Son, you understand very little about me," Sloate said. His bald head and imperious face gave him a look of a Roman senator. Ted could imagine him hiding daggers in his crisp suit. "You might recall that I am innocent of all charges made against me."

"You were found not guilty," Ted said. "That doesn't make you innocent."

"And you came trespassing on this property. That does not make you a hero."

"Does it make me a prisoner?" Ted questioned.

"Why, no," Sloate said with false concern. "If I give that impression, I must apologize."

"What about Samson over there?" Ted nodded toward the big man.

"Naturally he was concerned about a strange figure skulking about the grounds at night. I might say it is lucky your neck wasn't broken."

"Get to the point, Sloate. I know I won't be leaving until you've had your say."

Sloate turned to Elinor. "You were quite right, my dear. Our young man here has lost the social graces his mother diligently attempted to impart to him."

Ted felt a fresh rush of anger. "I wouldn't mention my mother if I were you." The thought that Sloate had swindled her still filled him with rage. How many others had he done the same thing to? Ted wished he had the gun in his hand. It sat on a table near Elinor.

"Young man," Sloate said, "I have spent a great many years in halls of influence, in courtrooms and offices of those who have the sort of power you can only dream of. I daresay I know something about what makes men tick when it comes to the rub. I know this about you. Despite what you think of me, you will listen carefully to what I have to say because you know that not doing so might be very dangerous in the long term."

"Dear," Elinor chimed in, "how can I prevail upon you to be cooperative?"

Her words struck Ted as odd, yet fitting. Elinor was a calculating woman, but she did not have the native intelligence of the born conspirator. Sloate had that, in spades.

"What's the game, Sloate?" Ted said.

"Decidedly not a game," Sloate said. "Elinor has told me of your recent conversation. Was there anything not made plain to you at that time?"

"I think I see things pretty clear," Ted said. "You're not over the fact that Kit Shannon is practicing law and showed the town just what sort of man you are."

Sloate paused, a slight sneer on his face. "You can see that for yourself, sonny. I am here and I will not go away."

"And you want to destroy Kit."

"Whatever gave you that idea?" Sloate said.

Ted looked at him carefully, Sloate's face reflecting an odd calm. Could this man ever be trusted to tell the truth?

"I will not involve myself with Miss Shannon," Sloate said. "Except as an advisor to the district attorney. Someday, perhaps, I will assume that very position. Now, however, I am content to help them seek justice."

"How can they even allow you?" Ted said.

"Son, I have told you I know what makes men tick. John Davenport wishes to be successful, like most men. He knows my experience is unmatched. I can help him. I can also help you."

"That I do not believe."

"Let me explain. Elinor has already made it clear that a scandal involving Miss Shannon is not in anyone's best interests. In fact, I wish her well. She is a very talented young woman. Perhaps, in time, she will learn the art of compromise."

"You don't know Kit."

Sloate shrugged. "What is it the poet says? 'A woman is a foreign land of which a man will ne'er quite understand.' I'll grant you the mystery of women"—Sloate looked at Elinor—"but we men understand one another. We can weigh on the scales what is good, bad, or indifferent and come to a rational conclusion."

"I'm listening," Ted said through clenched teeth.

"I am merely suggesting the least possible trouble for all of us," Sloate said. "Your being here tonight, that is trouble. I do not want this to happen again. If you will behave yourself, I will promise you that I will have nothing to do with Miss Shannon. Ever."

"Why should I trust you?"

"I do not see as you have a choice. You will also stay away from Miss Shannon, and in return, I will not have you arrested and tried for attempted murder."

Ted shook his head, but the whole thing was beginning to make perverse sense. Sloate, as always, had found a way to manipulate matters to his benefit.

"I have your gun as evidence," Sloate said. "And the testimony of Caleb." Sloate motioned to the large man, still standing by the door. "I am willing to forget about all of this, but I will keep the revolver as insurance. Do we understand each other?"

"All except the rock," Ted said.

"I am afraid I don't understand."

"The rock you live under."

Sloate paused, then smiled. "I have been insulted by better men than you, son. And I've seen a number of them buried. Now, if there is nothing more, you are free to go."

Ted struggled to a standing position. Sloate, adding insult to injury, handed him his crutches. There was nothing more to say to the man. As he started for the door, though, he paused to look down at Elinor.

"I warned you," he said. "When you make a deal with the devil, there is hell to pay."

For a moment she looked like a lost little girl. "Someday you will understand me," she said.

"I don't think so, Elinor." Ted left without a further word.

———

Kit fell to her knees and poured her heart out to God. *You alone know what I should do*, she prayed. *I have tried always to live according to your will. I have tried to follow your Word. Now I am at a loss. What should I do?*

In her room at the Westminster, with the window open to the night, Kit could hear the clack of the occasional carriage, the horse-mounted police, the clang of a distant trolley as it made its way down main streets.

But the sound of her beating heart was louder still, a rhythm of fear.

*I am representing a guilty man who wishes to confess. That is your will for all sinners, is it not? How can I prevent it? How could I hope to continue, knowing that my skill and training would ultimately thwart justice?*

*I am lost, Father. Please show me what to do.*

Then she thought of Ted. Where was he? How was he? Kit felt awash in sorrow so strong, so powerful, that she felt her body drain of strength. She could see his smiling face, the exhilarated expression when he spoke of flying.

But that was the Ted she'd first met upon arriving in Los Angeles. That Ted no longer existed. That Ted had died in the crash.

She hoped he might be resurrected by the saving grace of Jesus. She prayed that in time he would be restored—that his hope and dreams would once again be renewed. But maybe he no longer cared about those dreams. Maybe those dreams wouldn't include her.

She would have to face up to that. Her heart cried out against it, but her head told her to keep still. Rely on God, always. He will show you the way.

A tear trickled down her cheek. *Then show me, Lord. Show me.*

# Chapter 35

*Los Angeles Examiner*
July 6, 1904

### HANRATTY DRUNK, WITNESS SAYS
#### Gun Drawn, He Went Looking for Chausser
#### Kathleen Shannon Shocked
#### by Tom Phelps

*Yesterday, in the courtroom of Judge Andrew Cartwright, the case against Officer Edward Hanratty was made in terms even the cleverest of lawyers would not be able to overcome.*

*Otto Balsam, resident at the Braxton Arms Hotel, told a hushed gathering of his encounter with the murderous Edward Hanratty on the stairway of said lodging. "He had been drinking quite a lot," the witness said. "That man was drunk and danger-ous."*

*In the stunned courtroom none appeared more aghast than the defendant's lawyer, Kathleen Shannon. So shocked was she that she did not ask the witness any questions on cross-examination. Miss Shannon appeared visibly shaken as she conferred with her client at the counsel table.*

*The preliminary hearing continues today and should be completed in short order. District Attorney John Davenport has proved once again that the people of the county of Los Angeles are being well served . . .*

*Enough,* Freddy thought. *I cannot read any more. Kit, oh Kit, why have you done this to yourself? To me?*

For some odd reason Freddy was hot this morning. Even though the breeze through one of the great windows was pleasant and full of orange blossom, it did not matter. She was stifled in her own house.

She dared not venture to the courthouse to see her niece humiliated. If only Kit would have asked Professor Stillwater for help and advice! But she was stubborn, like her father had been, and closed to the prospect of the spiritual world. Oh, she had her Christian beliefs, which were fine for keeping one from becoming vile, but there was so much more.

Benjamin could have told her about this policeman from the start, told her to stay away from the case. Told her what was obvious to everybody else: that he was guilty, and she could do nothing for him.

That was why Benjamin's work was so important, and why she was going to see it carried on. Someday, Freddy hoped, Kit would see it, appreciate it—embrace it. But until then . . .

Why was it so hot in the house?

"Jerrold?" she cried. She noticed her hands were shaking, causing the newspaper to rustle.

Presently Jerrold entered the drawing room. "Madame?"

"Have you a fire going in the house?"

"No, Madame. Shall I start one?"

"Heavens, no. Why is the house so hot?"

"I haven't noticed. Perhaps the new fan should be turned on?"

"Oh, I suppose," Freddy said. "I simply am mystified. This house always seemed so . . ."

She felt short of breath, unable to complete the thought. "A chair," she said suddenly. "Jerrold, I need . . ."

Before she could finish she felt a vise close on her body and a burning in her chest that was unlike anything she had experienced before. Helpless, she heard herself exclaim, "Oh, dear!" before falling into darkness.

———

This morning the walk to the courthouse was, like the city itself, veiled in a cloudy gray. Kit's very step was slower, plodding, as if she did not want to arrive at all.

And she did not. This had all the feeling of a march to a funeral.

She had not felt any firm direction from God, which in her mind made it plain that He wanted her in just this circumstance, though the lesson of it was not yet clear. In other words, He wanted her to endure it. That was the only answer she could come up with, and it offered little comfort.

Carrie Hanratty's face kept coming into Kit's mind, like the baleful remnant of a bad dream. There was nothing Kit could do, legally or ethically. She had a client who had confessed and wanted to come clean. In fact, it seemed the best solution for all concerned, considering what might happen at a trial.

Why, then, did Kit feel like a traitor?

Perhaps this was the lesson she needed to learn. She always let her heart get invested with the fate of her clients. Earl Rogers had told her on several occasions the best lawyer was one who did not care about his clients, only about winning.

She could never be that kind of lawyer. She knew that. But she would have to learn that sometimes the right decision would be gall to her and those close to the case.

Plodding up the hill to Temple Street and the courthouse, Kit kept a prayer in her heart. *If I'm missing anything, please, Lord, bring it to mind before it's too late.*

At the top of the courthouse steps Kit was greeted by a few reporters, men who had come to treat her with the deference, if not respect, due to an ongoing source of publicity. Tom Phelps, smoking a cigarette to one side, gave her a nod. She ignored it.

"What's the score, Kit?" one of the reporters, a man from the *Times*, asked.

She ignored him, too, and her look must have signaled the others that this was no time to be asking her questions. No one asked another.

Feeling like she'd walked across a desert, Kit finally made it to the courtroom, where the crowd was gathering. Now would come the worst part of all. Now she would have to inform Davenport and Judge Cartwright of Ed Hanratty's decision.

John Davenport sat at his table reading a newspaper. Kit did not have to look to know it was the *Examiner*.

"We need to see the judge," she said. Davenport put the paper down and did not even inquire as to the reason. It must have been apparent from Kit's face that this was of the utmost importance.

They were ushered into Cartwright's chambers by his young clerk.

"Are we ready for the session?" he asked.

"Not quite," Kit said. Cartwright motioned for them to sit. "My client," Kit said, "is considering changing his plea."

Judge Cartwright and Davenport exchanged looks. When Cartwright spoke, it was cautiously. "He wants to plead guilty?"

"Perhaps. But I should like to know what the court's inclination is concerning sentence."

Cartwright leaned back in his chair, his hands behind his head. "John, what do you think of all this?"

For his part, Davenport looked stunned, as if capitulation were the last thing he ever expected. "I think the People would defer to Your Honor's judgment."

*A true politician*, Kit thought.

"Well, now," Cartwright said, "I guess you're not feeling as high and mighty as you thought."

"I beg your pardon?" Kit said.

"You came into my courtroom with such airs. You knew this case against your client was strong as steel. It was a waste of time for everybody."

"This is a preliminary hearing," Kit said in protest. "Any defendant has the right to—"

"And don't lecture to me about rights. We all know what the game is. You should have told your client to plead right away and things would have been a lot easier on him."

"Easier? You mean you will hold it against him that—"

"You just listen for a change, young lady. No one has ever accused Judge Andrew Cartwright of being unfair. John, you agree?"

"Of course, Your Honor," Davenport said.

The judge pointed at Kit. "I told you once I didn't like the idea of a woman in court. You're the weaker sex and inclined to do things without due consideration. That's what you've done here. You've let your emotions run roughshod over the facts." He turned to John, "Seen my wife do that a thousand times over." He turned back to Kit, stroking his chin. "But like I say, I'm fair, and this time I am not going to visit the sins of the lawyer on the client."

Kit squirmed in her chair, which seemed suddenly smaller than when she'd first sat in it. Had she come to this court with an undue sense of pride? Was that what God was trying to teach her—to humble herself before God and man?

"So I'm willing to make the sentence fair and fit the crime. Life in prison."

The sentence hit Kit with the force of a boulder. Though she knew this was a normal term for murder, she had hoped the judge would consider something less. "Your Honor," she began, finding it hard to breathe, "Officer Hanratty is a man who has served this city honorably. He is throwing himself on the court's mercy. He has a wife and family."

"So did Jay Chausser," Davenport injected.

Kit ignored him. "If Your Honor would give him a twenty-five-year sentence, he might have a chance to get out, with good behavior, before he dies."

"He's not getting the gallows," Cartwright said.

"Your Honor," Kit stammered, "surely you can . . ." She stopped, looked back and forth between the two men. Their eyes were resolute and unmoved.

Cartwright's clerk stuck his head in the door. "Excuse me, Judge Cartwright, but there's a man out here asking for Miss Shannon."

"What is this about?" Cartwright asked Kit.

"I don't know," Kit said.

"He looks rather upset," the clerk said. "He's an older man, I think he said his name was Jerrold."

Kit stood up immediately. "Your Honor, this is a family matter, I believe. I shall have to confer with my client. May I have a stay of the proceedings until I do?"

Judge Cartwright looked to Davenport, who seemed unconcerned. "I have no objection," Davenport said, "so long as the answer comes today."

"I'll want your client in here for his plea at four o'clock," said Judge Cartwright. "I firmly suggest that you be prompt."

# Chapter 36

JERROLD CRIED ALL THE WAY to the hospital. But
he managed to tell Kit about Aunt Freddy's fall and how a doctor
had said she was almost lost.

Kit held the old man's arm and patted it gently, if only to keep
from bursting into tears herself.

Suddenly, with all else that was swirling about in Kit's life, Aunt
Freddy might be at death's door. There was so much to say, so
much that had been unsaid between them in the last months. Her
desperation to see Aunt Freddy grew with every hoofbeat of the
horse drawing the carriage.

Sisters Hospital, at least, was the finest in the region. Kit had a
sudden remembrance of her meeting Dr. Jeffrey Kenton, the man
she almost married, there. Indeed, each time she passed the brick
edifice off Beaudry Avenue she had a pang of loss and betrayal. But
it came and went quickly, for she had more pressing matters on
her mind.

When the carriage stopped in front of the hospital, Jerrold would not get out of the carriage. Kit insisted that he come with her to see Freddy, but he demurred. "It would not be fitting for the servant until the family has been to see her, and then only if he is requested."

"She will ask for you, Jerrold. I know it. And thank you. I'll be all right from here."

Aunt Freddy was in a room on the third floor. In keeping with her social station, it was a private room with a large window. But when Kit entered Freddy was not alone.

Benjamin Stillwater rose from a chair and gave Kit a cool glance. Kit felt the heat rush to her cheeks and was about to tell him to leave when she heard a weak voice from the bed. "Oh, Kit . . ."

Kit rushed to the bedside. Aunt Freddy seemed wan and old, without a hint of the vibrancy that was at one time her greatest social asset. Her eyes seemed more deeply set and her breathing came in short, labored huffs.

Taking her aunt's feeble hand, Kit placed it to her cheek. "Aunt Freddy, I came as soon as I heard."

"How . . ." Freddy said.

"Jerrold came to court. Faithful Jerrold."

"Court . . . you have a case . . ."

"Don't try to talk, Aunt Freddy. I am here. I will stay as long as you want."

Then, from the other side of the bed, Stillwater whispered something that sounded like *tut* and wagged his index finger at Kit. Her anger returned in a burst, but she held it in check for Freddy's sake.

"Aunt Freddy," she said, "I would like to confer with the doctor for a moment. I won't be but a moment."

"Come back soon," Freddy said.

Kit kissed her hand and gently placed it back on the bed. Then she flashed her eyes at Stillwater in a fashion that he would not be able to mistake. *Get out into the hall now*, they said.

Stillwater paused at the bedside. "I shall return forthwith," he said, loud enough that it might have been directed at Kit.

Out in the hall it took all of Kit's strength not to scream in Stillwater's face. "How dare you tell me what to say to my aunt?"

"You do not know her condition," Stillwater said with detached assurance. "I do."

"I am her niece, and I want you to leave us now. I wish to be alone with her."

"I am afraid that won't be possible."

Kit felt iron jaws of rage clamp down on her.

"You see," Stillwater said, "I have become a great comfort to your great-aunt, and that is precisely what she needs at this time."

"She needs me, sir."

"You are petulant and inconsiderate. Freddy is dying."

The words struck Kit like fire. Her entire body shook with anger and shock. She wanted to push this fraud aside and rush to Aunt Freddy. But something told her to hesitate, that Stillwater, for all his bile, was right about Freddy needing comfort just now. A row would only make matters worse for her.

A doctor approached them. He was an older man with a serious expression. "Professor," he said to Stillwater. "We can talk now."

"Excuse me," Kit said.

The doctor gave her a curious glance.

"I am Freddy's great-niece. You may talk to me."

"But I was given to understand that Professor Stillwater is—"

"Professor Stillwater is not family," Kit said. "You will address me."

The doctor cleared his throat. "I must say, that is, well, your aunt, you see, has requested Professor Stillwater. I am at a loss."

The hallway seemed to close in around Kit. She was determined to push it back, along with these men. "If I have to go to court," she said, "I will do it."

"Miss," the doctor said, "your aunt is in a very delicate condition. Her heart is weak. If she were to experience emotional stress it could be fatal. What she needs is complete comfort."

"Are you telling me," Kit said, "that I do not have a say in my aunt's situation?"

The doctor looked at Stillwater, who said, "That is Mrs. Fairbank's wish. And I am not going to see that frustrated. I will allow you to see her—"

"Allow me?"

"—allow you, but I am not going to leave her side. What I will *not* allow is for you to say anything to upset her in any way."

Kit's instinct was to fight, but her head told her Freddy's condition was more important. She would wait for a more opportune time.

"May I see her now?" Kit asked the doctor.

"So long as you do not disturb her," Stillwater answered. And by his look Kit knew he meant to enforce the prohibition.

She walked back into the room.

"Is everything . . . all right?" Aunt Freddy asked. Her eyes were heavy lidded, as if she were starting to fall asleep.

Sensing Stillwater's presence, Kit said, "Just fine. It's you I'm concerned about."

"Oh, fiddle. Don't make a fuss."

"No fuss," Kit said. She gave a sideward glance at Stillwater, who had returned to what seemed like his perch at the window.

"Aunt Freddy, I want you to know something."

"Eh?"

"I want you to know," Kit said, "that I shall be praying for you each day."

"Yes?"

"And that Jesus our Savior is watching over you." Kit sensed Stillwater come to attention at the window. In a moment he was on the opposite side of the bed. Kit did not look at him.

Freddy said, "Benjamin, he will take care of it . . ."

"Jesus," Kit repeated. "Call out to Him."

"Benjamin will . . ." Freddy's eyes closed. She began to breathe steadily.

"She had better rest now," Stillwater said. "Time for you to go."

Kit lingered over Aunt Freddy for a long moment, then leaned over and kissed her forehead. Then she stood and faced Stillwater. "I will be back," she said.

"I will be here," he replied.

————

So many emotions were running through Kit as she walked back to her office that she thought she might burst out with an unseemly scream. She wanted Corazón. She needed her comfort and counsel.

Her faithful friend was waiting for her in front of the building. Kit had missed their lunch appointment.

"I am so sorry," Kit said immediately, embracing Corazón. "Aunt Freddy is in the hospital."

Corazón looked shocked. "She is very sick?"

"Yes. We must pray for her. We must protect her."

"Protect?"

"I will explain later. Now we have to get ready for court. Our client is going to plead guilty."

As if this were the second shot out of a double-barreled rifle, Corazón stepped back. Then she shook her head vigorously. "No."

"Yes. He has changed his mind and I—"

"No, no."

"There is nothing to be—"

Corazón gripped Kit's shoulders. "Listen!" Her accent rendered the word *Lee-sen*.

"What is it?" Kit asked.

"A man. You must go to him."

"What man?"

"He is waiting."

"But we have to—"

"Now, Kit." *Keet.*

The urgency in Corazón's voice and the very manner of her ordering made it plain to Kit this was not something to argue about.

"All right," she said as Corazón took her arm. "Take me."

# Chapter 37

HEATH SLOATE SAVORED the wine. It tasted like victory. He raised his glass to John Davenport and Judge Andrew Cartwright. "Gentlemen," he said, "to a job well done."

Cartwright and Davenport responded and the three drank. They were in the private dining room at the Nadeau Hotel. Sloate had arranged the lunch.

Davenport carved his steak. "You were right about Shannon, Sloate," he said. "Temperamental. It got the better of her."

"I second that," Cartwright said. "This idea of a woman trying a criminal case—it's preposterous."

"It won't last," Sloate said. "In fact, this will be a ruinous adventure for women pursuing the profession. When they see what has happened to Kathleen Shannon, do you think they will want to follow suit?"

"I don't know," the judge said. "I can't understand my wife, let alone the entire sex."

"They are not difficult to figure." Sloate dabbed at his lips with his napkin. "What is it Mr. Bierce says? 'He gets on best with women who knows how to get on without them.' "

The three men shared a hearty laugh.

"Still, one wonders about her resiliency," Davenport said.

"How's that?" Judge Cartwright said.

"It's the look of her," the District Attorney observed. "The set in her eyes. Stubborn. Not an attractive quality, I grant, but something that gives one pause to count her out."

Sloate shook his head. "I shouldn't worry, John. Her spirit can be broken, and it will be."

"What have you got up your sleeve?" Davenport asked.

"Let us just say," Sloate said, "that Miss Shannon has some unpleasant surprises coming her way."

"Nothing nefarious, I hope," Cartwright said. "I am an officer of the court."

"Gentlemen, let me assure you, everything is above board. I would hate to have my friend John prosecute me again."

Once more, the three laughed. Then Davenport said, "Anything to keep Clarence Darrow out of town."

"Then I shall be in the courtroom at four o'clock," Sloate said. "I never could resist a good execution."

———

Ted found Gus at the terminus of the Main Street trolley line. Gus, his coveralls splotchy with grease, was tinkering with a tangle of gears.

"You missed a spot," Ted said.

Gus whirled around, glaring. "What in the Sam Hill are you talkin' about?"

"On your clothes. I can see a spot that's clean."

Gus threw down his wrench. "You got nothin' better to do than bother a person?"

"Tell you the truth, Gus, I don't."

Outside the building a trolley clanged as it came to the turn-around. Gus looked out the window. "I got work to do," he said.

"So do I," Ted said. "And I need your help."

Gus squinted at him, like he was studying an odd insect. "Tell me what this is about."

Ted smiled, leaning on his crutches. "I came to apologize, Gus. I treated you wrong. I'm sorry."

The mechanic rubbed his hands on the front of his coveralls, as if he had no other response.

"Still love me?" Ted said.

"Ahh," said Gus.

"I love you, too."

"Will yer stop with that!"

"Help me."

"What is it?"

"If you clean yourself up, I'll explain it to you. You in or out?"

Gus looked out the window. "I got to finish this."

"How long will it take?"

"For most people a day. For me, ten minutes."

"I'll meet you outside."

———

At precisely four o'clock Kit walked into Cartwright's court-room. Her heart beat so loud she thought everyone in the room could hear it, like Sousa's band marching through the streets.

But she was resolute. She didn't care who heard her.

Ed Hanratty was seated at the counsel table, a deputy sheriff standing nearby. Kit slipped into the chair next to him. Davenport sat unconcerned at the other table, waiting for Cartwright to enter.

Kit leaned over to Hanratty. "You are not going to plead guilty," she whispered to him.

He whipped around to her. "But—"

"Listen to me. I will not allow you to throw your life away. For Carrie's sake. For the sake of your children. I want the chance to prove you innocent. I don't think you know clearly what happened that night. You were full of drink. But something has come up, and I want to move forward."

He shook his head slowly, looking at her as if she were crazy. "I cannot see how. They have the deck stacked."

"Let's make them show us the whole deck," Kit said. "Ed, give yourself this chance."

Hanratty paused. Then he looked into the gallery, toward his wife. Carrie looked back at him, a small, sweet smile on her face.

Finally, he said, "God have mercy on us both."

"He will," Kit said.

Judge Cartwright entered the courtroom as everyone stood. He gaveled for order. "I understand, Miss Shannon, that your client wishes to change his plea."

A buzz of voices sounded expressions of surprise. Kit stood, "Your Honor, my client does not wish to change his plea. He is not guilty."

The shock and anger on Cartwright's face could not have been more apparent if he had been a ham actor playing King Lear. He pushed himself to a standing position, as if he might spring across the bench and take matters—Kit—into his own hands.

John Davenport was equally stung. At least his openmouthed gape gave that impression.

"What is the meaning of this, Miss Shannon?" the judge said.

"Since we are on the record," Kit said, "and in the presence of an august gathering that includes the press, I shall place into the record the meaning of this. Mr. Hanratty is being railroaded, and this proceeding has not concluded until I put on my own case. And that is what I intend to do."

"You have tried this court's patience," Cartwright said. "You have lost us an entire day."

"For the record, Your Honor, this court gave me leave until four o'clock to confer with my client. I have abided by the court's schedule. I have conferred with my client, and he says to this court, and to the district attorney, that he pleads not guilty. We shall present our case."

Almost helplessly, Cartwright turned to Davenport. "Do you have any response?"

With an angry shrug, Davenport said, "This office is no longer surprised at the decisions of Miss Shannon, detrimental though they might be to the pursuit of justice. I suppose we shall have to continue."

Cartwright shook his head in disgust. "Then be here at nine o'clock tomorrow morning."

Then he banged his gavel so hard it seemed to split wood.

———

Kit and Corazón went directly from court to the hospital. When they got there, Kit saw Stillwater sitting next to Freddy's bed, speaking to her in low tones. He stood up when he saw her.

She ignored him and went to Freddy's side.

"Hello dear," Freddy said. She seemed tired but alert.

"I've brought Corazón," Kit said.

Freddy put up her hand to her former maid. "Good day, my dear."

"Madame," Corazón said softly, taking Freddy's hand.

"Do not look so sad," Freddy said. "Dr. Fyshe and Professor Stillwater are taking good care of me."

Kit bristled. "I've brought you something," she said. She took a small Bible from her briefcase and laid it on the table next to Freddy's bed. "A Bible."

She saw Stillwater look at her suspiciously, but he said nothing.

"How thoughtful," Freddy said. "I wish you would talk to Benjamin about these things."

"What things?" Kit said.

"Spiritual," Freddy said.

"The Scriptures are our guide," Kit said.

Stillwater interrupted. "What Freddy means to say is that we should have a discussion sometime. But not here or now."

"When?" Kit said, unable to hide her pique.

"I will be in touch," he said.

She wanted to have it out with him right there, but now was not the time, for Freddy's sake. Yet the time would come. And it would have to be soon.

Outside the hospital, Kit turned to Corazón. "This Stillwater is playing a most deadly game, and my aunt's eternal soul is in the balance."

"How does he do this game?" Corazón asked.

Kit shook her head. "I can't say that I entirely understand the hold he has on her. She seems to find something in him. She is quite willing to hear him out and practice whatever boneheaded methods he suggests, but she refuses to accept that being a Christian is more than applying the title to your name."

"She is lonely, I think. This man, he gives her friendship. Like you and me. She no has friends—they laugh at her. She can no be friends with the servants. She needs Jesus, yes?"

*Jesus.* The name hit Kit between the eyes. Freddy wasn't rejecting her at all, she was rejecting Jesus. Stillwater hated Kit because she belonged to Christ. Sloate hated her for the same reason. They couldn't bear the light of Christ shining through her.

"Corazón, you're right. Aunt Freddy doesn't understand, and

with people like Stillwater hanging over her every minute, she may never understand."

"God cannot deal with this man? He is more powerful than God?"

Kit could see in Corazón's expression a look that almost suggested amusement.

"We no face this alone," Corazón said. "We face this on our knees."

Kit nodded. "Always, my friend." She embraced Corazón and felt, for the moment at least, something she had not felt in some time—comfort.

# Chapter 38

THE NEXT MORNING in court, Davenport called his final witness, Edna Chausser.

This was the first time Kit saw the wife of the victim. She wore black, in the manner of a widow, complete with hat and veil. Her face was obscured until she raised it to take the oath.

"You are the widow of Jay Chausser?" Davenport asked.

"I am," she said. She had close-set eyes and small features, giving her a girl-like appearance.

"Were you present with your husband on the night of June seventh?"

"Yes, sir. And my son."

"Robert?"

"Yes."

"Can you describe for the court the events that transpired that night?"

She sat up. "We had just returned from the nickelodeon. Jay

loved it so. Moving pictures. We had ice cream after the show. We were very . . ." Her voice broke off in a stifled sob.

"Take your time, Mrs. Chausser."

The woman took a deep breath. "We had come back to the hotel and were getting ready for bed. I was in the kitchen preparing a cup of tea when I heard the noise."

"What noise was that?"

"A crashing sound. I was so startled I dropped my teacup. Then I heard the shots."

"Gunshots?"

"Yes."

"How many?"

Mrs. Chausser paused, then said, "Two. One right after the other."

"What did you do next?"

"I was frightened. I peered around the door and saw him."

Davenport said, "May the record reflect the witness has identified the defendant."

"It shall so reflect," said Judge Cartwright.

"What happened then?" Davenport asked.

"He, the officer, ran after my son. That's when I came out and saw Jay . . ."

"It's all right, Mrs. Chausser. Can you tell us what his condition was?"

"He was bleeding from the chest. He tried to . . . he struggled to his feet. I closed the door, but it was broken. I was afraid the officer might come back. I went to Jay and I asked him how badly he was hurt. He told me it would be all right. He stood there for a moment, smiling at me. Then all of a sudden he . . ." She paused, dabbing at her eyes with the back of her hand. "He fell to the floor."

"Mrs. Chausser," Davenport said softly, "I have only a few

more questions for you. Did your husband own a gun?"

"No, sir."

"Do you recall being asked about that gun?"

"Yes, sir. By a detective."

"Was this detective named McGinty?"

"Yes, sir."

Davenport turned to the gallery as the people stirred. "Your witness," he said.

Kit began carefully. Earl Rogers had told her that widows and children were the hardest people to cross-examine. There was a natural sympathy for them, and being rough could backfire.

"Mrs. Chausser," Kit began, "you said you were in the kitchen when the tragic events took place?"

"Yes, ma'am."

"And you came into the room where your husband was after you heard the shots fired?"

"Yes."

"Then you did not actually see who fired the shots?"

"It was the officer."

"I am only asking about what you saw with your own eyes."

Edna Chausser shifted a little in the witness chair. "If you put it that way, no. I did not see him fire the gun. But I came in and—"

"You have answered my question," Kit interrupted. Control of the witness was crucial here. "I will not take much more of your time. Just prior to the shooting, did your son and your husband have an argument?"

The witness slowly shook her head. "No."

"They did not raise their voices?"

"Well, they did a little."

"Why?"

"They liked to make speeches to each other. My husband was a very learned man. They were pretending to be Teddy Roosevelt."

Kit was deflated. If that was the source of the loud voices the maid had heard, then there was no basis for a motive of anger between father and son. And Maria Espinoza would not be able to rebut this characterization. Davenport would quickly show that her language skill was not to be trusted.

Kit had one final inquiry. "Mrs. Chausser, you said you were preparing to go to bed, is that right?"

"Yes, ma'am."

"Where did Robert sleep?"

"On the floor."

"And you and your husband?"

"The wall bed. It comes down."

"It was down that night?"

"My husband was on the bed, on top of it."

"But it was made up?"

"Oh yes."

"Thank you, Mrs. Chausser."

Davenport waited until Edna Chausser was seated once again in the gallery. Then he said, "The prosecution rests, Your Honor. We believe there is abundant evidence to provide the court with cause to bind the defendant over for trial."

Nodding, but with a resigned expression, Judge Cartwright looked at Kit. "I suppose you still wish to present witnesses?"

"I do, Your Honor," Kit said.

With a quick wave of the hand Cartwright said, "Then be quick about it."

"The defense calls George Ambrose."

———

From the look on Davenport's face, Kit could tell he had no idea who this witness was. But if he was overly concerned he did not show it. He was, after all, holding the winning hand. He and the judge were just waiting for Kit to fold.

George Ambrose wore a suit, though it fitted him poorly. He appeared more a laborer than a gentleman, and that is exactly what he was.

"What is your age, Mr. Ambrose?"

"Thirty-one," Ambrose answered.

"And what is your occupation?"

"I am a painter and wall man."

"How long have you been so employed?"

"Ever since I was knee high, like my father and his father before him."

"Your firm is Ambrose and Sons?"

"My little brother, Todd, and I work with Dad."

"Would you say you have a good reputation in the community?"

"Ask anyone who has seen our work."

At this point Davenport rose. "If Your Honor please, may we inquire into the relevance of this witness? What does Miss Shannon hope to accomplish with him?"

"Your Honor," Kit said, "I wish to qualify my witness in the same way Mr. Davenport qualified Mr. Balsam. I waited patiently for the relevance of that to be shown, and I ask the court and Mr. Davenport to do the same."

Judge Cartwright moved the chaw around in his cheek. Reluctantly, he said, "I'll allow a few more questions in this regard. But keep it moving."

"Mr. Ambrose," Kit said, "have you ever had any trouble with hotel owners?"

Smiling, Ambrose said, "Nah. I've done some of my best work for 'em."

"All right. On the night of June the ninth, did you have occasion to do work at the Braxton Arms Hotel?"

"Yes, ma'am. I was called in to paint part of a wall."

"Was this wall on the second floor?"

"Yes."

"Did you say part of a wall?"

"They only wanted a portion of it painted."

"Did you find that unusual?"

"A little, but I just do what I'm told."

Kit waited for the muted laughter of the gallery to quiet down. "Did the portion of wall you were to paint face one of the rooms on the second floor?"

"Yes, ma'am. It was across from Rooms 202 and 204."

"Did you have to prepare the wall for painting?"

"Always have to prepare. I roughed it over with sandpaper, and filled some of the flaws."

"Was one of the flaws a bullet hole?"

"Objection," Davenport shouted. "Leading the witness."

Kit could not help a slight smile. Davenport was getting a taste of his own medicine. She knew she shouldn't enjoy it, but she did.

"Sustained," Judge Cartwright said.

"I will rephrase," Kit said. "Can you describe the nature of the flaws?"

"The only one I remember was a bullet hole."

Davenport's face reddened as Kit glanced at him for a fleeting moment. "Mr. Ambrose, would you please stand and indicate for the court, on the wall behind you, about how high the bullet hole was in the wall."

Ambrose stood, turned and indicated with his finger a point on the wall.

"Let the record reflect," Kit said, "that the witness is pointing to a spot approximately six feet from the floor."

"All right," Judge Cartwright snapped.

"Your witness," Kit said.

Davenport was up like a shot. "Mr. Ambrose, you are a painter?"

"Yes, sir."

"Were you ever in the army?"

"No, sir. Bum leg."

"Have you ever served in law enforcement?"

"No, sir."

"Have you ever studied Miss Shannon's favorite subject, ballistics?"

"Ba-what?"

"Ballistics, sir."

"Never heard of it."

"Then you are not an expert in bullets, are you?"

Ambrose folded his arms. "I would say I have some experience."

"In bullets?"

"In bullet holes."

"How is that, sir?"

Looking at the judge, Ambrose said, "I don't know if I should say."

"You are under oath," Cartwright said. "Come out with it."

"Well," Ambrose said, "I have done a lot of work for Miss Pearl Morton. And let me tell you, there's bullet holes in those walls."

The audience laughed heartily. Kit remembered the help Pearl had given during the Ted Fox case. She was a madam, and her house of ill repute was no doubt like any other—with damage done by drunken men with guns.

Davenport quickly recovered. "Did you in fact recover a bullet from the wall?"

"No, sir."

"Then you do not know if it was in fact a bullet hole. It might have been made by any number of items."

"It sure looked like it to me."

"Without proof, Mr. Ambrose, this court is not interested in what things look like to you. I have no further questions."

# Chapter 39

"CALL YOUR NEXT WITNESS," Judge Cartwright said.

"With the court's permission," Kit said, "I would like to offer a demonstration."

"How's that?"

"Your Honor," Kit explained, "testimony has been presented here that needs further explanation. Surely the court would like to know the entire matter before it renders a decision."

"Get on with it, Miss Shannon."

"I thank the court." Kit made a motion toward the rear of the courtroom. Almost immediately the doors opened and two men entered carrying a large, framed door.

Amidst the roiling voices Judge Cartwright said, "What is this?"

The two men, as Kit had instructed them, carried the door through the gate and set it in front of the witness stand.

"This is a door of the same height as that in the rooms at the

Braxton Arms," Kit said. "If Your Honor please, this is highly relevant."

The judge threw up his hands. "You show me how it is relevant immediately."

"I shall have to call a witness. The defense calls Thomas Seldon."

It was a hesitant Seldon who came forward, eyeing Kit and the door, Davenport, and the judge.

"You are still under oath," Judge Cartwright said. Seldon nodded and took the stand.

"Mr. Seldon," Kit said. "Is this door that these gentlemen are holding the same size as that at your room at the Braxton Arms?"

"It appears to be."

"Would you please demonstrate for the court how you managed to look over the transom on the night of June seventh?"

"You want me to get up and do it?"

"If you please."

Seldon, somewhat slowly, came out from the witness box and stood next to the door. He looked it up and down. "I was standing on an armchair," he said.

Kit took her wooden chair from counsel table and placed it next to the door. "Will this suffice for the demonstration?"

Seldon shrugged.

"If you please," Kit said.

The witness stepped onto the chair, then reached up with both hands and placed them on top of the door. "I pulled myself up a little," he said.

"With your hands on top of the door, you pulled yourself up?"

"That's right."

"Could you have seen over the transom if you had not pulled yourself up?"

"No. That's just how it happened. I told you I could do it by standing on this chair. I do not see what is so difficult to understand."

"Thank you, Mr. Seldon," Kit said. "I have no further questions."

Davenport shook his head and said, "I have nothing more for my own witness."

Kit turned to the two men holding the door. "Thank you, gentlemen," she said. "And when you go out into the hall, would you please ask Martha Milligan to come in?"

"Who is Martha Milligan?" Cartwright said.

"My next witness," Kit replied.

———————

The young woman looked nervous. Her face was pale and freckled, her dirty blond hair stuffed into a less-than-fashionable hat.

"Miss Milligan," Kit said, "will you tell us where you are employed?"

"At the Braxton Arms."

"What are your duties?"

"I am a maid."

"How long have you been a maid at the Braxton Arms?"

"About two weeks now."

Davenport said, "I must object to this witness. She was not employed at the Braxton during the tragic events. What relevance is there?"

"Your Honor," Kit said, "if you will allow me to show the relevance?"

"I'd like to see it," Cartwright said. "And soon."

To the witness Kit said, "Before your employment at the Braxton Arms, did you work as a maid?"

"Oh yes. For seven years I've been workin' in hotels and inns."

"Now, Miss Milligan. Four days ago, did you have a conversation with my associate, Miss Chavez?" Kit motioned toward Corazón, who sat on Hanratty's left at the counsel table.

"Yes," Martha Milligan said.

"How did that come about?"

"She was outside that day, in the alley. I came out with the refuse, and she told me she wished to speak to me. She said she had been a maid herself, but was now working for a lawyer."

"Did she name the lawyer?"

"Yes, ma'am. You."

"Had you heard of me?"

"I'm afraid not, ma'am."

"That is something of a relief."

The boys in the newspaper section gave a good laugh.

"Miss Milligan, what did Miss Chavez say to you next?"

"She said she needed some information and would I be willin' to help her."

"And you said what?" Kit asked.

"I said I would help her if I could."

"What information did she ask for?"

"It was about dust, ma'am."

"Please explain."

Milligan shifted in her seat. "She asked me to look at the dust on the transom of Room 201."

"Did you do so?"

"Yes, ma'am. I took a stepladder and looked at it."

"What did you find?"

"Dust. A lot of it."

"In your opinion, as a maid, how long had it been since the top of that door was dusted?"

"Years, ma'am."

Kit turned toward Davenport as she asked, "And did you find

in that dust any finger marks, hand prints, or other evidence that the dust had been disturbed?"

"No, ma'am. It had not been disturbed."

Pausing, Kit felt the ripple of realization coursing through the courtroom. She had just demonstrated for the judge and everyone else that Seldon was lying about how he allegedly saw the shooting.

"And so," Kit said, "no one had placed their hands on the top of the door of Room 201 for a matter of years?"

"That's right."

Kit turned over the witness to Davenport. His questions were fast and angry.

"Miss Milligan, is that your true name?"

"Why, yes sir."

"Did you attend school?"

"School, sir?"

"Yes, as in education. Do you have an education?"

Martha Milligan looked at her hands and softly said, "Only a little."

"How much is a little, Miss Milligan?"

Kit objected. "Mr. Davenport is merely trying to shame this witness."

"Overruled," Judge Cartwright said. "I believe he is trying to establish her credentials for rendering an opinion. Is that right, Mr. Davenport?"

"Yes, Your Honor."

"Proceed."

Davenport said, "Well, Miss Milligan, how much education?"

"Only grammar school. I had to go to work. My mother died, you see, and—"

"Thank you, Miss Milligan, you have answered my question. Then you have not been educated in the fields of science or forensics, have you?"

"Why, no."

"And when you made this tremendous dust observation, you used no tools or instruments, did you?"

"No." She was beginning to look confused and somewhat scared, but Kit knew she would have to weather this storm herself.

"You had no one else with you to corroborate the observation, correct?"

"I didn't think . . ."

"Answer yes or no, please."

"No."

"And are we to believe you are here to testify for the defense out of the goodness of your heart?"

"I was just—"

"That is all I have," Davenport said dismissively.

Judge Cartwright gaveled the court into recess. Hanratty took Kit's arm. "Did that do anything for us?" he asked.

"A little, perhaps," Kit said.

"But not enough."

"The judge is not going to dismiss this case based on the credibility problems of one witness. Remember, all he needs is enough to let a jury decide. We will continue to build our case."

"On what?"

Kit sighed. She wasn't sure what her next move would be. She needed time to think. But worries about Aunt Freddy clouded her mind, and there was even a touch of longing buried deep within. She had not seen or heard from Ted. Her life suddenly seemed to be a series of impending losses—Aunt Freddy, Ted, and this case.

———

Corazón took all of Kit's burdens as her own. She desperately wanted to help, to vindicate Kit's confidence in her. So far she had done well, but the case was still a long way from being won.

After the court session ended, Corazón went to the telegraph office to see if any word had come in from the Indianapolis police. Nothing. Would there ever be news?

She then met Kit for dinner to discuss matters further. But Kit's heart had been filled with thoughts of Aunt Freddy, and she went to the hospital directly.

Corazón returned to her room at the Westminster. She tried to concentrate on the case but could not. Instead, she did as Kit would have instructed. She knelt at her bedside and began to pray.

She heard a *plink* at her window. The curtains were closed against the night, so Corazón couldn't see out. Her second floor room faced to the east, toward the hillside. Sometimes dirt and dust from the winds would hit the glass of her window like that. But tonight there had been no strong wind.

*Plink.* Someone was throwing pebbles at her window. Who could it be? Juan, her brother? Or a mistaken stranger?

She opened the curtains and raised the window.

"Corazón."

It was a man's voice, a familiar one. "Sí?"

"It's Ted."

"Señor Fox?"

"Come down. I want to talk to you."

Her heart beat a rhythm as she flew down the stairs and out the back door of the Westminster. Ted was waiting for her, leaning on his crutches in a dark corner.

"Come inside," she said.

"No," Ted said. "I wish to speak to you here."

"Yes? Everything, it is all right?"

"How is Kit?"

"Will you see her? She would like that very much."

"I can't. Not just yet. Tell me, is she faring well?"

Corazón breathed deeply. "She is sad, I think."

Ted put his hand on her arm. "Why is she sad? The hearing?"

"That is one thing," Corazón said. "She is fighting for Señor Hanratty. It is very hard. But there is more. Señora Fairbank, she is sick."

His grip tightened slightly on her arm. "How sick?"

"In the hospital. Her heart, they say."

"I am sorry to hear that. I always liked her, though she had her suspicions about me."

"She like you, I think. She say you are the charmer. But she is maybe dying, and Kit cannot speak with her as she like."

"But why not?"

Corazón told him about Professor Stillwater and his hold over Freddy, and how Kit could not get a chance to talk alone with her. Ted was silent for a long time after she finished.

"Thank you, Corazón," Ted said. "Please don't tell Kit we spoke. Not yet."

"But she want to see you badly."

"Keep me in your prayers." He turned, and like a shadow disappearing into the night, he was gone.

# Chapter 40

"SELDON LIED," Kit said. It was Saturday morning, and mercifully there were two days before court would reconvene. She paced her office while thinking out loud. She found it kept her from thinking about Aunt Freddy. For the time being, at least. She would see her later in the afternoon, even if it meant seeing Stillwater.

"What was his motive?" Kit asked. "Does he have something against our client? Is there a connection between Seldon and Officer Hanratty?"

Corazón looked deep in thought. Kit had come to rely on Corazón more and more. Her mind was sharp, agile. She was already a good investigator. Kit was confident she'd become a great one in time.

"We don't know much about this man Seldon," Kit continued. "I'd like to know more. And I would like to know where he was immediately before and after the shooting."

Corazón nodded, still furrowing her brow. "The man Seldon took many trips," she said. "Maria Espinoza say."

"Where were these trips?"

"Lankershim, she think."

Kit took a reflective breath. "What would he be doing out there?"

"To sell, I think."

"Theatrical goods? To whom? Do you know much about that place?"

"Sí. It is the place of the coaches. With the house."

"Coach house?"

"Sí. And many fields."

"I think we should take a trip out there," Kit said. "And where is Robert, the son? Why has no one seen him? The D.A. is hiding him, I'm almost certain. Waiting for trial."

"I think we are—how do you say?—behind the ball of eight."

Smiling, Kit said, "Your English is getting better all the time. Now, who shall we call as our next witness?"

"Is there a witness?"

"We have more work to do, don't we?"

"Sí."

"Then after I visit Aunt Freddy, let's do it."

———

Benjamin Stillwater held Freddy's hand and spoke in low, comforting tones. "You have nothing to worry about, my dear, nothing. All is well, and so will you be."

Freddy sighed, trying to find solace in his words. She was surprised that it should be somewhat difficult to do so. He had been nothing but a constant and loyal friend, advisor, and spiritual guide. Everything he had done for her had been for her own benefit. She thought she should be free of concern and doubt.

Yet she was not. Not completely. She kept thinking of Kit. There was still that part of her that worried for her niece and the path she had chosen for her life. But Benjamin had assured her that Kit would be looked after and advised. If only she could live to see the benefits of all that.

"You do think it is best, don't you?" Freddy said, surprised at the weakness in her own voice.

"Of course, dear," Stillwater said. "There is no question about it. I have seen it in your hands, in your spirit, and in the future. But this is all silly talk. You have many years left and will see it for yourself."

"No. I fear not, Benjamin."

"Do you not believe I can see this as well?"

That was truly what she should have been thinking, wasn't it? How could she not trust him when her own life was the subject? Oh, but it was all so troublesome. She wished Kit were here. She knew she would come later, but Freddy also knew her niece was troubled by Benjamin's presence. If only Kit could see that it was all for her good.

"You look tired, dear," Stillwater said. "Why don't you rest now?"

"Yes, you're right. I will rest. Thank you."

"No need to thank me, dear Mrs. Fairbank."

She closed her eyes but opened them again at the soft knock. A nurse was standing at the door.

"Excuse me," she said, "but there is a man here to see you."

"A man?" Freddy said. "To see me?"

"No, ma'am," said the nurse. "Mr. Stillwater."

———

Gus leaned against the auto, enjoying the feel of the sun on his face, when the man approached him.

"Are you the one asking for me?" the man said.

"Your name Stillwater?" Gus said.

"That's right."

"The one who can see things?"

"Would you mind telling me what it is you wish to see me about?"

"Gas."

"I beg your pardon?"

"Gas. The future of gasoline-powered machinery. Like this little fella right here." Gus patted the leather bench. "And up there." Gus pointed to the clouds.

Stillwater began to look annoyed. "See here, my good man, if you would like to make an appointment I would be more than happy to—"

"Appointment! I guess there are several people I can ask about investment who are ready to jump."

"What did you say about investment?"

"In the machines I build. What Henry Ford is doing in Detroit. The money is right there, ready to be made. And I'm the one who can make it. I just was told you were one who might be interested."

Stillwater put a finger to his chin. "Did you build this yourself?"

"I sure did. And a sweeter machine you're not gonna find. How about a ride?"

"You mean now?"

"A little ride to show you what I've got. And then maybe you can tell me if you think you'd like in."

Stillwater looked Gus's horseless carriage up and down. Then to Gus, he said, "How did you happen to get my name?"

"A man named Sloate."

"Heath Sloate?"

"Don't know any other Sloates. Are you riding, or do I go my way?"

Stillwater looked at the hospital for a moment. "Let's be quick about it, then."

"Don't rush progress," said Gus. "Hop in."

---

"Aunt Freddy."

Kit whispered the name. She did not want to wake her aunt but felt she needed to. The opportunity to speak with her without Stillwater present was too important to pass up. She didn't know how long she would have.

"Aunt Freddy?"

The old woman's eyes slowly opened. "My dear. How. Pleasant."

She looked so small now. Like a little girl. Kit could not help the tears, but she managed to keep them from streaming.

"It is pleasant just to be with you," Kit said softly. She sat on a wooden stool and held Freddy's hand. It felt like paper.

Freddy turned her head slowly. "Where is Benjamin?"

"I don't know," Kit said.

"He has been constant."

Kit said nothing.

"I do so wish," Freddy said, "you would get along."

Kit nodded, but remained silent.

"Why do you not?"

"Aunt Freddy, I know you have grown fond of this man."

"He does fine work. Won't you work with him?"

The thought was bristling. She did not want to disturb her aunt by contending with her about this man. But then she decided some things are worth disturbance. One thing most of all.

"Aunt Freddy," Kit said, "I do not believe in this man's work. I believe what he practices is not in accord with the truth."

Freddy's eyes, tired looking though they were, reflected a keen interest. "Are you saying he is a charlatan?"

"I will not judge his motives. I will, and must, judge his claims." Kit put her other hand on Aunt Freddy's and held it earnestly. "The truth is in Scripture, Aunt Freddy. That is what I believe."

With her eyes Freddy showed understanding. "I know," she whispered.

This was the opportunity Kit had been hoping for, but it had eluded her with Stillwater's omnipresence. How long before he returned?

"May I read to you?" Kit said.

Ever so slightly, Aunt Freddy nodded her head. Kit took out her Bible from her briefcase and set it on her lap. She opened to the Gospel of John. " 'Let not your heart be troubled: ye believe in God, believe also in me. In my Father's house are many mansions: if it were not so, I would have told you. I go to prepare a place for you. And if I go and prepare a place for you, I will come again, and receive you unto myself; that where I am, there ye may be also.' "

A serene look slowly passed over Freddy's pale features. When she looked at Kit, a slight smile came to her lips. It was the first time in months she had smiled at Kit, and Kit's heart warmed as if by a gentle fire.

Kit looked back at the page. " 'Thomas saith unto him, "Lord, we know not whither thou goest; and how can we know the way?" Jesus saith unto him, "I am the way, the truth, and the life: no man cometh unto the Father, but by me." ' "

They were quiet for a long time after that. Kit watched as Freddy's face showed her pondering the wonderful words of the Savior.

Presently Aunt Freddy said, "Do you think I shall be in heaven?"

Oh, if only she could throw her arms around Aunt Freddy now, and squeeze from her an assent to Christ. "Trust in the Lord with all of your heart, and you will."

Freddy sighed deeply. "Benjamin says there are ways, many ways."

"What does your heart tell you?"

"Oh dear." She began looking lost again.

"Aunt Freddy, do you remember when you used to tell me about Uncle Jasper?"

A wan smile. "My Jasper."

"Yes, and how he hunted for oil in the old days? He kept poking holes in the ground, you said, never giving up, until one day he did it. In Texas, wasn't it? He struck oil."

"Yes, dear. He was so happy."

"The other holes were dry, but he learned each time. Aunt Freddy, you have poked many holes over the years—spiritualism and fortune telling and the like. But all those are dry. Yet they've brought you to Christ. He is the oil you have been looking for."

For a moment Freddy seemed to look out over a vista with a view so beautiful it took away her breath. Then she came down from the mountain. "I can see why."

"Why what, Aunt Freddy?"

"Why you are what they say. A great lawyer."

The words were all the sweeter because Kit knew what they meant. Aunt Freddy was at last giving her blessing on Kit's profession. Holding Freddy's hand against her cheek, Kit said, "Thank you."

"May I come in?"

Kit saw Ted, and the emotions she was feeling intensified at his look. It had been so long.

"Who is it, dear?" Freddy said.

"It is Mr. Fox," Kit said.

"Oh, have the lovely boy come in."

Ted came to Freddy's bedside. "I heard you were feeling poorly," Ted said. "You look good enough to dance a jig."

"Oh, you are a charmer," Freddy said, smiling.

"How is it with you, Kit?" Ted said.

She felt the warmth of his eyes for a moment, then said, "You know me. Murders, mayhem, madness."

"Oh dear," Freddy said.

"I've been reading the papers," Ted said. "You've got it tough."

"A little." She longed for him to take her in his arms right then, tell her he missed her and that they would not be separated again.

Instead, he said, "I'll wager you have work to do."

"Yes."

"Would you mind, then, if I spent some time with your aunt? I'll watch out for her."

"You would do that?"

"Of course," he said, looking at Freddy. "We have some catching up to do."

Kit said, "I have more to say myself."

"Oh, run along," Freddy said, her feistiness beginning to show. It was a good sign. "Come back and visit with me tomorrow."

Kit stood, feeling a pressure inside her, wanting to stay but knowing she had better prepare for Monday. She kissed her aunt on the forehead. "Think about what I said, will you? I'll see you soon."

"Scoot."

Kit turned to Ted. "See me to the door?"

"Don't go anywhere," he said to Freddy.

Just outside the door, Kit said, "A man named Stillwater has been hovering around Aunt Freddy for months. I don't know where he is now, but I do not trust him."

"Would you like me to keep an eye on things here?"

"Can you?"

"Certainly."

"I am mystified as to why he isn't here now."

Ted smiled at her. "The Lord moves in mysterious ways," he said.

Kit could not help putting her hand on his arm. There was so much to ask him, to say to him, if only he would afford the opportunity. If only he would tell her what was in his own heart toward her. But he had chosen not to. For now she would have to accept that.

————

"Look here!" Benjamin Stillwater said. "I must go back!"

Gus put a hand to his ear. With the other he jockeyed the steering column as he negotiated the wooded path through the trees. He knew this stretch of Laurel Canyon well. Many times he had hiked it. It was a pleasant spot for a picnic or rabbit hunt. Treacherous, though, for a carriage without horse.

"I said I must go back!" Stillwater shouted. "You've shown me quite enough!"

"Ain't she a honey?" Gus shouted.

"Sir, I must insist!"

"How's 'at?"

"I insist!"

"Can't you see every person in Los Angeles in one of these doozies?" Gus let out a tremendous laugh, which was both heartfelt and theatrical. He was having great fun at this. He couldn't wait to regale Ted with the tale later on.

"If you do not turn back, now, I shall have you arrested!" Stillwater shouted.

The sputtering bang of the engine filled the canyon with noise. A flock of crows, angrily cawing, burst from a tree in mad escape.

"Do you hear me, man?" Stillwater screamed.

Gus did hear him but chose to attend to the sound of the open road instead. He laughed again.

# Chapter 41

THE CORTEZ COACH HOUSE stood in the crook of a pass through the Santa Monica Mountains. Here horses could be watered or liveried before the coaches moved east into town or north toward the old rancheros of the San Fernando Valley. The coach house was also a resting place for weary travelers who could get a good Mexican meal and a bed, all for the cost of a dollar-fifty.

"Señor Cortez?" Kit said to the roughhewn man at the oak desk. He wore a thin mustache and three-piece suit and was about fifty years old. He had the look of a native Angeleno who had prospered in the transfer from rancho to city. "May I address you in English?" Kit questioned.

"Of course. I speak gringo very well." His accent was not heavy, nor was his frame, and he stood up to offer Kit and Corazón chairs. The adobe inn was a cascade of reds and oranges, the brightest colors on Indian-style blankets that hung on the walls.

"I am a lawyer," she said. She waited for Cortez's widening eyes to normalize themselves. "I am representing a man who may go on trial for his life."

"*Es verdád?* This man, what has he done?"

"He is a police officer. He shot a man in self-defense."

"Why does he have trouble?"

"We have no witnesses we can rely upon. There was a son, but he is missing."

Cortez ran his index finger along his mustache, as if stroking a pet. "Why do you come to me?"

"We believe," Kit said, "that a man named Seldon has traveled through here on his way to do business. We wonder if he might have stayed the night at any time."

"Many people, they come. They go."

Kit took a picture of Seldon she had clipped from the *Examiner* and showed it to Cortez. His response was immediate.

"Sí, I know this man."

"Can you be sure?"

"I think. What name you say?"

"Seldon."

Shaking his head, Cortez said, "No, that is no the name. But he look like him."

"What name did he call himself? Do you have a register?"

"No. I take the money and give the bed. I do not think it was as you say, Seldom."

Kit did not correct him. "Is there anything else you can tell us about him? What he did while he was here, that sort of thing?"

Suddenly Cortez broke out into a huge smile and looked shyly at the ground. And then he laughed, the sort of laugh a man tries to hide. "He was with a woman," Cortez said. "I think they have a honeymoon." He smiled again.

"What did this woman look like?" Kit said.

"Oh, very beautiful," Cortez said. "Her face it was—" He made a circular motion in front of his own face, searching for the words.

"Made up?" Kit said.

"Sí. Her hair, it was long and the color like yours. No, more red."

"Did you find out her name?"

Cortez squinted hard, as if trying to remember. "I am no sure. I think he call her Ra . . ."

"Rachel?"

"Sí, I think."

Kit looked at Corazón, whose face must have mirrored her own. They were getting close, but to what? Did Seldon have a wife? Even if he did, she might have nothing at all to do with this. Was all this just a waste of time, a chasing after the wild quail that lived in the hills?

"Mr. Cortez, is there anything more you can tell us? What sort of luggage did this man have with him? And the woman? Did they have cases, trunks?"

The innkeeper pondered a moment, then froze, looking at something over Kit's shoulder. She turned around.

A man with a gun, shaking slightly in anger or nervousness, faced them. He pointed the gun at Kit.

"Shut up, Cortez," he said.

"Hello, Robert," Kit said.

The man, whose short brown hair was dry and wild, shook his head. "How did you find me?"

Behind the desk, Cortez said, "Please no shoot."

"Do not point the gun," Kit said. "We can talk."

"Don't tell me what to do!" Robert Chausser's voice was strained and desperate. "Everybody's always telling me what to do!" With his free hand he ran fingers through his thatch of hair, as if trying to remove something foul from his head.

"Are you all right?" Kit said, taking a step forward.

"Just don't you move around," Robert said. The gun was unsteady in his hand.

"We must talk."

"I don't wanna talk. To nobody. And nobody talk about me, you hear?"

This was a desperate man who was liable to do a desperate thing. Kit had seen the look before, of men pushed to the brink of civility, with one foot over the line that holds back violence.

"Robert, you're in trouble," Kit said. "Let me help."

"What do you know about it?" he yelled. "Leave us alone!"

"It won't do anybody any good to have you shoot that gun. You don't want a murder charge."

"They told me about you," Robert said.

"Who, Robert?"

"They warned me."

"Is it the *Examiner*? Is that who knows where you are?"

"They said Mr. Hearst promised I wouldn't have to talk. They gave me money."

"Robert," Kit said quietly, "you know what really happened that night your father was shot."

"He killed him! That lying cop!"

"You know it wasn't murder, don't you, Robert? You know, and they've made you afraid to tell."

Robert's eyes veered from humanity into animal rage. Something like a growl issued from his throat as he pointed the gun at Kit's feet and fired.

The sharp report set off every nerve inside her. In front of her feet, wood chips exploded from the floor.

"Robert, listen to me," Kit said softly. She was concerned not only for herself, but also for Corazón and Cortez. There was no telling if Robert was intent on killing, and if he was, if he would stop with her.

Robert, seeming almost surprised the gun had fired, was silent. But he did not lower the revolver.

"You need protection," Kit said. "You have nothing to fear from the truth. You only have to fear those who would use you for their own purposes."

Robert began to shake his head, as if trying to bring his jumbling thoughts into some sort of order.

"Why don't you tell me what happened in your room that night?" Kit said. "I may be able to help you."

Sneering, Robert said, "How can you help? How can you know?"

Kit saw something move just outside the coach house door. A shadow. Behind Robert.

Kit said, "You will have to come forward sometime. The truth has a way of following you around until you look at it, face to face."

Robert rubbed his head with his free hand. "Stop talking! I have to think."

The movement behind Robert was a man, obviously a worker from the coach yard. He was short but had a massive chest and arms. He was only a few feet from Robert's back.

Kit kept her gaze on Robert's face. She put her hands up to try and steady his nerves.

The man took another step. The floor creaked.

As soon as Robert spun around, the man jumped at him. Both went down with a crash. The gun fired again. Kit grabbed Corazón by the arm and rushed her behind the counter.

The two men continued to struggle. Robert screamed and cursed. The other man issued a stream of words in Spanish.

Another shot, and the sound of a window exploding into fragments of shattered glass.

A third shot rang out, followed by a wail of pain. Then heavy footsteps.

Kit waited a moment before raising her head. By the door the worker lay writhing, holding his leg.

Kit ran to the man, followed by Cortez and Corazón. Cortez knelt by him and began to comfort him.

Then Kit heard the sound of hoofbeats. She raced outside in time to see Robert riding like wildfire on horseback, toward the hills.

---

The sun was almost gone now, the trees beginning to take the form of ghosts. Silence surrounded them as Gus tinkered with the engine.

"Well?" Stillwater demanded. He had not stopped pacing since the auto had quit half an hour ago.

"Can't seem to figure it," Gus said. "It was fine this morning."

"It's getting dark! How are we to get back?"

"You can walk if you like," Gus said.

"Walk! How far is it?"

"Twenty miles maybe, as the crow flies. 'Course, we ain't crows."

Stillwater's face contorted in several directions at once. "Surely there is a road nearby. We can stop someone."

"Where was that road?" Gus said, putting a finger to his chin. "I'd hate to get lost looking for it."

A distant howl arose, echoing eerily through the canyon. "What was that?" Stillwater said.

"Coyote, most likely," Gus said. "These hills are filled with 'em."

"What are we to do?"

"Well, sir," Gus said with a nod, "you can thank your lucky stars you're with Gus Willingham. I'm gonna build us a fire and show you how to make a lean-to."

"What is that?"

"Why, it's our home for the night."

Stillwater's pitiful squeal was matched by another distant howl.

————————

"Is that all?" Freddy asked.

"That is all," Ted replied. "Mr. Morgan made it as plain as day to me. When I made the decision, it was like falling into strong, loving arms waiting for me."

The old woman closed her eyes for a long time. Her breathing grew slow. Ted said nothing, only prayed silently for her.

When she opened her eyes there was pain there. "Kit," she said. "I want Kit."

"Yes," Ted said. "I will get her."

"Wait." She grabbed his sleeve weakly. "I must tell you first. I have done something terrible."

Her grip, feeble though it was, increased.

"What could you have done that is so bad?" Ted said.

"Will you hear me?"

"Of course."

"Can you help me?"

"I will do everything I can to help you, Mrs. Fairbank."

A small tear formed in her eye and slowly descended her cheek. "Thank you, dear boy. Thank you." She took a deep breath. "Listen, please."

# Chapter 42

*Los Angeles Examiner*
July 11, 1904

### HANRATTY HEARING TO END SOON
#### Defense Tactics Futile
#### Will Not Avoid a Jury
#### by Tom Phelps

*The preliminary hearing of Edward Hanratty on the charge of murder will likely end in a matter of days. Thus far, defense attorney Kathleen Shannon has not been able to make the least dent in the ironclad case made by District Attorney John Davenport.*

*An increasingly desperate defense has sought to portray the tragic events of June 7 as a case of self-defense. No witness, however, has been produced to support such a theory, and it seems inevitable that Hanratty will have to stand before a jury of his peers for murder. . . .*

Judge Cartwright looked more impatient than ever. The two-day respite had apparently done nothing for his disposition. "Miss Shannon," he demanded. "How many more witnesses do you intend to call?"

Kit stood. "Two or three, Your Honor."

"How about two?"

"Or four, depending upon the testimony."

Throwing up his hands, Cartwright said, "Call your witness."

"The defense recalls Julius Seldon."

He looked dismayed as he came forward. "You are still under oath," Cartwright said. "Take the stand."

Kit approached him. "Mr. Seldon, isn't it true that you and Jay Chausser were more than mere acquaintances?"

"I don't know what you mean."

"Didn't you also propose a business arrangement for the sale of theatrical costumes and devices?"

"No."

"Isn't it true, sir, that along with a woman named Rachel Travers, you conspired to defraud Mr. Chausser?"

"Objection," Davenport said. "Incompetent, irrelevant, and immaterial."

"Do you have any basis for these questions?" Judge Cartwright said. "I assure you I am no jury to be swayed. You stay with the facts or move along."

Kit nodded. "Your Honor, I would like to ask Mr. Seldon a few more questions about this woman and her involvement. I believe she is an actress, Your Honor, and a companion of Mr. Seldon."

"You may ask," Cartwright said, "but I will not allow you to go beyond the witness's words."

This was a virtual invitation for Seldon to deny everything, but Kit wanted it all on the record.

"You are under oath, Mr. Seldon," Kit said. "You have denied knowing a woman named Rachel Travers. I ask you now if you are sticking to that story."

Seldon's face reddened as he shifted in the witness chair. "You leave her out of this," he said with a snarl.

Kit did not expect that. She thought he would continue to deny knowing this woman. Now his admission was before the judge. Kit saw Cartwright looking troubled at this.

"Mr. Seldon, what is the nature of your relationship with Rachel Travers?"

His face became a deeper shade. He wagged his finger at her. "You have no right," he said. "This is my personal business."

"Your personal business was entwined with Mr. Chausser's, was it not?"

"No," said Seldon firmly.

"Where is Miss Travers now?"

"Irrelevant," said Davenport. "Unless Miss Shannon is prepared to show a connection with tangible evidence, the whereabouts of someone who may not even be a witness has no bearing on this proceeding."

"That is what this proceeding is trying to determine," Kit said.

"No, Miss Shannon," Judge Cartwright said. "We are only concerned with relevant facts. This is merely a proceeding to find probable cause to proceed to trial on a charge of murder."

"And I am seeking to show reasonable doubt in that charge," Kit said.

"Reasonable doubt is for a jury to decide."

He was right. All of her efforts so far had perhaps put a dent in an eventual trial. But she was not near to proving self-defense.

"Then allow me to ask the witness this question one more time, Your Honor." To Seldon she said, "What is the nature of your relationship with Rachel Travers, Mr. Seldon?"

A hush fell on the courtroom. Kit watched Seldon's face closely. It twitched for a moment before he answered. "How dare you."

"I demand an answer," Kit said.

"She is my sister."

The hush was broken with voices. The entire courtroom buzzed.

Seldon continued, looking at the judge. "She has fallen on hard times, and I have tried to help her. I did not want to bring her into this matter, but now that she has been forced here, must I continue with this? I assure the court she has nothing whatsoever to do with any of this."

Kit was in a momentary state of shock, not so much at the answer—Seldon had lied before—but at the sheer confidence of Seldon in addressing the judge directly. Less surprising was the judge's response, all in accordance with what had been going on since the hearing began.

"Miss Shannon, I have heard quite enough from this witness. I am going to allow him to step down. You are finished."

With a self-righteous nod, Seldon left the witness stand, issuing a highly audible *harrumph* as he walked by Kit. Her anger flared, not so much at Seldon but at Cartwright. And there was nothing she could do about his heavy hand. A writ to the Court of Appeals would only put off the inevitable, a finding that in this courtroom Cartwright was virtually untouchable.

"I am giving you a final warning," Judge Cartwright said. "If you do not present relevant evidence immediately, I will declare this hearing completed. Is that understood, Miss Shannon?"

"Very well, Your Honor," Kit said. "Then I have but two witnesses left to present."

"I will hold you to that," Cartwright said.

Kit had no doubt of that. "I call Dr. Bernard Hirsch to the stand."

The bald, bespectacled Hirsch came forward. He was stout as a beer barrel, his ill-fitting brown suit straining at the buttons. Before he was sworn in Davenport said, "I ask the court to require an offer of proof from Miss Shannon. Of what possible relevance is this witness at this time?"

Judge Cartwright nodded. "Yes, Miss Shannon. Before we waste any more time, tell us the purpose of this witness."

"Your Honor, I intend to prove that the prosecution's rendition of events could not possibly have happened."

As if a curtain were rising on the third act of a play, the audience in the courtroom seemed to lean forward as one. Kit could sense it even as she faced the judge. Her mind suddenly flashed to the actor John Barrymore, Earl Rogers' friend who had been such a help in the trial of Ted Fox. He would have loved this moment.

But she also felt that she had taken a step from the stage out over the orchestra pit. Would she fall or regain her balance in time?

"Your Honor," Davenport said, "this is a preposterous attempt by Miss Shannon to muddy what is exceedingly clear water. We would request this matter be brought to an abrupt conclusion."

Kit's heart beat a path up to her throat. If the court were to halt the proceedings now, everything would come to a crashing end. "I will ask only a few questions," Kit said quickly, "and if Mr. Davenport is so confident about the clarity of the water, he may cross-examine."

The challenge to Davenport's pride had the desired effect. "I assure Miss Shannon that I will cross-examine."

"Get to the point quickly, Miss Shannon," Judge Cartwright warned.

Hirsch, seeming impatient about the brouhaha, was sworn and seated.

"Dr. Hirsch," Kit began, "would you tell the court your occupation, please?"

"I am teaching at the University of Southern California." His heavy German accent rendered teaching as *teachink*, and Southern sounded like *Zudern*. But his pronunciation was crisp enough to make him entirely understandable.

"What is your field?"

"I am teaching science"—*zience*—"and chemistry."

"And sir, are you informed about the science of ballistics?"

"Yah, I teach that, too."

"Have you read Dr. Schultz's treatise on the subject?"

Hirsch cleared his throat in a slightly indignant manner. "I helped him to write it!"

Kit smiled as several in the courtroom laughed. Davenport was not among them. Kit once more produced the German treatise and opened to a page. "I believe Dr. Hirsch's name is, yes, here it is. Would the court care to see it?"

"No, Miss Shannon," Cartwright snapped. "I trust we will see some relevance?"

"Indeed," Kit said. She plopped the treatise on her desk with a heavy thud and went to the clerk's table. She picked up the small box that contained the bullets, marked as a prosecution exhibit. She set the box on the witness box rail.

"Dr. Hirsch, I place before you two bullets, which the coroner testified came from the body of Jay Chausser. I would like you to examine these and tell the court if you find any differences in them."

Hirsch gave a quick nod and fished an eyepiece from his inside coat pocket. He removed his spectacles and placed the eyepiece, as a jeweler would, in his right eye. Then he leaned over so his head was just above the rail and began to examine the bullets.

Kit saw Davenport watching warily. But apparently the smell of victory was so thick in his nostrils he saw no reason to object.

Presently, Hirsch sat back, removed the eyepiece and said, "Not the same."

Kit paused, cast a glance at Davenport, then asked, "How can you tell, sir?"

"One bullet is made of lead, with a small bit of copper impacted into the nose. The other bullet has not the copper, but tin."

Having made her point, Kit handed the witness to Davenport. She observed the row of reporters, all vigorously taking notes. They did not yet know the full significance of the testimony. For that, Kit was going to wait for just the right time.

"Sir," Davenport said, "you have made a cursory examination of the prosecution evidence."

"It is enough," Dr. Hirsch said, puffing his chest out.

"Yet you performed no chemical test, did you?"

The witness pursed his lips. "No."

"And a careful ballistics examination for the properties of a bullet would include that, would it not?"

"I am always careful."

"Please answer the question."

"I . . . yes. But this is my preliminary finding."

"And this is a preliminary hearing, sir. When this case comes to trial I trust you will be more reliable."

Hirsch seethed under Davenport's glare. "One more thing," Davenport said. "You have not examined under a scope the marks on either bullet, have you?"

"I have not had that chance."

"And so you don't know if these bullets came from the same gun or not, do you?"

"No."

"In fact, isn't it possible for a gun to hold bullets of different kinds?"

"It is possible."

Davenport nodded, placed his thumbs in his waistcoat pockets and said, "I have no further questions, Your Honor."

Kit said, "I would like to ask questions on re-direct, Your Honor."

"To what purpose?" Cartwright said.

"To establish one other fact. I beg the court's indulgence." She needed it, but the judge's patience was wearing thin. Kit prayed silently for the judge to allow her to continue, for now the entire defense came down to these moments.

Yet Cartwright hesitated, his chaw rippling his cheek. Kit waited, watching him. And then she saw him look out toward the gallery. Instinctively Kit turned to follow his gaze. It seemed to be directed at the reporters. All of them looked back at the judge, as did every eye in the courtroom.

Then Kit thought she saw the slightest nod from Tom Phelps to the judge.

Before she could consider the significance of this, she heard Cartwright say, "A few questions only."

Kit brought herself back to the moment and moved quickly. She went back to the counsel table, where Corazón sat next to Hanratty. She put out her hand. Corazón opened a linen handkerchief, retrieved the bullet that was wrapped in it, and put it into Kit's hand.

"I now show the witness a bullet that we will mark as a defense exhibit," Kit said. "Dr. Hirsch, can you tell if this bullet is similar to either of the two bullets you examined previously?"

Once more Hirsch took out his eyepiece, but not before casting a disdainful glance at Davenport.

He examined the bullets for a full two minutes. Then he raised his head. "Yes," he said. "The bullet you have shown to me is mixed with tin, not copper."

"Is there any other similarity?"

"Yes," Hirsch said. "I do not need the chemistry to see this! There is a mark that runs along one side. The other tin bullet has an identical mark."

"Then is it your conclusion that these tin-mixed bullets were fired from the same gun?"

"Yes!" Hirsch practically shouted.

"Cross-examine," Kit said to Davenport.

Davenport approached the witness with his own chest thrust forward. "I have only one question for you, Dr. Hirsch. Are you being paid to be here today?"

After a pause, during which time Hirsch puffed several annoyed breaths, he said, "Yes."

Kit stood. "Your Honor, the court knows that witnesses with expertise are compensated for time they must take from their work. This is not relevant to the testimony."

"We will let the court decide what is relevant," Davenport said. "I have no further questions."

"The court will take a short recess," Cartwright said. "And when I return I will require the defense to finish its case."

Kit had one witness left to call, and that would be the one to decide the matter once and for all. She had carefully laid the foundation, as Rogers had instructed her, and now the structure would have to go up. She could not afford a single wrong move.

Ed Hanratty seemed to sense her disquiet. Just before the deputy sheriff took him away, he put his hand on Kit's arm. "Miss Shannon," he said, his eyes holding a slight mist, "I just want you to know, whatever happens, you have done right by me. You've brought me back to my senses, too. If I ever get to hold my Carrie and my girls again, I'll have you to thank."

If only she could give him assurance. But what she was about to do had only the slimmest chance of succeeding. A jury trial was a near certainty. The events of the night of June 7 might never be fully known. And that is why she made the decision then and there that if Hanratty were bound over for trial she would go with him. She would put the prosecution to its burden of proof.

That was the system of justice that protected the dignity of all men, a dignity conferred by God. She would be God's servant.

"Thank you," she said. Then Hanratty was taken out of the courtroom.

Kit felt Corazón's touch. "Jerrold is here," Corazón said.

Kit looked to the back of the courtroom, where Freddy's butler stood, his cap in his hand. She motioned for him to come to the rail.

"What is it, Jerrold?" she asked.

"I have a message from the hospital," he said. "Madame is asking for you."

Kit felt a sudden chill. "Is she. . . ?"

Jerrold's eyes filled with tears.

# Chapter 43

KIT FOUND, TO HER CHAGRIN, that Stillwater was outside the door to Freddy's room. "I have never been so rudely treated," he said.

"Excuse me," Kit said and tried to move around him. He blocked her.

"Your aunt is not thinking straight. She has been manipulated and confused, and I hold you responsible."

"You will please move from that door."

"I assure you I will not let this go."

For once, Kit wished she were a man. It would be unseemly for a woman to take matters physically into her hands. But, oh, for one good punch.

Corazón, standing behind Kit, suddenly issued a string of sentences in the fastest possible Spanish tongue. Whatever she said, and Kit could only understand a few of the words, it was incendiary.

Stillwater may not have understood any of it, either, but he got the message. With a huff he stepped away from the door, and Kit entered.

A nurse sat at the bedside. Ted was in a chair by the window. His look communicated relief that Kit was here at last. She also saw a protective streak in him. No doubt Ted's presence was why Stillwater was not in the room.

Aunt Freddy lay with eyes closed, her breathing quick, short, labored. Kit felt a sense of impending loss. It hit her hard, though she knew she shouldn't have been surprised. Now that the time was close, though, she could not prevent the knots from forming inside her.

As if sensing Kit's presence, Aunt Freddy's eyes opened slowly. They widened when they focused on Kit. A little smile appeared, too. Weak, but with a powerful peace behind it. Aunt Freddy's face was different somehow. Like a huge weight had been lifted.

"My dear," Freddy said in a barely audible whisper.

"I'm here," Kit said.

The little smile widened slightly, and then Aunt Freddy raised her arm, her elbow resting on the bed. She beckoned Kit toward her, looking as if she wanted to speak. Kit leaned over and put her ear by Freddy's mouth.

"I found the oil," Freddy said.

Like the sun breaking through storm clouds, Kit's spirit burst forth in an inexpressible joy. She took Freddy's hand and kissed it, then wet it with her tears. As she did, she saw Ted's own look of elation, and she knew then that he had been the final water on the seed. God had used him for this moment and had brought forth a final harvest in Aunt Freddy's soul.

*Thank you, Father.* Kit said it over and over again in her mind. *Thank you.*

And then she thought of court. She had rushed out so quickly, leaving Jerrold to communicate to the judge. But how long would the judge extend the recess? She had no idea, but she was not going to return. Not yet.

———

"Where the devil is she then?" Judge Cartwright boomed. He was in his chambers where Davenport and Heath Sloate had joined him.

"I was only told she was on an emergency call," Davenport said.

"Who told you that?"

"A butler, I think. He mentioned it concerned Miss Shannon's great-aunt."

"Miss Shannon herself did not see fit to inform the court of this emergency," Cartwright said. "I have a good mind to hold her in contempt."

Sloate put up a calming hand. "If I may offer a suggestion?"

Cartwright looked at him.

"A contempt citation," Sloate said, "might be construed by the press as a sign of the court's animosity toward Miss Shannon. With all due respect to Your Honor, that has been rather evident thus far."

"What are you suggesting, Mr. Sloate?" Cartwright said.

"A simple expression of regret that the court's schedule must be adhered to. Declare the proceedings at an end and take the matter under advisement. That will give the impression you are considering the matter."

"Am I not?" Cartwright said.

Sloate laughed. "I am certain Your Honor will see that justice is served," he added.

It took only a few minutes for Cartwright to break off a fresh chaw of tobacco and take to the bench.

"Ladies and gentlemen," he said, "in view of the absence of

Miss Shannon at this time, after almost an hour's delay, the court must proceed. This preliminary hearing has already lasted far longer than is normal, and an abundance of evidence has been presented. I must therefore declare this hearing—"

"Objection!"

The voice cracked through the air like a gun blast. Cartwright sat back, almost swallowing his tobacco. His anger flared. "Who was that?"

In the back row Earl Rogers stood, then made his way forward.

"I object, Your Honor," Rogers said, striding through the rail.

"What is the meaning of this?" Cartwright said.

"I am objecting to the court's ruling," Rogers said. "The law gives the defense the right to present witnesses at the preliminary hearing. Absent good cause, of course."

John Davenport stood up. "Your Honor, I am sure we are all honored by the presence of Mr. Rogers, but I would remind my worthy adversary that he has no standing here. He is not the attorney of record."

Rogers took out his lorgnette, put the glasses to his eyes, and looked over Davenport as if he were an attired mannequin in the window of the Broadway Department Store. "I am Miss Shannon's associate, as she will attest. I have been involved in this matter from the beginning."

"How so?" Davenport demanded.

"That is privileged. Suffice to say she has consulted me on several occasions. As my colleague knows, there is no requirement of formal agreement. All that is required is a declaration, which can be made orally. Now, shall we proceed to the merits of the objection?"

Cartwright felt helpless. "I have good cause, Mr. Rogers. Your associate, if that's what she is, did not return in time to begin."

"Ah," Rogers said. "A delay. But I am sure the court is aware of the holding of our state supreme court, in the Sumner Case of 1882, wherein it was stated that the rights of an accused cannot be abrogated by a *de minimis* time delay. That is what I suggest has occurred here. One hour is not enough time when the rights of Mr. Hanratty are on the line. Besides . . ."

Here Rogers paused until Cartwright was compelled to ask, "Besides what?"

Rogers smiled, his blue eyes sparkling, "We wouldn't want to deprive ourselves of seeing what the second best lawyer in Los Angeles has to offer, do we?"

The reporters roared with laughter. Rogers, ever the showman, had made the point. Cartwright also acknowledged Rogers knew the law.

"You find Miss Shannon," Cartwright said. "And have her back here at one o'clock. Otherwise, Mr. Rogers, you will have to finish the case yourself."

Rogers bowed. And smiled.

———

Elinor Wynn sipped her late morning tea on the veranda. She thought, in the pleasant shade of the large magnolia tree—the one she had loved as a little girl—that the old feelings were gone for good. No longer would there be the pleasure of innocence. The world had its consolations, and she would soon have plenty of that.

This was the Wynn way, though, wasn't it? She found herself thinking of her late father, who had told her this was a man's world, and then her mother instructing her she must learn to use all her feminine wiles and use men to her advantage. They were so predictable, her mother had said.

Young Elinor believed her mother, but such wisdom brought a moment of loss for her, too. She had always loved the stories of knights and princesses, of great deeds done for fair maidens out of love alone. She had imagined she was a princess and her knight in shining armor would someday come.

Now he would never come. She herself had slain him.

Ted was a prize catch, her mother had said. Elinor had found herself falling in love. Yet when her mother had discovered the truth about Ted's past, love no longer seemed sufficient. Instead, her discovery was a secret to be saved until such time as it was needed. That is when the love died, and Ted became more an arrangement than a fiancé.

The harshness that followed was not so great a shift. When Ted rejected her it was the tearing of a carefully woven fabric, one she had labored on for years. For that he had to be punished. It was strange to her how easily she sought to mete out that punishment upon Ted. Only a small part of her formed any pang of regret.

Yet the regret was persistent, for what might have been with Ted was like the last image of a dream that, upon waking, is never to be dreamed again.

And then there was Sloate, who had managed to coil like a snake around all of their lives. Her wiles were no match for him. No one was a match for him, as they were all finding out. But the Wynn creed had always been unambiguous—learn to side with the winners.

Elinor sipped her tea, which was getting cold. She would order a new pot. There was no business to attend to today, only to wait. Thus it was with relative indifference that she sat and gazed at the carriages passing on the street with the clopping of horses' hooves, and at the occasional gas buggies with their bang and sputter.

One of these offered a particularly irritating blast, right in front of her gate. It left in its wake a thick puff of black exhaust, which hovered in place for an instant, like a magician's ruse. She watched it, fascinated, as if a child in the front row of the Orpheum, ready to see a turbaned magi suddenly appear.

Someone did appear. He strode from across the street, even as the smoke dissipated, and his features became clear through the haze.

Sloate.

He threw open the gate with unceremonial harshness. He was angry, and Elinor knew it, for she had come to know Sloate's every mannerism. To know what men thought by how they moved, that was a Wynn knack.

Without a word of greeting, Sloate came up the steps. "Your young man has been sticking his nose where it oughtn't be."

Elinor felt her skin prickle, as if it wanted to retreat from Sloate. "Why do you insist on calling him my young man?" she said.

Sloate ignored her, turning his back to her as he looked out at the street. "He knows something. I shall have to deal with him harshly."

As if from a forgotten stream, a coldness arose in Elinor, a shock to her system. "What are you talking about?"

With a sudden calm—*The famous Sloate control*, she thought—he turned back to her and smiled. It made her skin crawl even more.

"Nothing to worry your pretty head about," he said. "Only be prepared. If Fox comes calling, you must stick to your guns. I can count on you, as always, I am sure."

"Of course," she said, in a voice that came from a dark cave.

"You sound less than sure, my dear."

Elinor met his gaze directly. "I am sure. And may I ask you the same? May I count on you, as always?"

"Whatever would give you reason to doubt me?"

"Because I know you well."

His smile disappeared. "Then we understand each other."

"I think we do," Elinor said.

"Europe, I think, would be a refreshing change."

"Europe? When are you going?"

"You seem rather anxious that I do."

"Nothing of the sort."

"You're getting to be less skilled in the art of the lie, my dear," Sloate said. "I sense a certain anxiousness about the eyes. To lie, you must deliver it coldly, without sign of hesitation."

He was playing with her now. How she hated him when he did that.

"I wouldn't think of a sojourn on the continent," Sloate said, "without your lovely company."

"I?"

"But of course, my dear. That is to be the arrangement."

His pronouncement left no room for disagreement. He was ordering her. And then, by instinct formed over generations of Wynn femininity, she put on her first smile of the morning. "Why, Heath, you are so silly sometimes. But that is part of your charm."

His reaction was swift. "Do not patronize me. I can withstand your vacuity, for I am somehow drawn to the package it comes wrapped in. But do not ever allow yourself to look down upon me. Ever."

Elinor found no response.

"Listen to me very carefully," Sloate said. "You have been bought. The price is the sum of money that we have discussed, and the sort of life only I can offer you. You are a pariah in this city as you are no doubt aware, and you are not getting any younger. Your prospects with the eligible bachelors of our fair township are as dry as the Mojave Desert."

All true, Elinor knew. Sadly, achingly true. But she still had the Wynn charm and resilience, didn't she? There was always San Francisco. Mother had talked of moving there. . . .

"But in Europe," Sloate said, "I daresay you might find yourself a handsome prince to bewitch with your charms."

*Handsome prince . . .*

"In France, they say, the rich young rulers are desperate for fair-skinned American women," Sloate added. "And they are so much more civilized about the arrangement we'll be keeping."

Her head snapped back, as if slapped. "What arrangement?"

Sloate shook his head. "Feigned ignorance does not become you, my dear. But lest you deceive yourself, I shall make it plain once and for all. You are to be my mistress."

Her entire body became cold.

"Don't look so shocked," Sloate said. "I told you that you were bought, for a price. That conveys ownership. I am your owner. And do not ever forget that. Those who ignore me, like young Fox and Miss Shannon, reap the whirlwind."

Sloate removed his watch, snapped it open. "Ah, time for me to get back to court. It shall all be over quite soon."

Over. The word was ominous. It was her life that was over.

Sloate bowed quickly and descended the steps as quickly as he had come. He walked down the path and through the open gate, not bothering to close it behind him.

# Chapter 44

THE GALLERY IN Cartwright's courtroom was packed to overflowing. Two rows of spectators stood against the back wall, resulting in several people being squeezed into each corner.

Even though she had expected a crowd, Kit was surprised. Word had gotten around quickly that the best show in town, now that the Fourth of July was over, was about to conclude.

Ed Hanratty seemed, at long last, relieved. "I know you've done your best," he told Kit after being marched out. "I'll take my chances at trial, if you'll defend me."

"There isn't going to be any trial," Kit said.

Hanratty's look asked the question. Before Kit could answer Earl Rogers approached. "Mind if I take second chair?" he asked Kit.

"You want to sit up here, with me?"

"Of course," he said, smiling. "I want a front row seat."

Before Kit could say another word, Rogers went to the last

chair at the counsel table, by Corazón. The large sack she had brought with her to court sat under the table.

Then the clerk entered and announced the judge.

Everyone rose in the courtroom until Cartwright instructed them to sit down. "I understand, Miss Shannon, that you are going to call one more witness?"

"Yes, Your Honor," Kit said. "If the court please, I will finish my presentation this afternoon."

"Nothing would please the court more," Cartwright said. "Call your witness."

"I call Edna Chausser."

In a flash Davenport was on his feet. "Your Honor, we protest. Mrs. Chausser has been through quite enough. Miss Shannon already has questioned this witness."

"In light of new evidence," Kit said, "I would like to recall Mrs. Chausser."

"What evidence?" Davenport demanded.

Kit turned to him with such force she almost knocked her chair over. "I find that question out of order and out of character, Mr. Davenport. Your office chose to keep all the evidence it could from me, waiting for this hearing. Now that I propose to present evidence of my own, you express indignation. Which is the official position of the district attorney?"

After a quick look at the press corps, Davenport said, "The official position of the district attorney is the truth."

A politician's answer, but one Kit was going to hold him to as long as he was in the office. "Very well," Kit said. Then she turned to the judge. "Your Honor, in the shared interest of finding the truth, I ask Mrs. Chausser to take the stand."

"Mrs. Chausser," Cartwright said to the gallery.

Edna Chausser rose with hesitation and moved slowly toward

the witness stand. Her face was pale and her braided hair even more girlish than before.

"You are still under oath, Mrs. Chausser," Cartwright said. "Do you understand?"

She nodded slowly.

"Would you like a glass of water?"

"No, thank you."

"All right. If you need a break from the questioning, please tell me, won't you?" Cartwright's eyebrows were knit with concern.

"Thank you," Edna Chausser said.

"Go ahead, Miss Shannon."

Kit nodded. "I know this has all been very hard for you, Mrs. Chausser."

The witness nodded. Her hands were folded tightly in her lap.

"It must be hard on your son, as well."

Edna Chausser did not answer. She looked at Kit with wondering eyes.

"Have you seen Robert of late?" Kit asked.

"I . . ." She stopped, looked at the judge. "Do I have to answer?"

"I am afraid so," Cartwright said.

"Yes," Mrs. Chausser said to Kit.

"Where?"

A pause. "I do not wish to say."

"You love your son, don't you?"

"Of course I do."

"You would have no hesitation in protecting him if you thought he were in danger, would you?"

"I am a mother, Miss Shannon. I look out for my son."

"Does your son own a gun?"

"Why, no. Robert is gentle and kind."

Kit paced in front of the witness. "Mrs. Chausser, you

previously denied that Robert and your late husband were engaged in a heated argument before the shooting, did you not?"

"There wasn't any argument, like I said."

"This would not be an instance of protecting your son, would it?"

Edna Chausser sat back in the witness chair, stiffening. "You are insinuating that I lied."

"It would not be the first time, would it, Mrs. Chausser?"

Edna's eyes widened for a moment, seemed to be searching Kit's face for a clue. At that moment, Kit knew her hunch was right. Everything fell into place now, and it was only a matter of getting it out before it was too late.

"Or do you prefer the name Rachel Travers?"

A shock wave seemed to hit the courtroom, starting from Edna Chausser and rolling outward toward all who were gathered. For a moment no one moved, as if everyone there were waiting for a temblor to pass, wondering if they should react.

Davenport reacted first. "Objection on the grounds of relevance, Your Honor."

Cartwright looked uncertain. "Yes, what relevance is this line, Miss Shannon?"

"Motive, Your Honor."

"Motive for what?"

"Murder."

The wave rippled again, this time accompanied by voices and the frenetic scratching of reporters' pencils on paper.

"May I continue?" Kit said to the judge, whose mouth was frozen in mid-chew.

After a moment's recovery, Cartwright said. "Get to the point quickly."

Kit nodded, then looked at the witness. "Do you deny using the name Rachel Travers? Remember, you are under oath."

Edna Chausser's chin trembled as words seemed to stick in her throat. "I . . ."

Kit reached into the pocket of her suit. "Your Honor, I have here a letter from the Indianapolis police department addressed to my associate, Corazón Chavez. It is a report of the arrest of Edna and Jay Chausser on the charge of grifting."

She placed the letter in front of Cartwright. He read it slowly, his cheek twitching. "That is what it says."

Now Kit looked directly at Edna. "And the police also note the use of several aliases by the Chaussers. I submit that Edna Chausser used still another alias, one unknown to her own husband. The name Rachel Travers. May I continue my examination, Your Honor?"

Cartwright quietly said, "You may."

"You are not, in fact, the sister of Julius Seldon, are you?" Kit asked.

"What of it?" Edna answered.

"You are in fact his lover, are you not?"

"I . . ."

"And you used the name Rachel Travers when you met him at the Cortez Coach House, isn't that so?"

Edna said nothing. Her chin trembled.

Kit said, "It would be a simple matter for us to summon Mr. Cortez for an identification. I repeat the questions. Did you use the name Rachel Travers when you met Seldon at the Cortez Coach House?"

The voice that answered came from the gallery. "Do not answer!"

It was Julius Seldon, standing in the middle of the crowd.

Cartwright slammed the gavel. "You will not interrupt, sir. Or you will be removed."

A deputy sheriff at the courtroom door moved toward Seldon.

He looked at the lawman, hesitated, then slowly dropped back in his chair.

Kit looked at Edna Chausser. "Are you and Julius Seldon lovers?"

"A woman can't help falling in love. Is that a crime?"

"When it leads to murder," Kit said.

"The only murder was of my husband. By that man." Edna pointed at Ed Hanratty. "I was there. I saw it."

"But you previously testified you were in the kitchen, making tea."

Edna swallowed but did not answer.

Kit let the silence linger as she walked to the clerk's table and took up the defense's bullet exhibit.

"Mrs. Chausser," Kit said, "we have had testimony that this bullet is similar to one of the bullets found in your husband, and further that it was fired from the same gun. I am prepared to testify that this bullet came from a gun fired by Robert Chausser."

Edna shook her head violently. "No!"

"Yes, Mrs. Chausser. The same gun you used to kill your husband."

In the gallery, reporters seemed to be falling all over each other as they scribbled. One even shouted, "What did she say? What did she say?"

Cartwright called for order once more. "Miss Shannon, that is a shocking allegation."

John Davenport looked too stunned—either from surprise or indignation—to say anything.

"With the court's permission," Kit said, "and with the witness still under oath, allow me to show the court what happened."

"Show the court?"

"If Your Honor please."

Cartwright threw up his hands. "We have come this far."

Corazón was up on cue, opening up the large sack from under the table. On top of the table she placed the items—a pillow, a revolver, and a copy of the *Los Angeles Examiner*.

Kit took the newspaper first. "Your Honor, this is the edition of the *Examiner* that ran a front-page photograph of the crime scene." She placed it on the bench in front of the judge.

"As you can see," she continued, "in the center of the room there is a bed made up for sleeping. Mrs. Chausser testified she was getting ready for bed. But as you can see, Your Honor, there is something missing from the bed."

Cartwright now appeared interested. "What would that be?"

"A pillow," Kit said. "There is only one pillow on the bed. There is also only one pillow listed in the inventory of Detective McGinty."

Shaking his head, the judge said, "And so?"

"Allow me," Kit said. She went to the counsel table and lifted the revolver. "This gun has been loaded with a blank cartridge, Your Honor. Mr. Seldon testified that Mrs. Chausser fainted when he entered the room, hitting the floor hard."

"Yes, I recall," said the judge.

"That would have produced a loud thumping noise. Such a sound was heard by a witness who did not testify in court. His statement to me is not admissible, of course, but it is consistent with Seldon's testimony."

"Then what relevance does it have to your case?" asked the judge.

"The sound was not a body at all," Kit said. "Edna did not faint, and Jay Chausser's body was already on the floor. He had been shot in the shoulder by Officer Hanratty. But that is not what killed him."

Kit took the pillow from the table. "The sound that was heard was this." Wrapping the pillow around the gun, Kit pulled the trigger. A muffled bang rang out.

"That was the sound, Your Honor. The sound of Edna Chausser shooting her husband through the heart."

Edna Chausser grabbed the rail of the witness box.

"And then you destroyed the pillow, now with a hole and powder burns, by burning it in your stove," Kit said. "You hid the gun—possibly in the pocket of your dress—and later gave it to Robert."

The witness shook her head.

"You testified you were making tea in the kitchen. Detective McGinty's inventory lists no dishes out in the kitchen. The stove, however, was hot. So hot that the detective had to remove his coat when entering the other room. It was hot because the pillow was in there."

"That is a lie!"

"Mrs. Chausser, shall we send a scientist to analyze the ashes in your stove? They can tell feathers from wood, you know."

Silence. Edna Chausser began to take on the look of a cornered animal. Her head started to shake. She looked from side to side, as if seeking a hole in the wall to run to.

The silence was thick around them as Kit kept her eyes on Edna, refusing to give her the relief of another question. For a long moment there was no sound at all in the courtroom.

And then, with tears beginning to stream down her face, Edna Chausser said, "He made me do it." She pointed to the middle of the gallery.

"Liar!" Seldon shouted. This time, when he stood up, he pulled a gun from his pocket and waved it wildly.

Women screamed. The scuttle of chairs scraped the floor as both men and women moved wildly, some diving to the floor, others massing this way and that.

The deputy at the door was pinned by the crowd and could not get to Seldon, who moved quickly toward the wall.

A smallish older man, looking frightened and confused, stood in Seldon's path. Seldon grabbed him by the collar and threw him aside. The old man crumpled to the floor like discarded newspaper.

"Stop him!" Cartwright yelled.

The words brought Seldon up short. He paused, then pointed the gun at Cartwright. The judge's mouth dropped open at the same time he dove behind the bench.

A shot cracked through the courtroom. Plaster exploded on the wall behind the judge's chair.

More screams. A greater crush toward the door, away from Seldon, who was inching his way toward the window.

*He's going to get away,* Kit thought. If she could only alert a policeman on the street. A policeman with a gun . . .

And then she saw Ed Hanratty jumping the rail. Seldon saw him, too. He pointed the gun and fired.

Hanratty fell upon Seldon, throwing his big arms around the man's body, pulling him to the floor.

Grunts and groans arose from the two. The deputy from the back, along with another man from the gallery, saw their opportunity and rushed at the duo.

Kit noticed the reporters writing furiously off to the side. Helping a man in distress was obviously not so valuable as a good story.

In just a few moments the deputy and his ally had Seldon on his feet, screaming and struggling. The gun was not in his hand.

Now several other men came to aid in the apprehension of Seldon. One of them shouted, "Get a doctor!"

Kit rushed through the gate and made her way around the bustle of people. Carrie Hanratty was already at her husband's side when Kit got there.

He was unconscious, a wicked bloodstain on his shirt.

"Somebody help him!" Carrie cried.

# Chapter 45

ARCH CROWLEY'S TIE was loose, hanging like a lazy noose around his neck. Tom Phelps did not have to be told what the matter was. The trouble was written all over his face, like a headline in bold type.

"You know what this means, don't you?" Crowley growled, pacing the floor of his office, littered as it was with cigar butts, crumpled papers, and several discarded pencils.

Phelps knew exactly what the outcome of the Hanratty case was. Not his exoneration, which was complete. But the reputation of the *Examiner* itself.

"Well, don't you?" Crowley repeated.

"The *Examiner* helped to free an innocent man," Phelps said, only half facetiously.

Crowley stopped dead in mid-pace. "What in the blazes is *that* supposed to mean?"

"Kit Shannon handed the judge our newspaper. It was part of the show."

"Show!"

"You bet it was a show. I don't think Kit is capable of doing anything ordinary."

Crowley ran his hand over his head, as if trying to squeeze all thoughts out of it. "You don't see it, Phelps! Hearst is going to have my hide! Did you see the *Times* this morning?"

Phelps shook his head.

"Otis is crowing!" Crowley said. "All about how he was right all along, and the *Examiner* is now hoisted on its own petard. And it's your fault."

"My fault?" Phelps felt indignation rising like fire.

"You didn't put enough pressure on."

"I wrote just what you wanted me to," Phelps said, feeling dirty about the whole business.

"You let this Shannon woman slip one over on us."

"What she did was one of the most incredible things ever seen in a courtroom," Phelps said. "And if we don't get on her bandwagon, we'll look like fools."

"We already look like fools. Mr. Hearst knows that. You've got to get something on this Shannon woman."

Phelps shook his head slowly. "Are you suggesting I make something up?"

"Don't sound so sanctimonious," Crowley said.

"But the facts are clear. Last night Edna Chausser confessed. Seldon's being held as an accessory. The sheriff is out looking for Robert Chausser right now. They will wrap this up quickly. And Kit Shannon is the reason."

Crowley shrugged.

"Those are the facts," Phelps insisted.

"Facts can be interpreted in a number of ways."

"And the *Examiner* way is to stretch them as far as they'll go without snapping."

"Sometimes snapping is called for. Like now. We can't let Mr. Hearst be embarrassed."

Phelps snorted. "I would think Hearst has enough money not to care."

Crowley lit a fresh cigar. "He cares. He wants to be president. Presidents can't look foolish."

"But reporters can."

Crowley glared at him through a haze of smoke. "Meaning?"

"Meaning I don't wish to be made a sacrificial animal for the reputation of the great man."

"Are you refusing?"

"I will not attack Kit Shannon anymore."

The editor shook his head. "What's she done for you? You're acting like a Sunday-school biddy."

"A little Sunday school wouldn't hurt me about now." Phelps turned and made for the door.

"Where you going?" Crowley said.

"To get my belongings," Phelps said.

"You're quitting?"

Tom Phelps nodded. "Cleaning house. And then I'm going back to Otis to see if I can get my old job back."

Crowley snatched the cigar out of his mouth. "The *Times?* Mr. Hearst won't like this one bit."

"Tell Mr. Hearst what he likes is no longer any concern of mine," Phelps said, walking out the door.

---

Carrie Hanratty held her husband's hand, her cheeks wet with tears. Kit's own cheeks were wet, not only for the joy, but the promise.

Hanratty—whom the *Times* had labeled a hero, and the *Examiner* a "fortunate man"—lay in a bed in Sisters Hospital, one floor below Aunt Freddy. His wound would heal, and he would once again walk a beat, but there had been a healing of a much deeper sort.

"I mean it, Carrie," he said. "With all my heart. I'm swearing off liquor. For you and for the girls."

He looked at his two daughters then. They beamed, joy bursting out of their smiles. Carrie squeezed her husband's hand.

Then Hanratty, with a glance at Kit, said, "Oh, and one other thing. On Sundays, I want all of us in church."

Carrie said, "Glory."

"Miss Shannon," Ed Hanratty said, "How can I thank you?"

"You just have," she said.

A nurse entered the room and walked straight to Kit. "You are needed upstairs."

Kit stood immediately, then felt Carrie Hanratty's hand on her arm. "We will pray for you," she told Kit.

Kit knew she would need that now, in large measure. She found Aunt Freddy as she had been an hour ago, sleeping with labored breath. The doctor, a kind man named Finley, was waiting for her.

"We are making her as comfortable as possible, Miss Shannon," he said. "She could go at any time."

"Thank you, Doctor," Kit said. "May I stay with her?"

"Of course. I can arrange a meal for you, if you like."

"You are most kind."

The doctor left then, and Kit took a chair by the bed. Her heart was full of the amazing grace God had provided. An innocent client cleared of all charges and Aunt Freddy calling on the name of the Lord. Kit could not help the tears of joy that formed, washing her cheeks.

———————

"You look as good as new," Gus said. "Too bad they couldn't do nothin' about that ugly mug of yours."

Ted stood on the street corner, the cane helping him steady himself. The wooden leg was harnessed to his thigh and would take a lot of getting used to. Dr. R. E. Milligan had lived up to the billing in his newspaper advertisement: "fine craftsman of artificial limbs."

"You're all heart, Gus," Ted said. He took a few more steps up the street. It would take the coordination of body and cane to get the right rhythm. His walking would never be smooth or swift. But he would make his way.

He could hardly wait to show Kit. But he knew she was with her aunt, and Ted wanted her to have the last moments with her alone.

"You look like you could kick a mule," Gus said.

"You'll do," Ted said, then quickly added, "but before that, what do you say we take a run out to the hangar?"

Gus's eyes widened.

"That's right," Ted said. "Let's see how I fit in a cockpit."

# Chapter 46

IT WAS IN THE EARLY morning hours of Wednesday that Kit awoke from a troubled sleep. She had been dozing on and off, praying in wakefulness, dreaming when she slept. The dreams had been disturbing.

In the last one, an array of dark forces gathered around her as she stood on the edge of a cliff. On the other side of a large chasm Aunt Freddy was walking away from her. Kit called out to her, but Aunt Freddy did not hear. She was being ushered into God's kingdom, but in the dream, Kit could not speak with her.

The dark forces were faceless, formless. They seemed to crouch near Kit, not striking, but waiting. Waiting until Aunt Freddy was gone from sight. Then, Kit sensed in the dream, they would strike.

Kit had at last woken with a start and saw that Aunt Freddy was looking at her. The old woman did not speak, but her eyes were full of meaning. They seemed to be offering comfort to Kit, assurance that all was well. There was thankfulness in the eyes, too.

Aunt Freddy did not make an attempt to open her mouth. It was as if she knew words were not needed.

Kit held her hand. It was weak yet warm. Physical life seemed to be giving one last hurrah.

"I'm here," Kit whispered. "I love you."

A smile came not to Aunt Freddy's mouth, but to her eyes. And then the eyes closed, and she slept again.

She did not wake up.

---

Like vultures, Heath Sloate and Benjamin Stillwater appeared at the hospital before Aunt Freddy's body was removed. Kit could only speculate that they had a nurse waiting to notify them.

Kit, lacking sleep, wanted to do what most did with vultures— shoot them. The law would have to see it as the ridding of ugly irritants.

They met her at the front desk. "My condolences," Heath Sloate said.

Kit did not answer him. His tone suggested the opposite of his words. Stillwater stood in silence behind Sloate, like some minion waiting to do his master's bidding.

"If there is anything I can do," Sloate added.

"No thank you, Mr. Sloate," Kit said sharply.

"Your aunt was a great woman."

What was he doing here? Had he come just to mock her? Or was it something more?

"If you don't mind," Kit said, "I must make arrangements." She tried to move past him, but he stepped in front of her.

"Ah, arrangements," Sloate said. "That has all been taken care of."

"Taken . . ." Kit could not imagine what he meant, only that it was sinister. Each breath she took was suddenly like a dagger.

Sloate was not going to be put off. But from what?

"Your great-aunt deserves a great funeral," Sloate said. "The arrangements have all been made."

Kit shook her head, as much out of aggravation as denial. "You will have nothing to do with any arrangements, sir. You will have nothing to do with Aunt Freddy at all."

The smile that came to Sloate's mouth was pompous and assured. It made Kit's skin tighten and her stomach clench. How had this man managed to insert himself into her life again, and with such invasiveness? Unable to manipulate Aunt Freddy in life, was he going to attempt to influence her in death? And what of Stillwater? His silence made it clear Sloate was running the show.

"Miss Shannon," Sloate said. "Perhaps we had best take this up at two this afternoon."

"I have no intention of taking anything up with you, Mr. Sloate," Kit said. She was tired from her vigil with Aunt Freddy and felt dangerously close to doing something socially unacceptable to the face of Heath Sloate.

"Do you know Miller Hitchens, the attorney?" Sloate said.

The name was familiar to Kit. He was not a criminal lawyer, but his name showed up in the newspapers. He was a lawyer for the well-to-do. "Yes," Kit said.

"Then be at his office at two o'clock sharp," Sloate said. "We have some matters to settle."

"What on—"

"Just be there," he said sharply. He turned quickly, his lap dog Stillwater following obediently behind.

Kit felt like wild animals were tearing at her soul as she walked back to her office. What should have been a day of quiet reflection was now a battleground of uncertainty. The only thing that was sure was that she would never be free of Sloate so long as she stayed in Los Angeles.

But she would not be run out by him. Somehow, some way, she was going to prevail.

When Kit entered her office she saw Corazón sitting and Ted Fox walking. On two legs. He held a cane in one hand and appeared to be showing Corazón how he moved.

"What do you think?" Ted said.

"It's . . ." Kit had intended to say *wonderful,* but the word caught in her throat. With tears, she ran to Ted and fell into his arms. He held her tenderly.

"She's gone," Kit whispered.

"Home," Ted said.

"Yes."

They stayed like that in silence for a long moment.

"I have something for you," Ted said. Kit stepped back, wiping her tears with a lace handkerchief.

From his satchel, Ted produced her father's Bible and held it out for her. "It's time you had this back," he said.

She took it, her heart warming within her as she thought of Aunt Freddy and Ted coming to love the Scriptures, and the Lord, as she did. "His Word has truly not returned void," she said. But as she set the Bible on her desk, the good feelings faded.

"What is it, Kit?" Ted asked.

Kit told him and Corazón about Sloate and Stillwater, of the meeting they had demanded that afternoon. "I do not have any desire to see them," she said, "but I feel I must."

Ted seemed oddly calm. "I will be going with you."

"But why?"

"I believe I know what the meeting is about."

"Tell me, please."

"Do you believe in miracles?"

She had no idea why he should ask her that. "Of course I do," she offered tentatively.

Then Ted smiled. "Let me show you something miraculous."

# Chapter 47

WHEN KIT ENTERED the offices of Miller Hitchens, attorney, she did not enter alone.

"What is the meaning of this?" Heath Sloate said upon seeing her company. Ted Fox, Gus Willingham, and one Nathaniel Thompson followed Kit inside.

"You know Mr. Fox," Kit said. "This is his associate, Gus Willingham. And with us today is Mr. Thompson, a shorthand reporter from the court."

Sloate's eyes narrowed as he removed his pince-nez from his nose. "You are memorializing today's meeting?"

"That is my intention."

"One would think you didn't quite trust me, Miss Shannon."

"In that you are perceptive indeed," Kit said. "Shall we proceed?"

"This way."

Sloate led them into a musty library, large enough to accommodate an expansive conference table. At one end of the table sat Benjamin Stillwater, looking like an anxious animal awaiting his afternoon meal. Next to him, at the head of the table, sat a distinguished-looking man with a full head of gray hair. He rose to greet them.

"I am Miller Hitchens," he said. "I was under the impression Miss Shannon would be alone."

Kit introduced her trio. Ted said, "Hiya," as he sat down. Gus joined him.

Stillwater practically fell out of his chair. He pointed at Gus. "That's the man who . . ."

"Who what?" Sloate demanded.

Looking sheepish, Stillwater said, "Nothing. Nothing."

Gus smiled and nodded. "Nice to see ya again."

Nathaniel Thompson took out a large pad from his case and several pencils. "Mr. Thompson is a certified court reporter," Kit said. "He will be transcribing for us today."

Hitchens looked at Sloate with consternation. "Why wasn't I told of this?"

"It is news to me," Sloate said. "It does not matter a whit."

"True," Hitchens said. "But I will tell Miss Shannon this expense is unnecessary, as you will soon understand."

"We shall see," Kit said. "Please proceed."

Hitchens cleared his throat and sat down. He folded his hands above a sheaf of papers in front of him. "The purpose of today's meeting is a notification of probate. Your great-aunt, Frederica Fairbank, left a will dated Three July, 1904, which revokes all previous wills and codicils. The original of the will is in the possession of the named executor, Mr. Benjamin Stillwater. This is a handwritten copy that I am going to read to you now."

"Got their ducks in a row, don't they?" Gus said.

Ted elbowed Gus in the ribs. "Quiet, you. Can't you see we're in the presence of important men?"

Sloate glared at Ted. Thompson, an impassive look on his face, transcribed away.

Hitchens ignored the interplay and began to read. " 'I, Fredericka Stamper Fairbank, being of sound mind, declare this to be my last will and testament. I hereby revoke all previous wills and codicils.' "

Kit sat back, folded her arms, and listened to the first paragraph as Hitchens read it, naming Stillwater as executor.

Hitchens continued. " 'To my great-niece, Kathleen Morgan Shannon, I leave the sum of one million dollars. I also leave to Kathleen Morgan Shannon my collection of books. I also leave to Kathleen Morgan Shannon the portraits that hang in my residence.' "

As Hitchens paused, Sloate smiled and nodded at Kit, as if to say how generous Aunt Freddy was. Kit held her feelings in check, waiting.

"To the Institute of Progressive Religion and Science, I leave the sum of twenty-nine million dollars, plus the residue of my estate, including the house at Angeleno Heights, provided that residence be used for housing the Institute of Progressive Religion and Science."

Hitchens placed the paper on the table. "That is the substance of the will," he said. "It was a point of courtesy to have you hear it so there would not be any misunderstanding when it comes to probate."

Kit said, "There is already a misunderstanding."

"How so?" Hitchens said.

"This will is a fraud." She watched carefully the expressions on the faces of her adversaries. Stillwater looked the slightest bit worried. Hitchens looked impatient. Sloate appeared to be without emotion. But it was Sloate who spoke first.

"This claim," he said, "was anticipated. Surely you do not think Mr. Hitchens would be involved in drafting a will that would not stand under scrutiny."

"I do not question his professionalism," Kit said. "He is, after all, only doing what you have paid him to do. He does not, I think, know the extent of your undue influence, through the agency of Mr. Stillwater, upon Aunt Freddy."

"You are claiming that Mrs. Fairbank was not of sound mind when she made the will?" Hitchens asked.

"I make a claim of undue influence," Kit said. "Stillwater took advantage of an old woman."

"You have any proof?" Hitchens asked.

Kit stood and faced Benjamin Stillwater, much as she would a hostile witness. "Mr. Stillwater," she said, "are you prepared to testify that my aunt, Frederica Stamper Fairbank, was of sound mind when she made this will?"

Stillwater swallowed, clearly unnerved at being suddenly questioned. He glanced at Sloate, who nodded assent.

"Yes, I am so prepared," Stillwater said.

"Surely you knew my aunt's condition, having been with her so often in the hospital these last days. Surely you must have known her true mental condition."

Sitting up straight, Stillwater seemed to gather confidence. "Her mind was as sharp as ever. I knew her well. She consulted me on a number of occasions before she took ill. Her mind never left her. I'll swear to that from now till doomsday."

"May be closer than he thinks," Gus whispered, loud enough for Kit to hear him. She almost smiled.

"You are quite correct in your assessment, Mr. Stillwater," Kit said. "Mr. Fox and Mr. Willingham will also swear that Aunt

Freddy's mind was sound during this period of time. They were witnesses."

Some hint of concern flashed into Hitchens' eyes. "Witnesses to what?"

Kit turned to Ted, who fished out a folded paper from his jacket and handed it to Kit. "Witnesses to the last will and testament of Frederica Stamper Fairbank."

As she handed the paper to Hitchens, Sloate shot to his feet, intercepting the document. He yanked it open. His eyes became round with anger. "This is a . . ."

"Holographic will," Kit said. "Written in her own hand, witnessed by Mr. Fox and Mr. Willingham and a nurse at Sisters Hospital."

"Let me see that," Hitchens demanded. Sloate, rather than hand it to him, stood silently as the lawyer took it.

"You don't believe you can get away with this, do you?" Sloate said.

"But Mr. Stillwater has stated, and Mr. Thompson has recorded, that Aunt Freddy was of sound mind. I am sure Mr. Hitchens will confirm that under California law, a holographic will, if it is written entirely in the hand of the testator, is valid and revokes all previous wills. Note the date."

"This leaves the entire estate to Miss Shannon," Hitchens said slowly.

For a moment nobody moved, as if the street of some Wild West town had come to halt as gunmen faced each other. Then Stillwater grabbed the paper from Hitchens' hand. He began to tear it into pieces.

"No!" Hitchens said. But Stillwater was like a man possessed. Sloate stood by, oddly frozen, as if suddenly detached from the entire proceeding.

"Let the record reflect," Kit said to Thompson, "that Mr.

Stillwater is destroying the last will and testament of Frederica Stamper Fairbank."

"You fool," Hitchens said to Stillwater. "That won't do any good. I've seen the will myself."

"I have a certified copy of the will in my office," Kit said, "transcribed by Mr. Thompson."

"That money is mine!" Stillwater cried. "I earned it!"

"You have just earned a felony complaint," Kit said. "I may convince the district attorney to ignore it in return for dropping any contest."

Stillwater, his mouth hanging open, began to shake. Then he pressed his face into his hands.

"He don't look too good," Gus said.

Heath Sloate, without a word, walked out of the library.

"It seems," Miller Hitchens said quietly, "that you have become a very wealthy young lady. What do you intend to do with all that money?"

Kit glanced at Stillwater, who was frozen in shock. "There is a struggling Bible institute here in the city," she said. "They could use a substantial gift."

A squeal issued from Stillwater's throat. He rushed out the door, slamming it behind him.

"It seems our meeting is over," said Hitchens.

"It seems so," Kit said.

"Just one question, if I may. How did you happen to secure this holographic will?"

It was Ted who addressed the attorney. "I was speaking to Freddy about God," he said, "and Stillwater was not around. I was reading to her from the Bible. I think I was reading Paul's words about love, in Corinthians, and she suddenly began to weep. She was desperate; she wanted to tell me about some terrible wrong. She told me about the will she had made at Stillwater's insistence.

She said she wanted desperately to undo that. I told her how she could."

"You knew about holographic wills?" Hitchens said.

"I worked in a bank," Ted said. "So, I had my friend Mr. Willingham here get a nurse and some paper and a pen and ink, and that was that."

Kit looked at Ted. "But why didn't you tell me about it sooner?"

"It was your aunt's request," Ted said. "She didn't want you to concern yourself with the whole business. She wanted you to succeed in court. I believe she was proud of you."

"I hope she was."

"Someday," Ted said, "you will get to ask her."

## Chapter 48

FREDERICA STAMPER FAIRBANK was laid to rest on a glorious Saturday morning. The cemetery was on a grassy hillside to the east of her beloved Angeleno Heights. It had a view of the Pacific Ocean. *"My little pond,"* Kit remembered her saying.

The eulogy was delivered by Kit's pastor, Reverend Macauley. A special prayer was offered by G. Campbell Morgan, who had been kind enough to come. Half of Los Angeles society, it seemed, had turned out. And they all got to hear about how Freddy found faith in the Savior before she died. Corazón was there, too, with her brother Juan. They stood next to Kit the entire service.

As did Ted. Kit held his arm and was comforted by the warmth of his touch.

Notable by their absence were Stillwater and Sloate. Kit didn't know what she might have done had they shown up. Without them, the service was perfect.

As the crowd dispersed, Kit received condolences for half an hour or so. Among the last were Morgan and Macauley.

"Miss Shannon," said Morgan, taking her hand, "my heart is full for you today and gratified beyond measure for what you and your aunt are doing."

"Thank you, Dr. Morgan," Kit said. "I believe Aunt Freddy is pleased right now, knowing that so much of her fortune shall be used for the advancement of God's Word here and around the world."

Morgan turned to Ted. "And I would like to speak to you, young man, as soon as possible."

Ted looked confused. "Me?"

"I am told you have banking experience," Morgan said.

"Yes, sir," Ted said.

"The Bible Institute will need someone with financial expertise. Reverend Macauley and I would like you to consider the job."

Kit watched as Ted's face jumped from incredulity to a grin as wide as the sea. "I will consider it right now," Ted said. "I accept."

They all laughed heartily. Kit looked up at the clouds and thanked God for making it a perfect morning.

Afterward, Ted gave Kit a ride back to town in Gus's automobile. He proudly showed Kit how he could work the pedal and the stick. "And this is how I'll fly the plane," he added.

Kit laughed for joy. "Yes, Ted! That is as it should be. You in the air again. With God all things are possible."

He drove her around the outskirts of the city. At one point he pulled to a stop on a crest looking east toward a succession of wild, rolling hills, one above another. Still further, they could see the rocky Sierra Madre range of mountains, its crest fringed with pine trees, which at this distance looked like blades of grass.

"It's beautiful," Kit said. When she turned to Ted, he was looking directly at her.

"Beautiful," he said.

He took her in his arms. His kiss was soft, warm, like the caress of a Santa Ana breeze. Kit rested her head on his shoulder. They stayed that way for a long time.

Finally they drove back to the city, talking of God and Aunt Freddy and flying in aeroplanes. They puttered down Beaudry Avenue, past Sonora Town with its Spanish buildings and gentle pepper trees, all the way to First Street. When they finally got back to Kit's office, they found Tom Phelps in front of the building, pacing. He seemed out of breath. He ran up to the auto, his forehead gleaming with sweat under his straw skimmer.

"What is this?" Kit said. She was cautious with the reporter after his angle of the case in the *Examiner*.

"I quit Hearst," Phelps said. "I'm working for Otis again. Got hired today."

"Congratulations," Kit said tentatively. "You came here to tell me that?"

He paused to catch his breath. "I figured I owed you some exclusive information after the way the *Examiner* treated you."

"What's happened?"

"Two hours ago Elinor Wynn shot Heath Sloate."

Kit's breath left her. She felt Ted take her arm.

"Dead?" Kit asked.

"As a doornail," Phelps said. "They got her down at police headquarters and . . ."

"And what?"

"She's asking for you."

———

Detective Captain Michael McGinty was hovering over Elinor Wynn, who was sobbing into her hands. She was seated at his spare desk in a hard, wooden chair. On the other side was District Attorney John Davenport. Neither looked pleased to see Kit.

Elinor looked up, her face puffy and red. "Help me, Miss Shannon. Please!"

"She won't say a word unless she talks to you," McGinty said.

"But we've got her dead to rights," Davenport said. "Found her holding the gun over the body. Best thing is if she confesses. It'll go easier on her."

Kit looked at Elinor, a pitiful sight. Reduced to this, the scandal of all scandals. Accused of murder.

Her first thought was that this was exactly what Elinor had coming to her. The consequence of her own selfish acts. But then, it was Heath Sloate who was killed. There had to be more to the story.

"Let me speak to her alone," Kit said.

Sweet relief washed over Elinor's face.

"I'm warning you," Davenport said.

"Of what, Mr. Davenport?"

"Don't try any tricks."

"Mr. Davenport," Kit said, "the right of an accused to talk to a lawyer is not a trick. If you like, we can ask a judge about it."

Davenport's face darkened, but he said nothing.

"Come with me," McGinty said. He showed Kit and Elinor to a tiny room at the end of the station. It had a small table and two chairs.

"I know you must hate me," Elinor said when they were alone. "You have every right to."

"Did you shoot him?"

Elinor bowed her head. "Yes," she said quietly.

"With what?"

"Ted's gun. It was left at my house."

"Why, Elinor?"

"I don't know," she said. "I was afraid."

"Did he attack you?"

"I thought he would."

"Tell me the whole story," Kit said. "And tell me the truth."

Elinor began sobbing. "I'm so scared. Can you ever forgive me for what I've done?"

———

*Los Angeles Daily Times*
July 12, 1904

### Around the City

*Kathleen Shannon, attorney-at-law, has been retained by Eli nor Wynn for her defense in the killing of Heath Sloate. District Attorney John Davenport has declared he will prosecute the case personally.*

*Miss Shannon recently faced Mr. Davenport in the court of Judge Andrew Cartwright, producing a stunning exoneration of her client, police officer Edward Hanratty, on the charge of murder. One legal expert, who has requested anonymity, states that the district attorney will not rest until he has bested Miss Shannon in court.*

*Thus begins another chapter in the young but heralded career of the first woman to practice criminal law in Los Angeles.*

Ted put the paper down and looked at Kit. "Do you really think you can do it?" he said.

"Do what?" she asked. They sat side by side at a table in Aunt Freddy's garden. Kit had invited him for a late breakfast. The perfumed aromas were a delight, the sky a brilliant azure dotted with puffs of white clouds.

"Defend Elinor," Ted said.

Before she could answer, a servant girl appeared with a silver tray of coffee and cakes. She poured two cups, then curtsied. Kit took a lingering sip of coffee, thinking about the question. It was one she had asked herself a dozen times. "I think of the Scripture that says God is rich in mercy, how He loved us even when we were dead in our sins. I realize He loves Elinor Wynn as much as He loves me. No, I won't hold back. I don't think she's guilty of murder."

"Even though she shot him point-blank?"

"Murder requires malice aforethought. That is a state of mind. Elinor told me she was in fear for her life. She was refusing to leave the city with him, and he attacked her. Knowing Sloate, that sounds not only possible, but probable."

"Elinor," Ted said slowly. "She brought this on herself."

"No one is beyond redemption," Kit said. "At one time, I thought Ed Hanratty might have been. And now look at him."

Ted took Kit's hand in his. "You are a remarkable woman, Kit Shannon."

Jerrold appeared in the garden, carrying something in his gloved hand. "This just arrived, miss," he said. He handed Kit a telegram.

"What news?" Ted asked.

"I don't know." Kit opened the wire. The city of origin was Washington, D.C. Kit read the text:

CONGRATULATIONS STOP JUSTICE WAS SERVED STOP IF YOU ARE EVER IN WASH DC SEE ME STOP T ROOSEVELT

From some distant place she heard Ted's voice. "Kit, what is it?"

Without a word she held out the telegram. He snatched it and read. Then he looked at her with a smile. "It appears I'm not the only one who finds you remarkable."

"I think," Kit said, "I am ready to be normal for a while."

Ted peered at the telegram again. He seemed to be thinking

about it. "Let's do that. Let's drop in on old Rough and Ready Teddy."

Kit looked at Ted's crazy grin. "Drop in? You and me?"

"We could stop in Washington D.C. after Niagara Falls."

"Niagara . . ."

"I understand it's a popular honeymoon location."

Kit's heart soared as Ted stood up. His hands took hers and he pulled her into a crushing embrace. He kissed her long and passionately. Kit melted against him, raising her hand to touch his hair.

Then she looked into his eyes, dazzling blue in the morning sun, and for one moment everything was perfect. There was no crime, no courts, no violence. There were no crooked cops or lawyers or politicians, no need for law and order because order and harmony were here now, the very fabric of life. The city of Los Angeles was Eden restored in this one moment, and two were together in paradise.